THE
REMAINDERS

MATTHEW ARNOLD STERN

Black Rose Writing | Texas

ISBN: 978-1-68433-830-6
PUBLISHED BY BLACK ROSE WRITING
www.blackrosewriting.com

Printed in the United States of America
Suggested Retail Price (SRP) $19.95

The Remainders is printed in Sabon

*As a planet-friendly publisher, Black Rose Writing does its best to eliminate unnecessary waste to reduce paper usage and energy costs, while never compromising the reading experience. As a result, the final word count vs. page count may not meet common expectations.

For Dad. I forgive you.

THE REMAINDERS

This book depicts suicide and physical abuse, which may disturb some readers. If you or someone you know is threatening to harm themselves, call your emergency service number (9-1-1 in the United States) immediately. For additional assistance in the United States, contact the National Suicide Prevention Hotline by calling 1-800-273-8255 or visiting https://suicidepreventionlifeline.org.

CHAPTER ONE

Dana Point

"Damn you, Dylan! Get out! Now!"

The night before, my stepdad Steven spoke in front of 18,000 at the Honda Center, urging them to live to their full God-given potential or some shit like that. That morning, he yelled at me in the front entryway of our house like I was some drunk who puked all over his $1,000 shoes. Behind him, Mom screamed at me uncontrollably. I couldn't make out a word she said. Just blasts of hateful air burning out of her lungs.

"You've humiliated us for the last time!"

I didn't know what I did. If it happened the night before, I didn't remember. I don't remember anything when I go out partying. I figure if I don't remember, I had a good time. But I wished I remembered that morning. If I had, I would have apologized for it. I wouldn't have meant it, but it would've stopped what happened next.

"You're 18 now, Dylan! We don't have to put up with your garbage anymore!"

I didn't want to put up with *their* garbage either. I was planning to move out after I graduated high school. Except I wasn't going to graduate. I was failing at Dana Hills High School. I did pretty well in elementary school. They even recommended me for the honors program. But I just got bored with school in seventh grade. Mom and Steven sent me to a military prep academy in eleventh grade and made Dad pay for it. When that school threw me out, I went back to Dana Hills until I dropped out. I was planning to go back and get a GED in the fall. If Mom and Steven would let me stay.

"If you don't want to be here and follow our rules, you can get out!"

1

And Mom said the only intelligible words I heard from her that morning, "And you can go live with your father, you ungrateful little shit!"

There was only one thing I could do.

"Where are you going!?" Steven stood between me and the stairway.

"Getting my stuff."

"Oh, no, buddy boy." He stuck his arms out to the sides as if he were making some magical invisible barrier. "Remember what I told you? Wealth is the sign of God's favor. You don't deserve God's favor or mine! You take what I give you! No Xbox. No MacBook Air. Nothing!" He then stared at the rectangular bulge in my front pocket. "And forget about using your iPhone. We shut off the service this morning."

· · ·

I stood in front of what was my house and watched my clothes get thrown out of a second-story window. Steven didn't look at me as he replaced the deadbolt on the front door.

They didn't take my keys. That meant I still had my Ford Explorer. Dad gave it to me for my sixteenth birthday, and there was no fucking way they'd take that away from me. When the last pair of underwear landed on the front step, I gathered up the pile one armful at a time and tossed it in the back of the Explorer. They didn't give me everything. They didn't give me my favorite Hundreds t-shirt. Or my Angels jersey with number 58 for Wayne Morgan. It wasn't any good anyway because they traded him last year to the Royals. I would've liked to keep my Dana Hills High School Dolphins sweatshirt. I didn't give a fuck about the school, but it was the warmest one I had.

When I threw the last of my socks in the back, Steven had already finished replacing the deadbolt and shut the door. The upstairs window had already been shut and the shutters tightly closed. The downstairs drapes were shut tight too. Perhaps they were watching me with their security cameras. Or maybe they didn't care to see if I left.

I thought about shouting a final "fuck you" and squealing the tires as I pulled out of their driveway. But I didn't care either.

CHAPTER TWO

Reseda

"These go on aisle 12." Quang pointed to a box full of books.

I never liked books. At least they weren't hard to stock. They fit neatly on a shelf and were easy to organize. We had a bunch of paperbacks and some hardcovers. All of them had a black mark across the bottom. Quang said they were remainders, which are the books other stores couldn't sell. Well, they couldn't sell them at full price. Perhaps people would buy them here for a dollar.

At Buck & Awesome, we sold the stuff they couldn't sell elsewhere. We still sell 2016 calendars, even though we're four months into the year. We sell generic breakfast cereals. Pumpkin spice Pop Tarts when it wasn't pumpkin spice season. The superhero toys that sort of look like Marvel Avengers, but the package said, "Marvelous Adventurers." Disney Frozen hairbrushes that were just regular hairbrushes with a Frozen sticker on it. I guess you can get little girls to sit still and have their hair brushed if Elsa's face is on it. At least until the sticker fades and falls off.

And people came from all over to buy our stuff. Things that seemed worthless at full price suddenly seemed worthwhile for a dollar.

If we had places like this in Orange County, I didn't know about them. Mom and Steven thought they were too good even for Target. "Tar-*zhey*," they called it with a sneer. Walmart would make them break out in hives. Macy's was as cheap as they would go.

But when I realized I was stuck in Reseda, I knew I had to get a job. Buck & Awesome hired me on the spot. It was the first job I ever had.

3

• • •

I didn't know why I wound up in Reseda, but I knew how.

After they kicked me out of the house, I had to drive around to my friends to see if they would take me in. My iPhone didn't have service, so I couldn't call them.

I went to Armando's first. He was my best friend, so I was sure he'd hook me up. He just rubbed the back of his neck and said he wasn't sure if they had the room. His family has a 6,000-square-foot five-bedroom house. They had a casita off to the side where we used to blaze. And he was an only child. I assumed his answer was no.

Then I went to Doug's. He said they were in the middle of remodeling. But there were no construction crews, stacks of wood beams, table saws, or any of the stuff you'd see at a remodeling site. I assumed his answer was also no.

Gabriel moved out right after high school, so I thought he would be cool with me moving in with him. He started getting real jittery when I asked him. He said his roommate didn't want anyone else living there. I assumed his answer was also no.

I stopped by Omar's, but his family wasn't home. I considered asking my ex, but her parents made it clear they didn't want me anywhere near her.

I went up Golden Lantern towards Lysander's house in Nellie Gail. I then remembered that one party we had at his place and knew I couldn't ask him.

Instead, I turned onto Oso Parkway and headed to the 5 Freeway. I decided I would see Dad in Lake Forest. He said I'd always be welcome to live with him.

My parents had a nasty divorce, but it was mostly Mom's fault.

Dad was a doctor, one of those general practitioners. You'd think he'd be super-rich, but he had lots of med school debt. Since he mostly worked with elderly patients, he always had to fight to get paid from Medicare. Mom grew up in Corona del Mar, so she was used to fine things. Dad got us a nice home and nice cars, but they weren't nice enough for Mom. They argued about money all the time, so Mom decided she would earn more money by returning to her old job as a hospital receptionist.

And that's how she met Steven. He was visiting a kid who had cancer. That video with him praying by her bedside went viral. What the video didn't show was what he and Mom were doing in a hospital storeroom afterwards.

She screwed Dad over during the divorce proceedings. They were supposed to get joint custody of my sister Muriel and me, but Mom got full custody and the child support that went with it. Not that I would have cared. I wasn't really close to Dad because he had to work all the time. Muriel was closer to him, but she was involved in sports and music. He would always go to her events, but he sat far away from Mom. I'm sure he would have gone to more of my events if I got involved in anything.

But since Mom didn't want me anymore, I figured I better get closer to him.

The freeway signs said that Lake Forest Drive was coming up. I moved to the right lane. I checked the gas gauge. I had a little over a quarter of a tank, but the Explorer got shitty gas mileage. I still had more than enough to get off the freeway and drive a few miles to his house. But would he really take me in?

Dad recently started dating again. I saw pictures of his new girlfriend on Facebook. She looked really pretty and athletic. They were always doing outdoor things like hiking and kayaking in the Back Bay. They even ran a 5K together. Dad wasn't into sports before he met her, except for watching Angels games. She had two kids from her previous marriage. They were ten and eight, and they were both in Little League and AYSO.

He wouldn't want some 18-year-old messing up his new life. Even if it were his own son.

I reached the Lake Forest exit, but I pulled into the lane to my left. I cut off a guy who gave me an angry honk.

"Fuck it." I stepped on the gas. I stayed on the 5 Freeway and kept going north.

I didn't know or care where I was going. I kept driving until I ran out of gas. I ran out of gas in Reseda.

. . .

Reseda wasn't what I expected. The way they always show it in movies and sing about it in songs, I thought it would be some rich place with lots of movie stars. It wasn't. Reseda actually looked kind of ghetto, like Santa Ana. But unlike Santa Ana that looked drab and run-down, Reseda was bright and colorful with murals and painted utility boxes.

Buck & Awesome was in an old strip mall on this boulevard called Sherman Way. In front of our store was a sign that said "Reseda Welcomes You. Hub of the West Valley." The street had a grassy median that still seemed green despite the drought. Palm trees lined both sides of the street. Someone wrapped some yarn around one of the trees. Yarnbombing, they called it.

The people in Reseda are pretty chill. Many of them are Hispanic. I get along with them well. I knew some Spanish. I took a semester of it in high school, but I learned most of it by hanging around my Spanish-speaking friends. They taught me useful words, like "cabrón" and "pendejo," instead of spending two weeks on how to conjugate "ser."

There are a lot of immigrants too. One of the people working the register is a Syrian refugee. Her name is Fatima. She always wears one of those headscarves. She smiles at everyone and always has a kind word. She encourages everyone to drop their change in the plastic coin box at the register. It has a sign that says "Buck & Awesome supports United Cerebral Palsy" with a picture of a guy with his arm around a smiling little girl in a walker. I heard it is our company's CEO and his daughter.

They say a lot of white people used to live in Reseda, and I still see a lot of them in the store. Mrs. Cimino is one of our regulars. She's short and thin with neatly curled gray hair. She's in her seventies, but she moves well and has good posture. She says she stays in shape by gardening and taking yoga classes. She'd tell us stories about what Reseda used to be like when they had department stores, the abandoned movie theater down the street actually showed movies, and bartenders wore crisp white shirts and black bow ties and made drinks like

Manhattans and Gin Rickeys. It's interesting to talk to her, but I couldn't when Quang was around.

•   •   •

One Sunday morning, I remembered why.

I saw Quang in front of Annabelle's register. She was drunk. I could tell. I had seen plenty of people that shitfaced at parties. But I figured a 54-year-old woman like her would know better than showing up drunk at work. I knew she was 54 because she kept telling us that, especially whenever she was asked to lift a box, sweep the floor, or basically do any work at all.

Quang was at a level of pissed I had never seen before. I had seen him get pissed before. He got pissed at me the first time I stocked a shelf wrong. He has this way of stepping up and shaking a finger at you. Even though he was only five-foot-two, he made me tremble. I didn't stock a shelf wrong again. I couldn't afford to get fired.

I knew Annabelle wasn't going to get off for what she did. Quang stood rigidly. He loosened his brown and beige tie, which he always kept neat and straight. Veins popped on his forehead.

I turned towards a side aisle and looked for a display to straighten up. I knew what was coming and didn't want to be caught up in it. But I couldn't ignore the shouts.

"You know the rules, Annabelle!"

"I didn't take drugs."

"What do you think alcohol is!?"

"I just had one drink."

Quang stared at her, disbelieving. He must have known she had more than one drink. It was so obvious. I could smell the liquor on her breath from where I stood.

She protested, "I need it for my back!"

"You drink for back pain!?"

"I can't afford meds with as little as you pay us!"

"Then you don't have to worry about me paying you anymore!"

Then a soft voice came from behind me. "It's just as well."

I turned around and saw Mrs. Cimino. I could feel my face burn from embarrassment.

"I'm sorry, Mrs. Cimino." I stammered as quietly as I could. "You shouldn't have to hear this…"

"I've heard it before."

"Here? At this store?"

Mrs. Cimino stood silently for a moment and then said, "Annabelle is an unhappy person. I know. Unhappy people do things that cause them greater unhappiness."

She then looked directly at me. I felt a little creeped out at first, having an older woman look at me like that. But she gave me a small smile.

"I hope you don't do that to yourself, Dylan. You have too much of your life ahead of you to make yourself miserable. One foolish mistake can ruin your whole life."

She returned to her cart and continued down the aisle. I waited until she turned away and got out of earshot before I could exhale.

I looked back at the front of the store. It didn't take Quang long to get rid of Annabelle. She had already stormed out of the store, paperwork crumpled in her hand. Quang watched her leave. When she was gone, he tightened and straighten his tie. He went back into the office and took out a sign, "Now Hiring/Se Aceptan Aplicaciones." Without a word, he carried the sign to the front window and put it on a ledge next to another sign, "Notice: This is a drug-free workplace./Aviso: Este es un area de trabajo libre de drogas."

I went back to cleaning up the shelves.

• • •

At five, I hung up my green work apron in the office. If someone was around when I left, I'd wish them a good day. I never said "goodbye." For some reason, that word freaked Dad out. Fatima was always there because her register was close to the door to the office. I always wished her a good day, and she'd reply with the biggest smile. She always smiled. I couldn't figure out how she could smile with what she went through in Syria and what she had to deal with every day at work.

8

From the moment I stepped out the door, I started walking. I couldn't drive the Explorer since it has no gas and had been sitting for a month. I wasn't sure if it'd even start. Fortunately, it wasn't hard to find my way around Reseda. All the streets were a neat grid. They didn't bend around, go at funny angles, or changed names like they did at home. I still called my old place home, even though I knew I wouldn't be welcomed back there again.

Over the past month, I learned the places to go in Reseda.

There's a restaurant a few blocks down on Sherman Way called Mamá Frieda. They serve kosher Mexican food. No chicharrones, but delicious chicken albondigas and noodle soup. It was owned by this woman named Magdalena. She's really chill. When I first came to Reseda and didn't have any money, she'd give me whatever leftovers they had. If she didn't have any leftovers, she'd let me wash some dishes in exchange for a free meal. I was glad I now had money to pay her, even if I could only afford a taco. She still threw in the rice and beans for free.

The guy who worked at the gas station on Reseda and Sherman Way was chill too. His name was Reza, and he let me use the bathroom whenever his boss Carlos wasn't around. Carlos was a bit of dick, and he didn't want "homeless scum and drug dealers" hanging around his gas station. And he packed a .38, so he was serious. But Carlos wasn't there until seven, so I knew when it was safe to go there.

After a couple of weeks, I found the library. It took a half an hour to walk there, but it gave me a safe place to hang out for a while, especially since it was near the police station. They had computers where I could check the Internet and outlets where I could charge my iPhone. I thought about selling my iPhone, since I couldn't use it without service. But I had reasons for not letting it go.

It took me another week before I could get up the nerve to check my Facebook. What did people say? Did they miss me? Did they care that I'm gone? Did they want me to come back? Did Mom and Steven want me to come back? What about Dad?

The first time I checked, it broke my heart. No one posted anything about me. No one asked where I went. No one messaged me. No one. It was as if I no longer existed. My friends posted pictures of themselves.

The usual duck-faced selfies. Pics of parties I was no longer invited to. And my friends—or people I thought were my friends—had the droopy, glazed eyes I used to have in my photos. My ex posted pictures of her new boyfriend. He's the starting second baseman on the Dana Hills baseball team. He's Black. I'm not sure how well that went over with her parents. Then again, they didn't like me, and I'm white. But they had their reasons for not liking me.

I didn't expect Mom and Steven to post anything about me. Steven used Facebook to post photos and videos to promote his books, speeches, and his non-profit organization, Face Time for Healing, which supposedly "used the healing power of Christ to bring hope to the poor and disadvantaged." Mom posted pictures of sunsets and flying eagles and mountain peaks with inspirational quotes like "No problem is so great that God cannot handle it." Bullshit. She considered me a problem, so she threw me out of the house. I guess she didn't trust God enough to handle me.

Dad posted more pictures of his new girlfriend and her kids. One was a picture of them at the beach. Dad's girlfriend rocked a bikini. Maybe he posted it to taunt Mom, showing her how good he was getting it. He didn't post anything about me.

But Dad usually emailed me. It took me a few more days to get up the nerve to check.

Sure enough, there was an email from him:

Son,
I heard from Mom and Steven about what happened. I really wished you would have called me. You know you're always welcome to live with me. I haven't heard from you in weeks. Please call me or email when you can. I love you very much.
Love,
Dad

I didn't reply, but I didn't delete the message either. I kept it in my inbox. Every time I would come to the library, I'd look at it, trying to figure out how I'd reply. I didn't know what to say.

I then got another email from Dad.

Son,

We're all getting very concerned about you. We hope you're OK and nothing happened to you. Please, Dylan, if you get this message, reply or call me. We just want to know if you're all right. I love you very much.

Love,

Dad

I stared at that email for a moment, puzzled. What did he mean by "we"? Did he mean him and Muriel? Or him and Mom? He certainly couldn't mean him, Mom, and Steven. Or maybe it was him and his new girlfriend. But why would she be concerned about me? She doesn't know me! Or was he just saying "we" to make me feel better, like other people cared about me when they really didn't? And why did he write to me at all? So he didn't feel guilty if something happened to me? And why the fuck would he care what happened to me, anyway? He doesn't really know me! And if he cared so fucking much, he would have fucking tried to spend more time with me!

"Dude, are you OK?"

I looked over my shoulder. It was some kid in a maroon Abercrombie & Fitch t-shirt. I stared back at the screen.

"Yeah, I'm fine."

"Then," he mumbled, "I'm sorry, but if you don't mind, like, are you done? I really need to use the computer for homework."

I clicked the button to log off from the computer. "Go ahead."

I unplugged my iPhone charger from the outlet and started making my way home.

•   •   •

Home was my Ford Explorer.

I had parked it behind the abandoned movie theater. I don't know why I chose that spot, except it was where the Explorer started sputtering and stalling as it used the last drops of gas. Maybe I knew I'd be left alone there. Maybe it was because the theater was a crumbling old building, a piece of shit sitting there to rot. It had no value. Worthless. A remainder.

Just like me.

I didn't feel that way at first. I was pissed for a long time. I hated Mom and Steven for kicking me out. I hated Dad for going on with his life with a new woman and family. I hated Muriel for being so perfect in everything and then doing the perfect thing by going off to college so she'd get away from our fucked-up family. She wouldn't know that I was sleeping in an SUV in Reseda. Or care. I hated my fake friends who were "ride and die" with me when I had money and weed, but they weren't there when I needed them. I hated Orange County. I hated its shopping malls, its Starbucks, its beaches, its fake girls with their fake tits and fake tans. I hated having to get a new iPhone every year because you weren't cool if you didn't get one the day it came out. And you had to get the right case, and the right wallpaper, and the right apps. "Are you on Fleekchat? Everyone's on Fleekchat now." Fuck you!

Then I started hating myself.

I didn't come right out and say it, but it showed up in weird ways. I'd accidentally leave the doors of the Explorer unlocked at night in case someone wanted to steal my shit and slit my throat. When I heard some people talking about the Orange Line, I thought about stepping in front of one of those trains. I learned these are buses on their own special roadway, but stepping in front of one would still do the job. And if I couldn't find that Orange Line, I'd just step in front of one of the cars rushing by on Sherman Way. I wondered if anyone would notice or care. If anyone would miss me.

In truth, I'd been feeling that way for a long time. Even when I was little. But I'd blaze or take some bars, and the feeling would go away. For a while, anyway.

But I had no money for drugs. Not even skunk weed. And I had no connects. I couldn't trust anyone in Reseda. They could be with a cartel. Or an undercover cop. Or just some guy who rolls you and takes your money. And because I couldn't get drugs, I was stuck with all those voices telling me what a worthless piece of shit I was, and I should do the world a favor and end myself.

The only reason I didn't was because of people like Magdalena and Reza. And getting the job at Buck & Awesome helped too.

•   •   •

But I still felt my stomach clench whenever I walked past that abandoned old theater with strands of dead neon tubes hanging off the tall Reseda sign and the empty marquee. Especially when it had gotten dark. Even with the streetlights and the headlights of the oncoming cars brightening the sidewalk, it still seemed dark and sketchy.

I had to go around the theater and neighboring buildings by turning on a side street named Canby Avenue. As I got closer to the parking lot, I wondered if the Explorer was still there. Perhaps it was stolen or towed away. I started getting more jittery. Canby was darker than Sherman Way, with fewer streetlights and fewer cars driving by. I reached the driveway to the parking lot. I took a quick look around the corner of the building by the driveway. It was dark there, with only a small dim lamp over a doorway on the back of a building. When I knew it was clear, I rushed into the parking lot and walked quickly down the alley. I recognized the dark outline of the Explorer next to the abandoned theater. I gave a deep sigh.

I stopped using the remote to unlock the car. I doubted that it worked anymore, but I also didn't want the sound to give me away. I unlocked and raised the tailgate. This weird funk came out of it, like the stale smell of polyester pants when you've been sweating in them all day. The funk would go away after a moment, and I'd crawl inside.

I sold most of my clothes. They took up space where I needed to sleep, and I needed the money more. I only had $45 in my pocket when Mom and Steven kicked me out of the house. I left the house with $300 the night before. I had gotten money from birthdays, when I sold weed before I got busted, and cash I took out of Mom's wallet.

I tried making a withdrawal from the ATM when I got to Reseda, but I found out that Mom and Steven closed my bank account. I thought you couldn't do that to an 18-year-old. Steven always said, "Wealth is the sign of God's favor." I guess he wanted me to have as little of it as possible.

I used the $45 and what little money I got from the clothes to buy some things at Goodwill I needed. Like a sleeping bag and a black plastic tarp to cover the windows so I can sleep. When Dad first gave me the Explorer, I found instructions online on how to install a latch to open the lift gate from the inside. I sort of borrowed the tools from Steven, but I'm not sure if I returned them. I put in that latch so my friends and I could hotbox in the back. I never imagined I'd need it to sleep in my car.

So, I'd be pretty fucked if the Explorer was stolen or towed away. I'd lose everything, including the money I got from my paychecks that I stashed in the center console. And where would I sleep? On the streets, I suppose. I've seen people sleeping in doorways or curled up against the side of a building.

I used to see them in Orange County too. They'd stand at the exit of the Costco parking lot where they held up cardboard signs. Usually, they brought their kids with them. But we always drove past them like they weren't there. I once heard Steven huff, "Lazy bums. Wealth is the sign of God's favor. Perhaps they'd get His favor if they got off their butts and worked." I wanted to ask why he didn't take the money he raised and "the healing power of Christ" to help them. But I sort of agreed with him. Being homeless was their fault.

But here I was, just one step away from sleeping in doorways or holding a cardboard sign in a parking lot. How could Mrs. Cimino tell me not to make myself miserable when my life was as miserable as it can get?

That's when I took out my iPhone. It was now nothing more than an alarm clock and an occasional flashlight. I had to make sure the charge lasted through the night, which is why I never tried looking for Wi-Fi and getting online. Sometimes, I'd look at the photos. The duck-faced selfies I used to take. And my friends, back when I really thought they were friends. And my ex. There was even a picture of Mom, Steven, Muriel, and me at The Cheesecake Factory in the Shops of Mission Viejo. We were sending Muriel off to Minnesota for college. And we were all smiling. Even me. Perhaps it was because I took a bong rip before we went to dinner. Still, our smiles seemed real. I'd like to think there was a time, even if it were a moment, when we were all happy together.

I took a deep sigh and turned off the phone. I had work in the morning.

CHAPTER THREE

Lake Forest

"Did he ever write back, Oliver?"

I shook my head.

Rachel put her arm around my shoulders. She was both firm and soft. Taut deltoids and biceps and silky skin. She exhaled deep.

"We should let her know..."

I sighed. "I don't know..."

"It has been a month."

I turned to her. She stood next to my chair, but I didn't have to look up much to see her face. But packed into her four-foot-eleven frame was a powerhouse of strength and energy. She was in the Israeli Army, proficient in Krav Maga, and played every sport they offered in school. She looked younger than 38. Her dark olive skin was smooth, and she only had a few wrinkles around the eyes. She told me she got her youthful skin from her Ethiopian father, who also gave her curly black hair and full lips.

At that moment, those lips pursed tight. They forced another sigh from my lips.

"But Muriel's about to start her midterms for the quarter..."

"Still, she should know. Maybe she heard from him."

"They weren't that close."

"They're still brother and sister."

I nodded because I knew Rachel didn't yet understand. David and Moshe were just kids. They still fought over silly things like whose turn it was to use the iPad or that one called the other a "stinky poo-poo butt" when they weren't saying probably worse things in Hebrew.

Rachel never stood for that. I don't know what she did, but it got them to stop. I knew things would be different when they were teenagers. Like it was for Muriel and Dylan. And my brother and me.

"I can't write her now. It's late in Minneapolis."

"You can write her in the morning."

• • •

One 145-milligram tablet of fenofibrate for my triglycerides. One 50-milligram tablet of losartan for high blood pressure. One 81-milligram tablet of low-dosage aspirin for heart health. And one 5-milligram tablet of Cialis for an awful 17-year marriage. Because of that marriage, I used to take other medicines. Because of Rachel, I stopped needing to take them.

I swished around a capful of spearmint mouthwash and spit it out. Then, I put a dab of whitening toothpaste on my Sonicare toothbrush.

Soft and firm arms wrapped around me.

When Rachel and I first started dating, she could barely reach around me. Now, she could reach past her wrists, thanks to her forcing me to go on daily workouts.

But I had to spit out.

"Always the romantic," she joked.

I turned around in her embrace. She wore one of my old Angels t-shirt as a nightshirt. She had a glint in her eye and a mischievous smile.

"Try to grab me." She fluttered her eyelids.

"We'll wake your kids…"

"They can sleep through anything. Come on." She let go of my torso and took my hand. She led me into the bedroom. I closed the bathroom door behind me. She released my hand and dashed to the other side of the bed.

"Hey!" I couldn't call out too loud for fear of waking the kids.

Rachel didn't have such a worry. She giggled out loud. "You got to grab me!"

I chased her to the other side. She scampered over the bed, stirring the comforter. I was about to follow her, but I turned and rushed around the bed towards her. She may be faster, but I could outsmart her! As she headed towards me, she froze and started to giggle. Perhaps she outsmarted me because she knew I would go that way.

I grabbed her by the waist and threw her on the bed. Though she weighed about 90 pounds, there was a time I could barely lift her. And was afraid to. Not because I was afraid of hurting her. She was a soldier, after all. I was afraid of hurting myself. I worried that either my lower back or heart would give out. Since she got me to start working out, I didn't feel afraid anymore. I tossed her on the bed like a doll and pounced on her. Her giggles turned into a deep, body-shaking laugh. She flailed her arms at me in a half-hearted attempt to resist. I grabbed her wrists and forced them on the bed. She squirmed in a mock struggle. That's when our eyes locked. Her green eyes staring into mine. The giggles stopped. Her breathing became deeper. My lips pressed against hers. I grasped her wrists tightly, just the way I knew she liked it. My lips pressed against the side of the neck and traced down to the gap between her clavicles. I let go of her wrists and reached under the Angels shirt. My fingers glided up her defined torso, around breasts that were still firm. I pulled the Angels shirt over her head and flung it across the room. Rachel looked so beautiful without her clothes. Sculpted as if crafted from stone.

She grasped the tops of my sleep pants and briefs together and yanked them down. I was hard. That was a relief. It was difficult at the beginning, especially when I had to put on a condom. I was afraid of losing it and losing her for losing it. After a while, I felt more comfortable, especially when we stopped using condoms. We had been monogamous long enough, and she had been using birth control. It was one less thing to worry about.

I slid off her panties and entered her. She lubricated easily. We both moaned as her vaginal walls pulled away for me. I grabbed her wrists again and forced them deep into the comforter. She struggled this time, her body writhed against mine as I slid up and down her.

I was better about waiting. That was difficult too. The first time we made out, even before we had intercourse, I came in my underwear. That was embarrassing. Fortunately, she didn't know or chose not to say.

I could hold myself until I knew she was ready. Her moans got deeper. She tilted back her head and closed her eyes. It felt so good to let go. My whole body shuddered as every muscle pushed to ejaculate into her. When she climaxed, her body seized before she let out several hard and long moans before letting every part of her body relax.

. . .

I washed off in the shower. Rachel had fallen into a deep sleep. I slipped on my briefs and tucked myself into bed.

As I stared into a blissfully sleeping Rachel, I couldn't believe that I made love to such a beautiful and strong woman. I thought my sex life was over when I split up with Teresa. Actually, it ended long before then. It wasn't the only reason we broke up, but it was a factor.

Still, I felt numb for the longest time after our marriage ended, especially since it happened right after Mom's death. The divorce proceedings were a blur. I knew I was getting screwed over, but I didn't care how much Teresa took as long as she was out of my life. I figured the kids would be OK with her. She was a good-enough mother, and Steven seemed an upright fellow. Well, for an adulterer at least. Muriel turned out all right. Dylan? I knew he had problems. I agreed with Teresa and Steven that Pacific Military Academy would straighten him out. But I guess it didn't. In many respects, I really didn't know that much about him, even though he's my own son. I certainly didn't know how bad things had gotten until I got that call from Teresa.

Maybe she was right. Tough love was what he needed. He's an adult, after all. He's not her responsibility anymore. Or mine. I have a new life now, and possibly a new family with Rachel.

Still, I couldn't stop worrying about Dylan.

CHAPTER FOUR

Reseda

I got up at six because I knew Carlos would be at the gas station at seven. I cut across the parking lot to get to the station. All the while, I prayed no one else was in the bathroom or Carlos didn't come in early.

I was lucky on both counts. Reza gestured to the door.

I turned on the water in the sink to get it warm. I pissed. Then I took off my t-shirt. I washed my face, armpits, chest, and hands. If I had enough time, I'd wet a paper towel and washed my ass and that nasty cheesy shit under my nut sack. I used the paper towels to dry myself.

I knew I had to be quick. I wasn't sure who else would be waiting for the bathroom or if Carlos would come. I also had to be neat. I couldn't leave the bathroom a mess, or Reza would get busted. If I couldn't use this bathroom, I don't know what I'd do. I couldn't go to work all gross. Or piss in the corner of the parking lot. I grabbed another paper towel and wiped off the sink and floor and shoved the paper towels deep in the trash container by the door.

I opened the door and looked around quickly. Fortunately, Reza was still there alone, reading a Persian-language newspaper.

"Later, dude," I said.

He smiled back. "Have a good day!"

I still didn't understand while every Middle Easterner I met was so happy. Maybe that's why whites like Mom and Steven and my ex's parents didn't trust them. They're weren't as miserable as they are.

.　.　.

I finished the rest of my morning routine back at the Explorer. I shaved, using the selfie camera on my iPhone as a mirror. I tried growing a goatee when I got out of military school, but it never grew in right. I figured if I shaved, I wouldn't look like a homeless bum.

Then I brushed my teeth. Even though I slept in a car, I still had to take care of my teeth, especially after all the money Dad spent at the orthodontist for me.

That was how I got my job at Buck & Awesome. I went in there to buy more toothpaste, even though I was down to my last dollar. That's when I saw the "Now Hiring/Se Aceptan Aplicaciones" sign. Quang said I had clean teeth and good breath. He said that he gave up smoking when he came to the United States because he didn't like what it did to his teeth and breath. He said Americans have good teeth, and they took pride in taking care of them. So, he wanted to be a real American too by taking care of his teeth.

When I couldn't take care of my teeth anymore, that's the day I'd step in front of a car or an Orange Line bus.

·   ·   ·

It took me about five minutes to walk along Sherman Way from the Explorer to work. But I had to allow for extra time because I was passing Mamá Frieda. And Magdalena.

"¡Hola, Dylan!"

Magdalena spoke with a heavy slur. She had a stroke a few years ago. She had trouble speaking at times, and she walked with a cane. But she still had plenty of energy for a woman in her fifties, and she always had a broad, though slightly crooked smile. She seemed to know when I was coming. She stepped out of the front door of her restaurant holding a bag of fresh pan dulces.

"You should eat."

She once told me she came from a Jewish family in Mexico City. The Mexican part of her made the most amazing pan dulces. The Jewish part of her insisted that I eat them. She handed the bag to me without me even asking.

"Thank you, Magdalena."

She gently patted my cheek. "You're a good boy. Don't forget that."

The first time she told me that, I nearly cried. No one ever told me I was good. And hearing her say it that morning, it brightened me up more than a double espresso.

"Thank you." I nodded.

"Have a good day at work."

I smiled. She smiled back. And with a smile like hers, I thought nothing would ruin my day.

.   .   .

That was until I saw the lifted black pickup truck in the corner of the parking lot. They always hung around the donut shop next to CVS.

I knew their type. We had them in Dana Point too. They sat in the back of the Dana Hills High School parking lot in the same type of black lifted pickup truck with the skull trailer hitch cover with the eyes that glowed red when they hit the brakes. They always took up two parking spaces. They wore muscle tees that showed off their badly drawn tats. They didn't make the football team because they didn't have the grades. So, they spent their time yelling at gays, Blacks, and Hispanics. They tell girls they'd give them the best sex they ever had, even though the 'roids kept them from getting boners. They'd bump that twangy country music or some shit.

And these guys in front of the donut shop had bumped their twangy country music really loud.

I just walked past their truck and ignored them. We couldn't ignore the music. We could hear the muffled thumps inside the store. Quang stood by the front windows staring at them. Kishana, our assistant manager, stood next to him.

"Stupid trailer trash," Quang grumbled. "They have nothing better to do but sit around and disturb everyone with their hillbilly music."

Kishana said softly, "You remember what the police told you."

He folded her arms and gave a hard sigh. "It's ridiculous. Stupid people have the right to be stupid, and hard-working people have to shut up and let them."

Fortunately, the shitkickers in the lifted black pickup didn't start shit. They fired up their loud growling engine and drove off, trailing their equally loud and obnoxious music off with them.

CHAPTER FIVE

Lake Forest

I had been up since four thirty a.m. when Avicii's "Wake Me Up" blared out of my iPhone.

My hand reached out of the covers and slapped on anything until the music stopped. When I opened my eyes, the bedroom was already lit up. And Rachel stood by my side of the bed in her sports bra, yoga pants, and Nike running shoes.

"Come on, slowpoke!"

I fumbled out of bed and pulled on my black jogging shorts. I hated wearing shorts, partly because I had been traumatized by those embarrassingly short shorts I wore in PE at El Toro High School in the eighties and partly because I felt uncomfortable about my legs and everything else about me. Somehow, I felt more comfortable in front of Rachel. I threw on a Wayne Morgan t-shirt I had relegated to the junk clothes pile since he got traded from the Angels. Then, I slipped on some low-rise socks and my Nike running shoes.

We ran along a trail that went behind her housing complex and up and down the foothills. The first time I ran, I slogged far behind Rachel. I feared I would die on the first hill. Now, I could keep up with her. Barely.

When we got home, she made us soy protein shakes with her Vitamix. It was supposed to be vanilla flavor, but it had the chalky taste of a barium milkshake I once had for an upper GI. I had to admit that it woke me up better than the double-shot espressos I used to have.

Rachel and I took turns with the shower. She put on her hospital scrubs. I shaved and put on my slacks and dress shirt and tie. By the time we were finished, David and Moshe were up.

"Boker tov, Ima," they chimed to Rachel.

David and Moshe were born in the United States after Rachel and her ex came here, but they spoke Hebrew at home. I learned Hebrew when I was studying for my bar mitzvah, but I forgot most of it. I still knew parts of the alphabet and "Ayfo hashayrutim," which would be useful if I ever visited Israel.

"Good morning, Dr. Glass," they said to me.

"Good morning." I gave her kids a big smile. They smiled back.

David and Moshe didn't know what to call me. They couldn't call me "Dad" because I wasn't their dad. "Oliver" was too informal, and Rachel thought it was disrespectful for children to call adults by their first names. "Dr. Glass" was too formal, but there was nothing else they could call me. And Rachel and I hadn't been together long enough for her children to see me as something other than a doctor.

She gave David and Moshe a bunch of instructions in Hebrew. Rachel promised to help me brush up on my Hebrew, but she hadn't gotten around to it. I doubted that she ever would teach me. She usually spoke Hebrew to her children when she had something she didn't want me to hear.

"Kayn, Ima," they dutifully agreed.

When Muriel and Dylan were that age, they instantly agreed with anything Teresa and I told them. Dylan had a habit of agreeing with us and then going ahead and doing what he wanted. I still thought he was a good kid. What happened? Was it because of the divorce? And why didn't I know what was going on with him?

The kids slipped on their backpacks. Rachel grabbed her purse. I slipped my iPhone in my pocket and picked up my briefcase. We all headed out the front door, and I walked with them to her car. Rachel had a big SUV, a four-year-old GMC Yukon that used to belong to her ex. She never could fit it in her garage, so she parked it outside. She was kind enough to let me put my new Lexus SUV in the garage.

"David and Moshe have practice today at four," she said, "And I'm on call late today. Do you think you can take them?"

"Sure. My last appointment is at two thirty."

She pressed the button on her remote. The doors of her SUV clicked open. "See you later."

I gave her a hug and a kiss. "See you."

I knelt and hugged her kids. They felt comfortable with me doing that.

• • •

My office was just a few minutes' drive from the house. The landlord just upgraded the paint and carpeting so the building didn't look so dated. My waiting room still had the same corduroy sofa and coffee table I bought 13 years ago. My patients didn't mind. They probably felt old furniture meant I wasn't overcharging them.

"Good morning, doctor." Alison had been my receptionist since I opened the office. "Your nine o'clock, Mr. Garcia, said that he'll be a few minutes late. Mrs. Chen asked if she could reschedule for four today."

"I have another commitment." Since I started dating Rachel, I had gotten better about not letting work interfere with home. "Do we have any openings tomorrow morning?"

"The ten thirty cancelled. I can call Mrs. Chen and see if we can fit her in."

"Sounds good. Thank you, Alison."

I stepped away from her desk.

"Oh, and Dr. Glass?"

I stopped. She gestured towards my office.

"You got a call from your ex. It sounds urgent. I forwarded her call to your voicemail."

"Thanks."

• • •

I didn't rush to the office because I didn't want to alarm my staff. But my heart pounded with every step I took. The past few years, the only time I would hear from Teresa was if something terrible happened, like when she and Steven kicked Dylan out of the house. Otherwise, I wouldn't hear from her. Or would want to.

As I stepped into the office, the red message light was blinking on my phone. I quietly closed the door behind me, set down my briefcase, and lowered myself into my desk chair. I took a deep breath and pressed the Message button.

"You have one new message. First message."

Then Teresa's voice blared out the speaker. She did sound upset.

"Listen, Oliver. I don't know what you heard or saw, but it isn't true! Believe me, it isn't true!"

The calm automated voice came back.

"End of message. To delete this message, press…"

I punched the seven button hard. My shoulders trembled as I exhaled.

CHAPTER SIX

Reseda

The rest of the morning was pretty uneventful. We got a new shipment of Easter chocolates because Easter ended. For the start of baseball season, we got a shipment of Wiffle balls and oversized plastic bats for the toy aisle, baseball night lights where the red paint wasn't exactly painted on the stitches, and blue caps that were supposed to look like Dodger caps, except the L and A were screen-printed side-by-side. I stocked those next to the real Angels caps with the real Angels logo because nobody around here likes the Angels.

I also had shopping cart duty. I went out to the parking lot to gather our carts and made sure I didn't accidentally get the carts from the supermarket next door. The worst part was when someone stuck a cart between two parked cars. I had to be careful not to scratch the cars as I pulled out the cart, even if the car had faded paint, half the rear panel scraped off, a missing front bumper, and bungee cords to keep the trunk closed. Those were the people who complained the loudest if they got a new scratch on their precious ride. I then had to insert the carts, one into the other, into a long line and push them to the front of the store. And I had to make sure I didn't go too slowly and hold up waiting cars. Or have the carts veer into the back of a parked car because a cart had a stuck wheel. It was hard, annoying work, and I was glad to step back into the cool, air-conditioned store.

"Do I really have to piss in a cup?"

I turned to my side. Sitting on the bench just inside the front entrance was this young woman. I looked at her. She seemed annoyed.

"I said, do I really have to piss in a cup?"

"What do you mean?" I said.

"Oh." She looked away for a moment. She then looked at me again. If she was embarrassed, she didn't show it. "I mean, do you have to take a drug test to get this job?"

She pushed her brownish blond hair back over her shoulder. She wore a short blue dress. It seemed a little baggy, drooping at her shoulders with folds of fabric hanging on her chest and sides. It seemed a size or two too big for her. She had nice legs, though. I'm not supposed to pay too much attention to how women looked when I'm working, but she had these deep-set pale blue eyes.

I had to ignore them and answer her. "No. At least I didn't have to take a drug test."

And that was a big relief to me when I applied. I didn't see the "This is a drug-free workplace" sign until after I turned in my application. When I saw it, I was sure I was fucked. I hadn't taken drugs since I got to Reseda, but I hadn't been here long enough for the drugs I already took to get out of my system. My friends used special mouthwashes and drinks so they could turn out clean on their drug tests, but those were $45. I heard apple cider vinegar worked too, but I didn't have the money for that either. Fortunately, Quang hired me anyway. I didn't have to piss in a cup.

Quang was heading towards this woman. I knew it was time for me to get back to work.

"I gotta go," I told her. "Good luck."

She nodded but didn't smile.

I headed towards the toy aisle. It was a mess. A bunch of kids must have run wild there while I got the carts. I glanced back to the front of the store. The woman stood up and shook Quang's hand. The dress was too big on her. It slid down as she stood up, hiding the shape of her body. She had nice legs, though.

I went back to picking up the toys.

· · ·

"Excuse me, young man?"

I stood up and turned to Mrs. Cimino.

"Do you know where I can find facial tissue?"

"It's on aisle three. We just moved it." I said, "I'll show you."

I walked to the aisle with Mrs. Cimino following right behind me. When we got to the shelf with the neatly stacked no-name facial tissue, I picked up a light blue box and handed it to her. It wasn't just because I wanted to be a gentleman. I didn't want to spend another ten minutes redoing the display.

"Thank you, Dylan."

"You're welcome, ma'am."

She smiled. "I thought about our talk the other day, Dylan, and I'd like to give you something. Something I feel you need."

She tucked the box of facial tissues under her arm and reached into her purse.

"This saved my life." She pulled out a paperback book and placed it in my hands. "Have you read this?"

I glanced at the cover.

"No. I haven't."

"You should." She smiled.

I stared at the cover again. *Face Time with Jesus* by Dr. Steven Dimity, with my stepdad with his perfect hair and self-satisfied smile staring back at me.

CHAPTER SEVEN

Lake Forest

Getting David and Moshe to Little League practice required coordination that would challenge the most adept hospital scheduler. They played in different divisions. David was moved up to AAA this season while the coaches recommended that Moshe play another season of Single A. David was the better athlete of the two and enthusiastic about going to every practice and game. Rachel could punish him by threatening to take away practice time. Moshe didn't seem that interested in sports.

They reminded me of Muriel and Dylan. Muriel threw herself into every activity we signed her up for, whether it was softball, choir, or ballet. We tried lots of things with Dylan from sports to Scouts. He'd stick with them for a while and then give up. Except Rachel wouldn't let Moshe give up on anything. The parenting books Teresa and I read when our kids were young said that it was wrong to keep kids in things they didn't like. With the way things turned out with Dylan, maybe they were wrong, and Rachel was right.

Still, it was difficult to get both of her kids to practice. David's practice was at Heroes Park at Jeronimo and Los Alisos, and Moshe's was in Foothill Ranch, 15 minutes away. I dropped David off first. His manager, Coach Hoyt, offered to watch him after practice if I was late after picking up Moshe. Then I drove Moshe to his practice. I knew he would be late, but Moshe didn't seem to mind. Especially since his coach was usually late too.

We stopped at the signal at El Toro and Jeronimo. On the corner stood a man in an Army jacket and faded jeans. Next to him was a shopping cart filled with stuffed black trash bags and a rolled up sleeping bag. He held up a cardboard sign. "Homeless Vet. Iraq War. Married, Two Kids. Anything Helps. God Bless."

"Dr. Glass," Moshe asked, "Why do they do that?"

"Some people are unlucky, I guess."

The signal turned green. I drove past the man.

• • •

"C'mon, Mo. Nice even swing."

The coach stood in the middle of the infield behind an L screen. He tossed an easy pitch towards Moshe. He swung too early and too low. The ball bounced against the backstop.

"C'mon, Mo. You can do it!"

The coach tossed another easy pitch. Moshe swung again. This time, the metal bat made a muted ping as it brushed the underside of the ball. It flew off foul and rolled to the edge of the backstop.

"That's better, Mo. Keeping working on it." He turned to the dugout. "Batter up!"

Moshe tucked his bat under his arm. He peeled off his batting gloves as he walked towards the dugout.

"Hi-i-i!"

I only knew her as "Jimmy's mom." Her clinically obese body was squeezed into a black t-shirt with "Baseball Mom" in glitter and the "o" in "Mom" in the shape of a heart with baseball stitches on it. Her baggy denim shorts bared her fleshy and spray-tanned thighs. She was the loudest of the moms on the bleachers.

"I never see you at practice." She spoke with a honey-and-nicotine drawl. "Which one is yours?"

I glanced toward Moshe as he made a leisurely jog towards the outfield.

"Oh! You're Mo's dad!" She used the nickname his coach gave him.

I didn't know how to answer her. Rachel and I chose not to talk about our relationship. Most of these women go to the same church. We weren't sure how well our housing situation and personal arrangements would go over with them.

31

But Jimmy's mom didn't give me the chance to answer. "Your wife usually takes him, right?"

Again, I didn't know how to answer. And again, she didn't give me a chance to answer.

She leaned in close and lightly touched my arm. She spoke softly, well, softly compared to her usual booming voice.

"Now, your wife, she's Mexican, right?"

"Uh..." My voice tensed. "No. She's Israeli."

Her voice boomed again. "Oh, bless my stars! I get so confused. Everything is so diverse and politically correct nowadays, it's hard to keep up."

I decided that I shouldn't correct her about anything else she said, especially that Rachel wasn't was my wife, and we weren't living together under the bonds of holy matrimony.

PING!

"That's it! That's it!" The coach watched the ball jet into the outfield towards Moshe. He ran towards it but stopped when he got close to it. He let it go right past him.

"You got to go for those, Mo!"

Moshe said nothing.

Jimmy's mom patted me on the shoulder. "He's just learning."

I could tell she mastered the art of the kind insult, especially when she followed up by looking towards the stands.

"Caren!" She bellowed at a peroxide blond in too short shorts climbing onto the bleachers. "When did you get here?"

She turned towards the bleachers, but she stopped when she remembered her manners. She turned and gave me a fingertip wave.

"Nice to meet you, um..."

"Ollie." I figured it would better not to mention I was a doctor. Or have a Jewish last name. Even "Oliver" seemed out of place here.

"Well, see you around, Ollie."

Freed of her obligation to me, she waddled back to the bleachers, arms waving at Caren, and no doubt filled with enough gossip about me to satisfy the other mothers.

I knew how the game worked. I spent enough time around bleachers in Muriel's leagues and Dylan's season in Little League.

And nobody played the game better than Teresa.

There were many long drives after softball games when she would give me the tabloid-style rundown of who was sleeping with whom, whose kids were caught smoking pot, and whose house sheriff's deputies pulled up to because an argument went out of control. I just kept my eyes on the road and said nothing. That was because I learned things too. When we men hung around the outfield fence, we'd also gossip. That's how I learned things about Muriel that I wished she would have told me herself. Things I should have told Teresa but didn't.

•   •   •

"One, two, three, Lugnuts!"

Moshe raised his hand high with his other teammates. He cheered with enthusiasm, probably because practice was over.

I waited by the opening of the dugout as he put away his glove and unclipped his bat bag from the chain-link fence along the back of the dugout. He emerged from the field with his bag over his shoulder, head slightly down, the bill of his cap concealing his face.

I patted him on the shoulder. "Let's go get your brother."

He said nothing. He didn't say a word as we walked to the car. I tapped the remote to unlock. I opened the lift gate and put in his bat bag. Moshe opened the rear passenger-side door.

"Do I still have to use a booster seat?" he grumbled.

"You know what your mom said."

He climbed up on the seat and shut the door. I closed the lift gate and got into the car.

"Did you put on your seat belt, Moshe?"

"Yeah."

I put on mine and pressed the Start button. I kept my foot on the brake as I shifted into reverse. The backup camera showed Jimmy's mom, her friends, and their kids laughing and chatting as they ambled from one side of the screen to the other. When they were safely out of the way, I slowly let off the brake and pulled out of the parking space.

Moshe's distraught voice floated from the back. "I don't think they like me."

"What makes you say that?" I shifted into drive.

"They always talk to each other. They never talk to me."

"Do they say anything worth hearing?"

Silence. Then, "I dunno. I just don't like to be left out, you know."

I knew. There were so many stories I could tell him about how I felt when I was growing up. Stories that might help him. But he was too young to hear them. I didn't tell them to Dylan when he was younger. I should have when I had the chance.

"Dr. Glass?"

"Yes?"

"Why do I have to call you Dr. Glass?"

"Because that's my name."

"But it makes me feel like I'm going to the doctor."

I smiled until Moshe asked me his next question.

"Are you and Mom ever gonna get married?"

"Well...I suppose...You know, your mom and I...well, we've been dating for a short time...and..."

"You can leave anytime."

Silence filled the car. I could promise that I would never leave with the hope it was true. But it wasn't true when my dad said it to me. Or when Teresa said it to our kids. How do you tell an eight-year-old that love is temporary, even under the best of circumstances? My mom loved me, but her love was temporary too. It ended when her life ended. All that was left of her was silence, like the silence that filled the car.

I cleared my throat. "You want to listen to the Angels game? It's about to start."

"Can I listen to Radio Disney instead?"

"Sure, Moshe."

The silence was broken by the cheerful bounce of an Ariana Grande song.

• • •

We arrived at Heroes Park. A long driveway wound around the baseball fields with parking spaces along the sides. It was nearly hopeless to find a parking space on game day. If we couldn't find a space in the lot or on the street, we'd park at the Target on the opposite corner and hope we didn't get towed.

On practice days, the lot was nearly empty since most parents dropped off their kids. We had to go to the AAA Field, which was at the end of the driveway. I drove slowly because of the speed bumps. Even at slow speeds, each bump jostled the entire SUV. At the end of the driveway was a black lifted pickup truck.

As soon as I opened the car door, I heard Coach Hoyt's growl.

"C'mon, boys! Let's dig, dig, dig!"

I helped Moshe get out of the booster seat, and we made our way to the field.

Heroes Park was essentially a bowl, which is why it always filled up when it rained and would take days to dry out. A concrete path led from the parking lot down to the fields below. I started down the path, but Moshe started scampering down the slopes.

"Slow down there, Moshe," I called to him.

"All right." He continued racing down the slope.

Coach Hoyt stood at home plate smacking balls to the kids on defense. David played second base, his favorite position. Coach Hoyt smacked a ball up the middle. A player, who filled in as a base runner, took off from first. David rushed towards the ball, leaned forward, and extended his glove arm. He stopped the ball and brought the glove towards his chest. He picked up the ball with his right hand, his throwing hand, but froze. The base runner made it to second, and no one on defense was there to cover.

"Alfonso, where are you!" Coach Hoyt's voice rattled through the whole bowl.

The shortstop muttered something inaudible.

"You're supposed to cover second!"

Alfonso's shoulders slumped.

Coach Hoyt kept up the loud growl. "Let's try that again! Francisco, back to first!"

Another coach tossed Coach Hoyt a ball. He caught it with one hand and smacked it again. This time, the play seemed to be executed perfectly. David made the stop, Alfonso covered second, and with a quick throw from David, Francisco was out. Francisco, still running, turned in front of second.

"Francisco!"

He froze at Coach Hoyt's bellow.

"You were supposed to slide!"

Francisco said, "But coach, I was out..."

"You slide at every play! The fielder could have dropped the ball. Let's do it again!"

The players reset and ran the play again. I could see why Coach Hoyt was one of the league's best coaches. His team won division last year, and he coached his older son's All-Star Team. But as Moshe stood stiffly by my side, I knew there was no way he could play for someone like Coach Hoyt.

• • •

I wanted to play baseball so badly as a kid. I grew up listening to Angels games on KMPC radio and rooted for Nolan Ryan, Frank Tanana, Rod Carew, Bobby Grich, Don Baylor, and Lyman Bostock. It was a shame what happened to him.

Dad bought me all the gear: a bat, a glove, cleats, and a batting helmet. Mom signed me up for Little League. Grandma Dinah protested. She didn't like that they played games on Saturday, which was Shabbat. Even after Mom told her about Hank Greenberg and Sandy Koufax, she still wasn't convinced. "They aren't real Jews," Grandma Dinah grumbled. The fact they wouldn't play on Yom Kippur, even during a pennant race or the World Series, didn't change her mind. She didn't go to any of my games. Neither did Dad. He wanted to go, but he either had to work, or he was too sick or tired to go.

He always seemed to be tired. "Your dad had a long week," Mom would say. I knew he put in long hours as a surgeon. But every time I saw him, he was lying on the sofa. And when he wasn't there, he seemed to shuffle through the house, mumbling to himself. He seemed to be especially tired after one of his patients died on the operating table.

I loved playing baseball. I wasn't the best player, but I worked hard. My AAA coach, Coach Danny, said I was the most dedicated player on the team. We won the division championship that year. I didn't make the All-Star Team, but I didn't mind. The smile Dad gave me when he held my trophy was the happiest moment of my life.

"I wish you could have seen me play, Dad."

He put the trophy down on the floor next to the old leather sofa and put his hand on top of my dirt-and-sweat stained baseball cap.

"I wish I could have too."

"Do you think we can go to an Angels game sometime?"

"Sometime." He nodded and leaned back on the sofa. "Dad's tired right now. Goodbye."

When Dad said "goodbye," it unnerved me. He had a weird way of saying it, as if he were saying it for the last time. "Goodbye" made Mom turn away and cover her face.

He died a month later.

When we moved to Lake Forest, Mom thought about signing me up for the Little League there. By then, I had started studying for my bar mitzvah. Plus, Grandma Dinah imposed herself more in our lives since Dad—her son—had died. She never allowed us to violate Shabbat ever again.

I still loved baseball. But between Dad's death and Grandma Dinah's demands, I didn't have the heart to play it anymore.

•   •   •

"Your son's a good player, a smart player." Coach Hoyt kept his grumble even as we talked casually.

"Thanks." I didn't correct him for the same reasons I didn't correct Jimmy's mom.

I followed him up the walkway. He carried a five-gallon painter's bucket full of baseballs in one hand and a clutch of bats in the other with the barrels resting on his shoulders. One of his massive biceps had a Hieronymus Bosch-like hellscape surrounding a flaming human skull. His goatee was the color of straw and chewing tobacco with strands of gray. He was not the type of person I hung around with in high school. Yet, I trusted him with David.

"You should put him in travelball this summer. High school coaches won't even look at kids if they haven't played travelball."

"My oldest daughter did that with softball." It cost me a lot, especially since I was also paying her child support.

We reached the parking lot. Coach Hoyt stopped and turned towards me.

"I'm putting together a travel team this summer after All-Stars. You think your son would be interested?"

"I'm sure he would, but we have to talk about it." I knew I had to clear it with Rachel.

He walked to the side of the black lifted pickup truck. He hoisted the bucket of balls and bats into the bed.

"Well, see ya around, uh…"

"Ollie." I smiled.

"Ollie." He reached out his massive hand and give mine a firm shake. He smiled before turning to the truck. He then called out to his son, "C'mon, Hunter."

I knew we had to go too. Moshe remained nearly tethered to me. David was running up and down the slopes with a couple of his teammates.

"C'mon, David," I called.

"Coming!" He waved to his teammates and started heading up the slope toward us.

Moshe's puzzled voice floated towards me. "Ollie?"

I glanced down at him and smiled. "Ollie."

From behind us, the engine of Coach Hoyt's massive truck growled like his voice. Toby Keith blared out his stereo. The huge mud tires of his truck plowed over the speed bumps like beer cans.

That's why I told him my name was "Ollie." Guys like him used to beat the snot out of guys with names like "Oliver." I was beaten up by a couple of them.

CHAPTER EIGHT

Reseda

My stepdad's self-satisfied face stared back at me as I looked at the book. I was at the Carl's Jr. on Sherman Way. I didn't feel right about reading the book at Magdalena's restaurant because she's Jewish. And I couldn't go to the library in case they think I took it from them. Carl's seemed as good a place as any to go. I ordered a small fries and got a cup for water, and they pretty much left me alone. And this one was open 24 hours, so I had some quiet time to sit.

I didn't tell Mrs. Cimino that Dr. Steven Dimity was my stepdad. I'd then have to tell her all sorts of things about him that would make her think less of him, especially when she said his book saved her life. And it was true that I never read his book. With all the times I had to listen to the same bullshit stories, I didn't have to.

But since Mrs. Cimino asked, I had to read it anyway.

My face time with Jesus began in Iraq...

I was ready to put the book down right then. It was a story I knew by heart because I heard it too many times. Still, I had to continue.

I was with the Third Infantry Division heading into Karbala...

And when he was clearing out the neighborhoods, he found himself surrounded by Iraqi troops.

39

As we entered the neighborhoods in the south of town, we ran into heavy resistance from the Iraqi Republican Guard. We thought we found an opening on a side street near the Imam Hussein mosque. Then our sergeant, Antoine, took several rounds in the shoulder. That's when we saw the sniper on the minaret above us. Bullets whizzed around us. Two Republican Guards were in the house across the street. Three more down the block. We were trapped!

I missed some details, but this was basically the story he always told. It was at this point of the story he started talking about his shitty life growing up.

With almost certain death facing me, I thought about my life up to that point. I was always a troubled kid. I grew up tough in a bad part of Cleveland. I was the only white kid in a poor, run-down neighborhood. My dad moved out when I was three. He was arrested for armed robbery a year later. He joined a white supremacist gang in prison and was shanked by a rival gang. Mom did the best she could by working two jobs and collecting food stamps...

I knew he had it tough growing up, but he never told me about his dad being stabbed in prison. And if he had so many problems growing up, why couldn't he be more understanding about mine? I got more frustrated the more I read.

I turned to crime because that was basically what everybody did. I did little things at first. Boosting candy bars at the supermarket. Shortchanging clerks by paying with a dollar bill, and when I got my change, I said I paid with a five. When they wouldn't give me the money, I started crying and throwing a fit until the manager gave me the rest of the money. I had my first sip of alcohol when I was ten and smoked my first joint when I was eleven.

I didn't do most of the shit Steven said he did. I never stole or cheated anyone. Except for money I took from Mom's wallet. But she had so much cash, she never kept track of it. And she spent it on new designer handbags instead of me. I didn't drink or smoke weed until I was thirteen. And it was only because Mom and Dad were breaking up. I had to do something to quiet those hateful thoughts in my mind, which were screaming at the time. Thoughts that caused me to spend too much time around the kitchen knives and wonder which one would be long enough to pierce my heart.

I looked back at Steven's book. I didn't want to read anymore. I already knew the rest of the story. How he was arrested for dealing. How the cop who busted him didn't send him to jail but encouraged him to go to church. Which is the kind of thing that happens to white kids when they get busted. And what happened to me. If Steven or I were Black or Hispanic, our stories would have a different ending. We would have definitely gone to jail, if the cop didn't shoot us or beat us to death. It's amazing what cops can get away with and claim someone was "resisting arrest."

But Steven's story turned out better than mine. He managed to stay out of trouble, finish high school, and after 9/11, decided to join the Army. Which is how he wound up fighting for his life in Karbala. And meeting Jesus.

We found ourselves surrounded by Muslim terrorists. Bullets flying inches away from me. My buddies wounded and bleeding. And I gave a silent prayer, "Lord Jesus, if you deliver us from death, I promise that I will devote my life to serving you. I will spread your Holy Gospel and inspire others to live purer and better lives..."

And—spoiler alert—Jesus saves him and his fellow soldiers. As an added bonus, Steven got a Purple Heart and Bronze Star.

The first time Steven told me his story, I really liked it. And him. He wasn't an ordinary doctor like Dad who stuck his finger up old men's assholes and told them to eat right and exercise. Steven was a real war hero! As soon as he told me the story, I wanted to see his medals. Steven explained that he didn't have them with him. He had to put them in storage so his ex-wife wouldn't take them. It didn't matter to me at the time that I didn't see the medals. Just being around a war hero was cool enough.

I stared back at the book. I only had gotten through the first twenty pages. I thought about reading more, but my fry box and water cup were empty. And it was getting late. I tucked the book under my arm and headed out.

• • •

Steven's book was supposed to inspire people, but it just made me feel more depressed. He was a loser who made something of his life, and I was just a loser. No wonder why he kicked me out and Mom called me an "ungrateful little shit." I was worthless to them. And myself.

As I walked along Sherman Way, I kept looking at the cars and wondering which one I could step in front of. I then looked at the two-story building on the corner. It wasn't tall enough, but if I landed the right way, it would do the trick. And it had a flower shop on the first floor in case anyone wanted to make an impromptu memorial. Not that anyone would.

Then I thought about how disappointed Mrs. Cimino would be if I ended myself after reading the book she said had saved her life. So, I kept walking.

I could have cut across the gas station to get to the parking lot behind the theater, but I worried that Carlos might be there. If he saw me, he might have the Explorer towed. Or he might shoot me with that .38 of his. It seemed strange that I was ready to step in front of a speeding car or jump off a two-story building, but I was afraid to get shot. I guess if I was going to die, I wanted to decide when and how. If I couldn't control my life, at least I could control my death.

I stopped in front of the old theater for a moment. I wondered why they hadn't torn it down. What else are they going to do with it? I hated seeing movies anyway. Always the same shit. Superheroes. Sequels. Sequels about superheroes.

There was only one movie I saw that ever moved me. It was a DVD that someone's mother gave me as a birthday gift. It was a Disney cartoon, but it wasn't about princesses, singing lions, or some shit like that. It was about this kid named Jim. No one understood him until he met this guy named Silver. Even though Silver was supposed to be the bad guy, he believed in Jim. He saw the good in him when no one else did. There was some science fiction shit with aliens, and robots, and planets that blow up. And even though it was set in outer space, it had old-style sailing ships. Still, the cartoon moved me. It showed that no matter how big a loser you are or how worthless you feel, you can still be a hero. I wanted to be a hero. I wanted someone to believe in me too.

Why didn't Mrs. Cimino give me a book like that?

I sighed and continued my walk to my Explorer, where I would sleep alone.

CHAPTER NINE

Lake Forest

"Did you see this?"

Rachel handed me the front-page section of the *Orange County Register*. I rarely read that section. By the time I got to read the paper in the evening, the stories were already old news. But something caught Rachel's attention. She tapped a story on the front page with her index finger. I gave it a quick read and set the paper aside.

"I thought you would be more interested."

"It's not my problem." I noticed more bitterness in my voice than I expected.

. . .

"I'd stay away from her. She's just looking for doctor dick."

That was how Dr. Yvette Kim described Teresa Llewelyn. Yvette and I started our internship at UCI Medical Center in Orange in the fall of 1994. We were friends, nothing more. Not that I didn't want something more with her. She was sexy and brilliant. She was also Korean and Catholic, and I knew Grandma Dinah would never accept that. But Yvette had just gotten engaged, so we could safely remain just friends.

Teresa worked as a receptionist. I'd see her every morning as I walked into the hospital. I didn't give her a second glance, but she looked different at that holiday party. She wore a short and form-fitting slip dress with black sequins and spaghetti straps. They were clearly designer, and there was no way Teresa could have afforded that dress on a receptionist's salary.

I headed back to the buffet table. I never felt comfortable at parties, especially work parties. We had to come up with small talk when we already knew more about each other than we probably should. The only thing good about parties was the free food, which was better than the late-night Cup of Noodles I'd have to get from the vending machine after the cafeteria closed.

"You like sushi?"

I looked up. Teresa stood next to me. Her blond-tipped bangs arched over her smooth brow. Her eyes had the right amount of shadow. Her cheeks had the right amount of blush. Gazing into her gray-blue eyes, I forgot about Yvette's warning.

"Yeah." I nodded awkwardly.

"Do you like it with wasabi?"

"Uh, yeah."

I had no idea where she was going with this. Especially when she took a plate, picked up a couple California rolls, and scooped up a large green mound of the spicy stuff.

I stammered, "That's a lot of…"

Before I could answer, she sheared off half of the mound with the top of a California roll. She held it up towards me so she could show me the green pile on top. She then popped it in her mouth. I expected her to gag and beg for a glass of water. But I just watched as her jaw muscles shifted. Her metallic red lips unfurled into a wide smile.

"I like things spicy."

For a moment, I could only stammer. Then I blurted out an introduction.

"I'm…"

"Oliver Glass." She smiled. "I see you every day."

"And…" I realized that although I saw her every day too, I didn't know her name.

She opened her Yves Saint Laurent clutch and took out a piece of paper and a Montblanc pen. Another thing she couldn't afford on a receptionist's salary. She presented me with a name and a phone number.

"Call me." Teresa smiled and walked into the crowd.

• • •

And I did.

I soon found out how Teresa could afford all those expensive things on a receptionist's salary. She lived with her parents, and her parents were loaded. Her father John was the fourth generation of a family that owned large tracts of land throughout Southern California they sold off to build planned communities. Her mother Pauline was an actress who played damsels in distress on TV detective shows. She got paid a lot of money to wear short dresses and get tied up. She gave Teresa her good looks.

I told Teresa that I wanted to keep our relationship low-key. But soon, the whole hospital was abuzz about it. The male doctors would rib me and ask how good she was. And she was good. As she said, she liked things spicy.

Yvette became quiet with me. During our rounds, we wouldn't talk about anything besides medical charts. Afterwards, she kept her distance. Late one evening, we had finished assisting with an ureteroscopy. Yvette and I were washing our hands.

"I think that went well," I said.

"I agree. He'll be better in no time." She finished drying her hands and turned to me. "But you, you're suffering from cranial rectosis."

"What's that supposed to mean?"

"You're a fucking idiot." She crumpled up the paper towels and tossed them hard into the trash.

• • •

"Have you written to Muriel?" Rachel put her arms around my shoulders.

"About to."

I had been staring at the same blank mail message on my MacBook Pro for the past five minutes. I had composed the email in my mind, but I couldn't bring my fingers to the keyboard.

Rachel rested her chin on my shoulder. "What's wrong?"

I exhaled. "What if Dylan doesn't want us to look for him?"

"Don't you want to know if he's OK?"

"Of course, I do. It's just…"

"What?" She turned her head slightly.

I exhaled again. "He needs to grow up. He's 18. He's supposed to take care of himself, right?"

Rachel let go of my shoulders. She moved out from behind the chair and leaned against the desk. I turned towards her. She was still in her shorts and tank top from our evening workout.

"In Israel, kids had to grow up. The way things are there, you had to be tough."

"You're definitely tough."

I spoke with a smile and a low, soft voice that showed her I was interested. She wasn't taking it. She folded her arms.

"But here—I see it all the time with parents in school and sports—they treat their children like they're precious porcelain dolls. From the moment they're born, their parents record everything. They videotape every second of their first years on tapes they can't even play anymore."

I remembered the VHS tapes of Muriel and Dylan as babies I had stashed somewhere in storage.

"And parents do everything for them." Rachel unfolded her arms and started gesturing them in front of me. I knew she was getting upset when she started talking with her hands. "They organize play dates. They put pressure on their schools to put them with the right teachers. They sign up to be playground supervisors, room parents, and PTA officers. Not because they want to help, mind you, but because they can make sure their kids get the best treatment."

Now, I was getting upset. It was as if Rachel had found videotapes of Teresa and me when our kids were young and critiqued everything we did.

"And sports," she sighed angrily, "It's the worst! Parents yell at the umpire if he calls their kids out or gives them a yellow card. They yell at the coaches if they don't give them a good position or enough playing time. They threaten to sue the board if their child isn't picked for the All-Star team!"

Teresa came close to doing that when Muriel was left off the U10 All-Star team. Muriel cried about that for days. Not because she was left off the team. She didn't have a good season, so she understood why she wasn't picked. She cried because she thought we would embarrass her by complaining.

Rachel's hands trembled in front of me. "Parents overprotect their children, and then they can't understand why they're irresponsible and won't act like adults."

"You don't think Teresa and I overprotected our kids, do you?"

Rachel stared at me for a moment.

"If you don't know the answer to that, you probably have."

She stood up and left the study.

. . .

"We found these." The sheriff's deputy opened his hand and revealed several candy bars.

I was 13. My younger brother Maury was 10. He was the one outside the doorway standing next to the deputy. His head was down. His whole body trembled.

Mom and Grandma Dinah stood in the small tile entryway just inside the door. I stood in the living room, close enough to see, but far enough to get away from what I knew would happen.

"We're letting him off with a warning, but I made it clear that if this happens again, there will be consequences." The deputy nudged Maury towards the door. "I release him to you."

Mom nodded. "Thank you, officer."

"This will not happen again," Grandma Dinah interjected angrily.

"I'm sure that it won't." He gave a small smile. "Have a pleasant afternoon."

Mom watched nervously as the deputy turned from the doorway. Maury remained outside, slump-shouldered and trembling.

"Well, go on!" Grandma Dinah screeched at him.

Maury dragged his feet over the threshold and shuffled into the house. Mom closed the door behind him. We all stood frozen and silent. I didn't know what to say to him. If I did, I was afraid to speak up.

Outside, the squad car's engine churned. We stood silently as the grinding of tires over asphalt faded in the distance.

WHACK!

Grandma Dinah smacked Maury so fast, I didn't even see her hand move. Maury bent over, clutching his cheek.

WHACK!

Maury's hands covered his whole face. He sobbed hard.

"Mother Dinah, please!" Mom's soft voice pleaded.

Grandma Dinah kept her trembling hand high above her head. "The boy has to learn, Josephine!"

WHACK!

Maury collapsed face down into a fetal ball on the floor. He clutched his hands over his head, like in an earthquake drill.

I couldn't move or talk. I had been spared from Grandma Dinah's hand, but she had threatened me with it plenty of times. Maury had felt it before. The first time she hit him, I was doing my homework. I heard his cries, but I stuck to my work in fear of what Grandma Dinah would do to me. The second time, I was in choir practice at school. I only knew about it because he refused to let me look at his face. There may have been other times I didn't know about. This was the first time I saw it for myself. The weird thing was that I didn't feel bad for my brother. I just felt grateful that it wasn't me. And ashamed of myself for feeling that way.

Grandma Dinah raised her trembling hand up high again.

"Mother Dinah, stop it!"

Mom's shout made Grandma Dinah's hand freeze in place. Grandma Dinah then turned her fury-filled face towards her.

"Do you want to spoil the boy, Josephine!? Do you want to make him weak and immoral?"

"He's learned his lesson," Mom snarled. She then knelt next to Maury and put an arm around his shoulders. "Let's get you cleaned up."

She helped Maury to his feet. He kept his hands over his face, sobs seeping between his fingers. Mom shot Grandma Dinah a hateful glance as she led Maury down the hallway. Grandma Dinah remained fixed in place as she watched them. I didn't dare move, fearing I'd draw her attention and her wrath. But she knew I was there. She turned slowly towards me with the same hateful glare she gave Maury and Mom.

"If anyone at school asks you about this, tell them it's a lie. And if you say anything." She jutted out her open hand, "You'll get twice what he got."

She turned and walked down the hallway.

I reeled back and collapsed on the sofa. I was finally able to breathe, but my body was still shaking.

CHAPTER TEN

Reseda

I had just put on my apron when Quang walked into the office.

"Dylan, meet Pearl. She is our new cashier."

Her pale blue eyes stared at me. She was about as tall as me, but I wasn't very tall myself.

I reached out my hand. "Nice to meet you."

She gave me a brief smile and a firm handshake. I gave her a quick look. She wore a short paisley dress with long sleeves. It was a size too large. She had on her green apron, and it seemed too loose as well.

Quang stepped between us. "I want you to give her a tour of the store."

• • •

I took Pearl up and down each aisle. Past the tampons with rough cardboard applicators, cases and cables for long-obsolete smartphones, and candles for the least popular Catholic saints. Pearl didn't say a word. I didn't either when Kishana took me on a tour my first day.

I then showed her the bathrooms. Usually, the closing crew forgets to clean and stock them. Fortunately, they did the night before. They even remembered to dump the trash cans next to the toilets because we have customers who came from countries with sewage systems that can't handle toilet paper. I showed her the break room with the microwave and refrigerator no one has cleaned in months. I warned her about the coffee. No one had cleaned the coffee maker in months either.

Somehow, Quang and the other coffee lovers who work at the store drank it anyway.

Next stop was the warehouse, and I was instantly pissed. The closing crew had unloaded the truck, but they left the pallets still wrapped in the middle of the floor. I had to unwrap them and put the shit away. I wanted to say "shit," but I never swore at work. Quang frowned on that. But when he talks to himself in Vietnamese, I'm sure half those words are profanity. Even so, I didn't want to swear in front of a woman I just met.

When I had nothing left to show her, I said, "That's the end of the tour. Do you have any questions?"

She stared at me for a moment with those pale, deep-set blue eyes. "If you're homeless, how do you keep your teeth so white?"

I stared back at her for a moment. "What makes you think I'm homeless?"

"Your hair is greasy, your clothes obviously look like they haven't been washed in a month, and your shoes clearly came from a thrift shop."

I didn't know what to make of this woman. I knew plenty of girls back home who talked shit about other's looks, but those girls had the fashions, hairstyles, and manicures to be able to look down on others. But Pearl was talking shit about me in that dumpy, out-of-style, baggy dress of hers.

That dress.

I cleared my throat and deepened my voice to sound like I was in charge.

"I don't know if Quang told you this, but you shouldn't wear loose clothing. It can catch on things. It's a safety hazard."

Then, to make the point, I touched a fold of her sleeve and pulled it out. The fabric felt nice and thick, though. But I then realized that it was a bad idea for a guy to just reach out and touch some woman's clothing. Did I get myself in trouble?

But she pushed back her brownish blond hair and stared at me with those pale blue eyes. She gave a small smile.

"You're not a virgin, are you?"

I let go of that sleeve as if it were poisonous. I went from getting worried to getting pissed. I folded my arms.

"One other thing, don't ask me about my personal life. You wouldn't like the answers."

I turned and headed towards the warehouse door. Pearl didn't say a word as she followed me. I didn't either. I led her back to Quang, who was waiting by the registers. I figured he would train her how to use them. I headed back to the warehouse to put the stock away. The less I saw or heard from Pearl, the better.

.   .   .

Here's the answer I knew Pearl wouldn't like. I wasn't a virgin. And her name was Zoey.

I was 14. Her dad was a big deal city council member who got elected to the US House of Representatives. She made the varsity cheerleader squad as a sophomore, and she was an honor student. She was definitely out of my league.

Gabriel was the only one of my homies who drove at the time. I was hanging out with him and Armando, and then Lysander called us and said Zoey was throwing a party at her house. He said her folks were out of town again, and he could get us in. I was down.

Lysander told us we should put on something nice. I had my black dress shirt and slacks from my middle school promotion, and they still fit well. Dad bought me a pair of black dress shoes for Grandma Josephine's funeral. They were a little tight, but a couple bong rips made the discomfort go away.

Zoey's parents had the nicest house I'd ever seen. It even made Armando's look small. We pulled up on a long gray stone driveway. There were pillars in front of the house and large mahogany doors with etched and frosted glass. When we stepped in, the great room seemed to go on forever. Crystal chandeliers hung from the ceiling. And everything was white. White walls, white marble floors, white rugs, white furniture. I was afraid to touch anything.

Lysander patted Armando and me on the shoulders. "Told you this was awesome."

And overwhelming. It seemed every popular person in school was there. And everyone had a drink in their hand. I figured they were blazing in the back. I drifted alone through the crowd. All those people talking and laughing and drinking around me, and I felt like I wasn't there. Like a ghost walking through a wall of people.

"Hey."

Zoey was, in a word, stunning. Perfectly shiny and perfectly straight blond hair. Her makeup was on point with smoky gray eye shadow. Her cream-colored dress was super short, super tight, and super low cut and showed the most amazing cleavage and legs I had ever seen.

She also had a serious expression.

I expected her to throw out my homies and me right then and there. I knew I didn't belong there. So, getting tossed out wouldn't upset me that much, except I'd miss out on what was certainly primo kush.

Then her shiny red lips parted. "My whiskey bottle's too full. I need someone to help me empty it."

I was more into weed and bars than alcohol. But who would pass up a chance to hang out with someone who drank whiskey? Especially a hot-looking girl like Zoey.

I followed her into what looked like a home office. One wall was lined with mahogany bookcases filled with books. Another was filled with plaques and pictures of her father shaking hands with various politicians. The room had its own fireplace, which was lit even though it was a warm day. Over the fireplace was a gun rack with several rifles and shotguns. One looked like an assault rifle.

Zoey opened a cabinet between the bookcases. She took out two cut crystal glasses and set them on a low mahogany table next to a brown leather sofa. She opened another door and pulled out what looked like an ice bucket. But what she pulled out with the tongs didn't look like ice. They looked like gray, cube-shaped rocks.

"Ever seen whiskey stones before?"

I was too taken in by her beauty to answer.

I kept my eyes on her as she took out the whiskey bottle. It was definitely top-shelf stuff. She poured a shot in each of our glasses. She then took my hand and led me to the sofa. Her hand felt soft and warm in mine.

She smiled and took a sip. I smiled back and took a sip as well.

"This is good," I said. "Must be expensive too. Won't your dad be pissed?"

"He won't notice. He's in Washington. They're trying to repeal Obamacare again." She took another sip. "He calls President Obama the n word."

"Really?" I took another sip.

"In private, of course. Never in public. I don't know why everyone thinks politicians are so great. They're just middle school kids in suits."

She downed the rest of her drink. I downed the rest of mine.

She held up the bottle. "Want more?"

I nodded. She poured twice as much in my glass. She poured even more in hers.

"You're different from what they say you are at school." She took a long sip.

"What do they say?"

"You're a downer and a loser. But you're actually pretty cool."

"Thanks." I took a long sip.

"In fact." She flipped back her long blond hair. "I kinda like you."

And after a couple more glasses, she liked me so much that she took me to her bedroom. She flung the Disney stuffed animals off her bed and threw me on her *Tangled* comforter. Then we got tangled in each other. I pulled up her dress and saw she went commando. I fingered her while she unbuttoned my slacks.

I brought a condom with me. I wasn't stupid. I even paid attention in sex ed and tried not to giggle when the teacher put a condom on a banana. It was a different story when I was knee-deep in it, and drunk, and I was struggling to tear open the package and figure out which end goes first on while trying not to cum on Rapunzel's face.

"Don't worry about it," she puffed between breaths. "I can't get pregnant now. I just had my period."

And she was wrong.

We didn't know right away. We had been going out for a month when she noticed she didn't get her period. And a few weeks later, she started getting sick in the morning. She didn't tell her parents, but we knew she would have to at some point.

In history class the next day, we watched a video of the 9/11 terrorist attacks. It showed people jumping off the World Trade Center. They decided they wouldn't wait to burn to death or be crushed by the falling towers. They would take charge. Couples even held hands as they jumped.

It sounds sick now, but I thought how cool that would be. I could enjoy those last few moments while free falling through the sky. Air rushing by me. Perhaps that would be the way Zoey and I would go. We'd have to go to LA for the really tall buildings, but there were some in Irvine that were tall enough. She wouldn't have to face her parents, and I wouldn't have to face mine.

But Zoey had a crazier idea.

After that history class, she pulled me aside and drew me close. "Let's run away together. We can have this child. We'll raise this child together!"

"How?" I gasped.

"I have money. I have an uncle in LA. We can stay with him, finish high school, and get jobs. We'll be a family! It'll be so cool!"

"We don't know how to raise a child!"

"We'll figure it out!" She pulled me close and kissed me. Her normally cool face lit up with excitement. "I'm so lucky I met you!"

She held me close. A hug I thought would last forever.

But the next day, she didn't show up for school. Then the next. And I didn't hear from her during the weekend. I thought about calling her. But if she were planning something, I didn't want to tip her off to her family. So, I waited. Mom and Steven didn't know how nervous I was, but they were too busy planning some megachurch event in Orlando. I thought about calling Dad. But what if he didn't accept *me* being a dad?

Monday came. When I finally saw Zoey, she looked strange. She wore a high collared white and lace dress blouse with dark slacks. And she had this serene look on her face. She walked directly to me and put her hand on my shoulder. When she spoke, her voice was flat and robotic.

"You don't have to worry about it anymore. It has been taken care of."

"What?"

"It has been taken care of."

"You mean, you had an…"

"It has been taken care of." She then looked at me with dead eyes. "And my father says if you ever speak a word of this or come near me again, he will have you killed. He knows people who can do it and not leave a trace."

She turned and walked away. Although I'd see her around school, I never spoke to her or about her ever again.

I saw her father on TV just before I was kicked out. He was telling Congress to defund Planned Parenthood because they perform abortions. I guess he believes in the sanctity of life unless you're rich and have something to hide.

I can't fault Zoey for getting an abortion, though. She would have had to carry that baby and get shit for being a teen mom. She'd be kicked out of the cheerleading squad and lose her popularity. And God knows what her parents would have done to her. And who knows if her uncle would have really taken us in. But I wished we kept the baby. I would have liked to have known him or her. I would've loved that child. And that child would've loved me. And I would've had someone to care about. I would finally have a reason to live.

CHAPTER ELEVEN

Lake Forest

"Mr. Stromberg, didn't we talk about why you shouldn't depend on TV ads for medical advice?"

"But it said to find out from your doctor if this medicine is right for you!"

I gave a smile I hoped wasn't condescending.

"That medication isn't for your condition, Mr. Stromberg." I took out my prescription pad. "Let me give you a prescription for something else. This is for a stronger anti-inflammatory medicine. It's available in generic and is covered by Medicare."

"But people who use that medicine seem so happy. They dance, and scuba dive, and run through the sprinklers with their grandchildren..."

"And did you listen to the long list of side effects?" I tore off the prescription and handed it to him. "Give this a try. This should reduce the pain and increase your mobility. And if you don't see any improvement, come back and see me."

· · ·

I led Mr. Stromberg to the waiting room. He shook my hand. "Thank you, Dr. Glass. Goodbye."

I cringed, but I smiled and said, "Have a pleasant day."

As he went out the front door, I looked over the waiting room. It was empty. I walked to Alison, who was organizing some charts at her desk.

"Don't I have a one thirty?"

"She cancelled." She looked up from the charts. "I got a call from Ms. Martin's pharmacy. She wants a refill for Percocet."

"We don't give refills for that. Have her come in and see me. If she's in that much pain, I need to take a look."

"She told the pharmacist she needs the refill now."

"Then, she should come in right away. She can even come in now, if she likes."

"I'll give her a call."

I gently tapped the counter. "I better grab something to eat."

. . .

Before Rachel, grabbing something to eat meant running to a nearby fast-food place. Now, lunch was a sandwich on cracked wheat berry bread, romaine lettuce, avocado, heirloom tomatoes, cucumbers, and roasted pepper hummus. It was delicious, but I would kill for some bacon. I was never good about keeping kosher, even as a kid. When Grandma Dinah wasn't around, Mom would take Maury and me out for cheeseburgers.

I was glad to give up bacon and cheeseburgers to have the life I've had since I started dating Rachel.

Before that, I was a mess. I was adrift for years after Mom's death and the divorce. On top of that, my practice was in decline. I had to lay off one of my nurses. Other doctors I knew suggested that I move my practice to Irvine. "Patients don't want to come to some dumpy building in Lake Forest when there are new medical offices in Irvine. They have richer patients there too." I couldn't afford rent on a new place, especially when I had to pay child support, Muriel's softball, and Dylan's military school. Eventually, I had to drop the military school because I couldn't afford it, and it didn't seem to do anything for him anyway. I even had to sell my condo and lease an apartment because I risked foreclosure.

Then there were the meds.

I started with the samples. Anti-depressants mostly. They helped for a while, but then a few pills weren't enough. I started self-prescribing. It wasn't illegal if it wasn't a controlled substance, but I knew it wasn't right. But after a while, the medications I could self-prescribe weren't enough. I had a few friends who could. Yvette was one of them. She was getting prescriptions from another doctor for Ritalin to keep her focused during long shifts at the hospital. I learned there was a group of doctors who were prescribing controlled medications to each other. Some even sold them on the street. I knew I risked going to jail and losing my license by doing this, but I had to do something to stop those horrible voices in my head.

• • •

"Yitgadal v'yitkadash sh'may raboh…"

The gray men in the black suits didn't speak the crisp modern Hebrew that Rachel spoke. They said *oh* instead of *ah*, *oy* instead of *ai*, and occasionally used an *s* instead of a *t*. Their prayers sounded like murmured complaints.

"Ul'asokoh yot'hon l'khayay olmo…"

I stood in my own black suit, close to Mom. On the other side of her, Maury shifted uncomfortably. A hard grasp on the shoulder from Grandma Dinah got him to stand still.

In front of us was the mound of dirt where Dad was buried.

"Ba'agolo u'vizman kori, v'im'ru omayn."

• • •

"Your son was a fine doctor…"

"Josephine, we are so sorry for your loss…"

"I remember him in high school. He was my most conscientious student…"

I just sat frozen, surrounded by voices. And food. So much food. Bagels, lox, and cream cheese. Fruit trays with immaculately cut pieces of pineapples, cantaloupe, and strawberries. A dessert table with every pastry imaginable. A punchbowl with some reddish sweet drink with floating orange slices and some purplish sweet kosher wine for the adults. There is always food around when you're a Jew. We Jews had to have food for every occasion, even this one.

I couldn't eat. I sat in a chair in the corner of the reception hall.

"He looks just his father…"

"I hope those boys will be OK…"

"It's a shame they will grow up without their father in their lives…"

They talked about me, but not to me. It was like I wasn't there. I was as absent from that room as Dad was.

"He was gone way too soon…"

"Such a shame. He had so much promise…"

"He had his whole life ahead of him…"

They didn't talk about how Dad died. I didn't dare say a word, even though I was the first to find him.

·   ·   ·

At first, it seemed like some strange practical joke. His lifeless body hanging from the rafters in the garage between Mom's 1979 Datsun 510 station wagon and his brand-new 1981 Ford Thunderbird with the landau roof and opera window. He wanted a BMW 528i, but Grandma Dinah wouldn't allow it. It seemed strange to me she wouldn't permit German cars, but she found it perfectly acceptable to have one named after a man who published *The Protocols of the Elders of Zion* in his newspaper and received a medal from Nazi Germany.

And it didn't seem possible that Dad would kill himself after buying a shiny new car, regardless of make or model.

"Dad?"

It didn't occur to me he would never answer me again. I kept walking towards him.

"Dad?"

His body swayed slightly from the drafts in the garage. His arms hung limp by his sides. His feet pointed downwards, like on tiptoes. There was a smell, like when I had an accident before I could get to the bathroom. I wanted to touch him to see if he was still alive. But I was too afraid.

On the floor below him was a tipped-over step stool and a piece of paper. The paper had Dad's handwriting, but it looked neater and stronger than usual.

I'm sorry. It's not your fault. I love you all. Goodbye.

The doorknob turned behind me.

"Oliver, have you seen…"

Mom's scream ripped through the garage. It was a sound I haven't stopped hearing for 35 years.

·   ·   ·

"Dr. Glass, Ms. Martin is here."

Startled, I looked around the room.

"Dr. Glass?"

I turned towards the office door. Alison had it partially opened and stuck her head in the opening.

"Ms. Martin has come in, as you requested."

"Good. That's good. Have Joy get her vitals and take her to room one. I'll be right there."

"Yes, doctor." She pulled her head from the doorway and closed the door slightly. "Shall I…"

"That's OK. I'll be right out."

I looked over my desk. My sandwich was only half eaten.

I wished I didn't remember so many things. Life would be easier if I didn't.

CHAPTER TWELVE

Reseda

It took me about two hours to put the stock away and clean up the warehouse. Quang thanked me, but I knew the closing crew was going to catch hell.

As I stepped back into the main part of the store, I glanced at the registers. Pearl was still there with that baggy dress of hers.

I then looked down at myself. If Pearl thought I looked crusty earlier, I sure felt it that moment. But where would I find a shower in Reseda? Was there a YMCA I could go to? There's supposed to be a pool at a park down Reseda Boulevard, but it sounds far away...

"She seems like a nice young woman."

I looked up and saw Mrs. Cimino standing next to me. She was looking at the registers, so I guessed she was talking about Pearl. But "nice" wasn't the word I'd used to describe her.

Mrs. Cimino turned to me and smiled. "So, what do you think of the book?"

"It's good." I nodded hard to convince her. "It's good so far."

"Have you gotten to the second part? That's the part you need to read."

• • •

Jesus said, "For if you forgive others when they sin against you, your heavenly Father will also forgive you. But if you do not forgive others their sins, your Father will not forgive your sins." (Matthew 6:14-15) Why must we forgive others before we can receive God's forgiveness?

Because all of us are broken. All of us are flawed. All of us have sinned against God, each other, and ourselves. Until we see the grace in the brokenness in ourselves and others, we cannot receive God's grace.

As I sat in the back of the Carl's Jr., I took another bite of my Famous Star and puzzled over what Steven had written. It's easy for him to tell people to see the grace in others. Why couldn't he see the grace in me?

Perhaps I didn't have any grace. I didn't have Christ. I didn't have any religion, really. Dad's Jewish, and Mom's Lutheran. Dad once told me that when he and Mom got married, they decided to raise Muriel and me with both religions. We'd have Christmas and Hanukkah. Easter and Passover. We'd have a bar and bat mitzvah and confirmations. But instead of two religions, we wound up with none.

When Steven entered the picture, we became full-on Christians, of course. We joined one of those megachurches near our home. I liked it at first. I liked the singing and worship. I liked how the pastor told us how much Jesus loved us, that he died on the cross for us, and that he would forgive us for our sins.

I made friends there. That's where I met Armando, who was the son of the pastor who did the Spanish-language services.

And when Steven spoke, it was almost like God himself was speaking. I thought Steven was the coolest, most perfect Christian I had ever seen. Well, outside of the whole "You shall not commit adultery" thing.

But the more I knew Steven and other Christians, the less I liked church.

After service, we would go out on the patio to have snacks and hang out. It was called fellowship, but there was nothing fellowship-like about it. Mom would gather with her friends and gossip. Steven and his friends were even worse. There was a pastor at another church whose son died by suicide. Instead of caring about him and his family and praying for them like a Christian should, they'd talk shit about what a big phony and a lousy father this pastor was.

I guess that's what Jesus meant by hypocrites and Pharisees. And after listening to Steven and his friends diss that poor pastor who was grieving for his son, I was so done with church.

But in a way, I still missed church. It was the only thing outside of getting high that silenced the hateful voices in my head.

• • •

I made a point of getting to the gas station early the next morning. I shouldn't care what baggy-dress Pearl thought about my hair. But if she noticed how nasty it looked, I'm sure the other customers did too. And if they started complaining, Quang would fire me.

"You're here early." Reza lowered his Persian-language newspaper.

"I got a lot of washing up to do."

"They have showers at the Rescue Mission. It's at Canby and Parthenia." He pronounced it "Par-tee-nee-ya."

"I'll check them out."

I didn't know how far away Parthenia was, but if it were more than a few minutes' walk from the Explorer and work, forget about taking a shower there.

And when I stepped into the gas station bathroom, I realized I could forget about washing my hair there too. The sink wasn't big enough to put my head under it. Even if I could, I didn't have any shampoo. I had to do something about my hair. It had gotten so dirty, it looked brown instead of the usual blond. So, I cupped my palm under the running water and splashed it over my head. I realized what a big mess I was making.

KNOCK KNOCK KNOCK.

Shit! I had to wash my face and hands as fast as I could. But I had to clean up the water on the sink, floor, and wall.

KNOCK KNOCK KNOCK.

Shit! No time! I grabbed a bunch of paper towels and unlocked the bathroom door.

At the other side was a guy in a business suit and a scrunched-up face. He must have had too many cappuccinos before going on his commute.

I stood up straight. "Watch out for the sink. It sprays."

The guy dashed around me and slammed the bathroom door.

I looked at Reza and mouthed, "I'm sorry."

He waved his hand to say, "It's OK," and he went back to his newspaper.

• • •

Back in the Explorer, I opened the center console and pulled out the wad of bills and change. I had already cashed in my first paycheck at Buck & Awesome. I had to spend some money for food and toothpaste. I flattened out the bills and counted them. I was surprised to find I had over $200. This was more than enough to get gas. If I could get the Explorer to start, I could drive again. I could go to that Rescue Mission and shower. I could even drive back to Orange County and move in with Dad. If he would take me.

A part of me missed Orange County. I missed its wide streets and ocean breezes. The clean shopping centers. Wahoo's. I missed chilling at the beach and Dana Point Harbor. Mostly, I missed having a soft bed and a hot shower. I missed feeling safe. I missed having a home. Living with Mom and Steven didn't feel like home, but at least I had a roof over my head.

Reseda was chill, but the thing I hated about it was being homeless and alone.

• • •

But seeing Magdalena on the way to work lifted my mood. So did the bag of pan dulces and "Have a good day." It was a mood crushed by looking at that lifted pickup truck and hearing their shitkicker music. My mood definitely nosedived when I got to Buck & Awesome. Pearl was by the registers. However, she wore a better fitting maroon short sleeve button-down blouse and a short blue skirt.

I stopped by her. "You're not wearing a loose outfit."

"And you tried to wash your hair."

I looked at her green apron. "But your apron's too loose. I can fix it for you."

She said nothing but pushed back her brownish blond hair. I assumed she meant yes. I stepped behind her, untied her apron strings, and pulled them snug.

When I did, she let out a soft moan.

"That's not too tight, is it?" I said.

"No."

Her voice sounded like—No, we were at work. It couldn't be that. I finished tying the apron strings as quickly as I could.

Then Quang stepped out of the office. "Dylan, I need you to clean the bathrooms. The stupid closing crew forgot again!"

I stepped around Pearl. "Got to go."

I glanced back at her when I went to the office for my apron. Did she smile at me?

• • •

Reza got his payback and then some. The bathrooms were disgusting. In the men's bathroom, someone must have had massive diarrhea. There were shit sprays all inside the bowl, underneath the seat, and some on the floor. He must have drunk the coffee from the break room. And no one emptied the trash can from when I did it at four the day before. It was overflowing. And someone threw a diaper in it. It was filled with baby shit, and it stunk up the whole room.

The woman's bathroom was even more disgusting. Someone must have changed her tampon and didn't flush. The inside of the bowl looked like someone slashed her wrists in it.

I wanted to slash my wrists after Zoey broke up with me. That was the closest I came to ending myself. We were at home. Steven was in his office rehearsing one of his speeches. Mom was on her computer posting more pictures of eagles, sunrises, or some shit like that on her Facebook page. Muriel was in her bedroom studying. And I was in the kitchen staring at the knives. I took out one of the steak knives and put it on my wrist. The edge settled into my skin. Just a quick slice would end my suffering. But it would hurt like a motherfucker. And blood would be gushing before my eyes, and I hated the sight of blood! I washed the knife and put it back in the block.

As I walked past Steven's office, I heard him through the door.

"As it says in Psalm 34, 'The Lord is close to the brokenhearted and saves those who are crushed in spirit. A righteous man may have many troubles, but the Lord delivers him from them all.'"

.   .   .

It took me an hour to clean and disinfect both bathrooms. If I didn't need a shower before, I definitely needed it when I was done. All I could think about after getting out of the bathroom was finding a shower. Maybe Magdalena can let me use—No, she's done more than enough for me. Or maybe I could gas up the Explorer and go to that Rescue Mission. Or go to Dad's.

Then I heard a commotion up at the registers. I sighed. Did Pearl ask somebody one of her obnoxious questions?

But when I stepped closer to the registers, the shouting came from Fatima's register. Most of it came from this big bellowing guy wearing a cheap mesh snapback with "Need Beer" printed on the front. I had seen him before in that lifted pickup truck.

"I'm not givin' my credit card to no fuckin' terrorist!"

"Sir, the card reader is broken." Fatima stayed surprisingly calm for someone who had just been called a terrorist. "As I said, I can swipe your card at the register…"

"And as I said, I'm not givin' my credit card to a fuckin' sand ni…"

That's when Kishana stepped up. "Sir, if that's the way you're going to act…" She too sounded surprisingly calm for someone who was about to hear the worst possible word that could be said about her.

But Quang was far from calm. He rushed in, veins popping. "Get out of the store! Right now!"

I knew that being surrounded by that much melanin was going to make Need Beer lose his shit. I had to rush in. I ran down the aisle at full speed.

But Need Beer had already opened his yellow-toothed redneck mouth. "What the fuck is this place!? Ain't no real fuckin' Americans workin' here!?"

"We're *all* real Americans!" I puffed out my chest. "You either pay her or get out!"

I was proud of myself for not saying "get the fuck out."

Need Beer stepped up to me. He was at least six inches taller and a foot wider than me. His foot-long beard probably weighed ten pounds by itself, and that included the chewing tobacco juice stained in it. But I took up boxing in the military academy. If he were to throw down, I would step up. I wasn't going to let him fuck with my coworkers, especially Fatima.

He sniffed at me. "You smell like shit!"

I couldn't stop myself. "Sure you're not smelling your own breath?"

Need Beer cocked back his fist, but I was ready to swing back if he went first. There was shouting around me. Kishana grabbed my arm.

"Excuse me!"

We all fell silent and turned around. Pearl stood next to Fatima at the register. She held up a black credit card.

"Is this your credit card?"

"Yeah," Need Beer mumbled.

Pearl raised the plastic bag. "Do you still want this merchandise?"

"Yeah."

Pearl swiped the card at the register. We all watched as she rang up the order. The register drawer popped open, and Pearl shut it hard. She tore off the receipt. She handed it, the credit card, and the bag of merchandise to Need Beer with the snarkiest, most hateful sneer I had ever seen.

"Thank you for shopping at Buck & Awesome. Have a pleasant day."

Need Beer grabbed the items from Pearl. He gave her a hateful glare. She gave him a nastier smirk in return.

We all watched as Need Beer left the store. And we all exhaled loudly when the door closed behind him.

Kishana and Quang turned to me. Kishana spoke.

"Dylan, we all appreciate you..."

From the parking lot, the squeal of mud tires and "Sweet Home Alabama."

Pearl and I glanced at each other and cringed.

When Lynyrd Skynyrd finally faded out down Sherman Way, Kishana continued speaking to me.

"But we simply cannot allow you to fight in the store. As an employee, you would make us liable…"

Quang patted her on the shoulder. "It's all right. If anyone's butt needs kicking, I'll do it."

I couldn't imagine Quang taking down Need Beer, but I suspected he could do it.

He looked around the store. A young Hispanic woman with her children in tow pushed her cart towards the registers. I hate to think what Need Beer would have said to them.

Quang nodded and left the register area. Kishana followed him. The woman placed her items on Fatima's belt. Fatima struggled to smile.

"Welcome to Buck & Awesome," Fatima's voice quivered. "How's your day so far?"

I looked at Fatima's hands. They were trembling. She fumbled a can of generic baby formula. Pearl straightened the can and put her hand on top of Fatima's.

"I'll take your register," she whispered to Fatima. She then looked at me.

I nodded. "I'll take Fatima to the break room."

I put my hand on Fatima's shoulder. I know Muslim women aren't supposed to be touched by a man other than their husband. But there was no way she'd make it to the break room without help. Her whole body trembled as she put one unsteady foot in front of the other.

As we went past the register area, Kishana stepped over to us.

"It's all right," she said softly to me. "I'll take her from here."

I waited for Kishana to take hold of Fatima before I let go. I watched them head down the aisle. Fatima started to sob. My heart broke for her, but it then started to heat. If Kishana hadn't had stopped me, I would've fucked up Need Beer for what he did to Fatima. If he ever did that to her again, I would.

I glanced at the registers. The young Hispanic woman dropped some change in the clear plastic box and left with her kids. Pearl started ringing up the next customer, but she looked up for a moment and glanced at me. What was she thinking? It didn't matter. I had work to do.

CHAPTER THIRTEEN

Lake Forest

It was my day to make the rounds at the hospital. I had to check on Mr. Ferrera who was recovering from pneumonia, Ms. Vasquez who had a gall bladder removed, and Mr. McAllister who believed what he saw on a drug ad on TV, tried tango dancing with his wife, and dislocated a disk in his lower back.

As I walked through emergency, I was surprised to see Mr. Marchenko on his way to being discharged. Actually, I was not surprised. Mr. Marchenko was the type of patient who made doctors, hospitals, and drug companies rich. He would come into my office for the slightest complaint or ER if his complaint frightened him enough. That day, he looked especially frightened.

"Are you OK, Mr. Marchenko?"

"I guess."

His hands were still trembling. But at first glance, everything else about him seemed fine. His face and skin were a normal color. He seemed to be breathing normally.

"So, what brought you into ER?"

"I started exercising, just like you said I should." His outfit proved it. He wore a red-and-black tracksuit and a pair of running shoes. They looked brand new.

"Then what happened?"

"I started breathing heavily, and I got dizzy. I thought I was going to die!"

That was exactly the way I felt the first time I ran with Rachel.

"So, what did the doctors say?"

71

"They ran all sorts of tests. They said my heart was fine. I didn't have a heart attack, or stroke, or anything like that."

I smiled. "It was good that you started exercising and sought help when you had conditions that concerned you. I suggest that you start your exercise program gradually. Go with short distances at low intensity and then work up to more strenuous workouts."

"But I've got to get myself in shape! I don't want to wind up like my parents!"

"If you keep taking care of yourself, you can reduce the risk of having the problems your parents had." I patted his shoulder. "Take care of yourself, Mr. Marchenko."

"Thank you, Dr. Glass."

· · ·

The only thing that made the rounds bearable was seeing Rachel. She had just spent twelve hours helping a woman deliver twins. She shuffled down the hall in an exhausted gait. Her curls had tightened up, and some were plastered by sweat to her forehead. Her green scrubs were stained at her armpits.

"Why don't we meet in your office?" I spoke with a smile and a low, soft voice.

· · ·

I had her bent over her desk, her pants at her ankles, while I thrust away behind her. Even alone in her office, we had to keep our moaning to soft gasps. And we had to be quick...

Her phone vibrated on her desk.

"Damn!" I murmured.

She held up her right hand to tell me to be quiet. I froze in half-stroke, my glans still inside her.

She swiped the screen and brought the phone to the side of her face.

"This is Dr. Rosen... Hello, Gwen."

I couldn't believe she could be so professional and polite with my penis still inside her.

"You're sure your water broke?... OK, just go straight to the maternity center and have your husband take care of your paperwork. We'll bring you right in... You're welcome. See you soon."

She tapped the screen to hang up. She then thrust her hips forward to force me out.

"I have to go." She stood up and turned around. "Sorry."

"But..."

She looked down at my still hard and disappointed penis. She sunk to her knees. A few times rolling it around in her mouth and a strategically placed tip of her tongue gave me relief. She swallowed and cleared her throat.

In one efficient movement, she pulled up her panties and pants as she stood up and tied her drawstring. Then, she swiped her phone off her desk and put it in her pocket. She did it all before I even pulled up my pants.

"See you tonight." She kissed my lips.

$\bullet$　　$\bullet$　　$\bullet$

I waited until Rachel was out of her office before I stepped out. As doctors, we learned how to be discreet, especially when there were patients around. Before Rachel had her own office in this wing, we'd use any spare room or out-of-the-way space we could find. We once used a bed in the maternity ward. And the stirrups. Hours later, Rachel delivered a seven-pound four-ounce baby girl in the same bed.

"Sign this."

A death certificate was thrust into my face by Dr. Morelli. He was a short bald man with thick fingers, but the most precise surgeon in the ward. I looked at the certificate on the clipboard and then at him.

"Don't I get to see the body first?"

$\bullet$　　$\bullet$　　$\bullet$

I didn't need to read the death certificate to know how Leo Shelton died. I had been after him for years to do something about his health. I prescribed him medications he didn't take, suggested diets he didn't follow, and recommended exercise programs that he would stay on for a week or two before quitting. "You don't know what a busy, stressful life I lead," he always told me. I knew. I didn't know the details about his personal life, but I could see he had the same harried, anxious feelings I had. The sense of drowning, of not being able to keep up. That his best wasn't good enough, no amount of money would pay his bills, and life was a dark tunnel with no light at the end.

When Dr. Morelli pulled back the sheet, Leo looked as alive as the last time I saw him at my office. I walked around his corpse. There were no incisions. They didn't even shave away the heavy thicket of black hair that covered his massive, distended torso. ER probably determined he was too far gone, or he had already died. I looked at his face. The facial muscles still seemed knotted in a tense grimace. Not even death gave him peace. And he didn't live long. He was only 45, a year younger than me.

"He went into full cardiac arrest. The paramedics did what they could, but the poor son of a bitch was dead before they put him in the ambulance." Dr. Morelli wasn't known for his bedside manner.

"You have his EKG?"

Dr. Morelli pulled out the folded-up printout from behind the death certificate. It corroborated what he said. All flatline.

I looked up at Dr. Morelli. "What did you write down for underlying causes?"

"Advanced atherosclerosis and morbid obesity. That's because I can't write down, 'He ate too many fucking cheeseburgers.'"

I held out my hand and waved my fingers at Dr. Morelli. He handed me the clipboard and the death certificate. I reached into my shirt pocket for a pen.

"If you had put that down, you would have been fairly accurate."

I scribbled my signature and handed the clipboard and EKG back to him. I tucked the pen back in my pocket.

"You saw Dr. Rosen today, didn't ya?"

He smiled. I tensed.

"How do you know?"

He sniffed. "I know."

I exhaled and regretted not washing off.

74

He stared at Leo's corpse. "It's funny."

"What's funny?"

"You, banging an obstetrician. She sees them at the beginning, and you see them at the end."

CHAPTER FOURTEEN

Reseda

My shift ended. I hung up my apron in the office. Fatima and Pearl then came in to hang up theirs.

Pearl turned to me. "I'm walking Fatima to the car."

"I'll come with you." Since I'm off the clock and out of uniform, I could kick Need Beer's ass if he showed up.

Employee parking was in the back. I could tell that Fatima was still shaky from what happened earlier. Pearl supported her as we walked out the back security door to the parking lot. We led her to her car, a black Honda Civic. Fatima seemed to relax. She used the remote to unlock her car.

Pearl let her go. "If you need anything…"

"I'll be fine." Fatima's usual smile returned. "Thank you so much."

"See you tomorrow," Pearl said.

"See you." I added.

Fatima got in her car. "Thank you so much. God bless you both."

She shut the door. Pearl and I stepped aside as Fatima started up her engine. We watched as she backed up and kept her eyes on her as she pulled out of the parking lot. We didn't say a word until she was safely on her way.

Pearl then turned to me and looked me over.

"That redneck asshole was right about one thing," she said. "You stink."

"Guess so." I let out a small smile, knowing that I probably couldn't do anything about it.

"Come with me."

"What?"

"Come with me." She turned and started walking.

"Come where?"

She didn't answer. She pulled her keys out of her purse and pressed the remote. The taillights of a blue Kia Rio blinked. It must have been around ten years old. The paint had faded, and there were scuffs on the rear bumper. But her license plate showed that she got it not too long ago. It was a car somebody didn't want anymore. But Pearl did.

She opened the passenger door.

I stared at her. "Where am I going?"

She walked around to the driver's side and opened her door. "You're going to take a shower."

•　　•　　•

Everything felt strange. The sensation of riding in a car again felt strange. Whizzing through a town where I only knew a few streets felt strange. I had no idea where Pearl was taking me. I assumed she was taking me to her house. But why? We barely knew each other, and half the time she asked me those rude, sort of weird questions about me being homeless. Or a virgin. Still, Pearl seemed like a kind person. The way she helped Fatima when she was all shaken up. The way she would offer to help me.

I thought of all the times back home when we drove past homeless people. People standing at parking lot exits, or huddled in doorways, or pushing shopping carts down busy streets. We acted like they weren't there. Like they were invisible.

I should have been invisible too. But Magdalena offered me free food and kind words every day. Reza let me use his bathroom. Fatima gave me smiles. Quang gave me a job. And none of them had any reason to. Magdalena had recovered from a stroke, Reza risked his job to help me, Fatima was a refugee from war-torn Syria, and Quang came up from nothing to manage a store. Yet they all treated me like I was a human being. Even assholes like Need Beer acted like I took up space.

Reseda was indeed a weird place.

•　　•　　•

Pearl turned into a side street called Amigo Avenue. She then turned into a driveway that led to the front of a house. I was relieved that she wasn't going to leave me in the mountains to die. I hoped she didn't have any shallow graves in the backyard.

Pearl fished her keys out of her purse. When we both got out of the car, she pressed the remote and locked the car with a beep. I followed her to her front door. She put the key in the lock.

I had to ask, "You live here by yourself?"

"With my mom." She turned the key. "She takes her nap around this time, so be quiet."

I wasn't sure what Pearl meant by "quiet," because she tossed her keys on a side table by the door with a loud jangle and clack. I decided not to say a word.

I followed her past what they would consider the great room of the house, the living room and dining room together with a short wall separating the entryway from the dining room. But Pearl's great room was no bigger than a bedroom in Mom and Steven's house. Or a closet in Zoey's.

We went through a door and entered the hall in the back of the house. I followed her to a bathroom.

"The shower here heats faster."

I took my first slow steps into the first real bathroom I had been in for a month. A shower/bathtub, a clean toilet, and a sink. Even the vinyl floor with the fake tile pattern was a welcome relief from gray concrete.

"Leave your clothes on the floor," Pearl said. "I'll wash them."

All I could do is nod. I was too overwhelmed by the comfort and generosity to say, "Thank you."

• • •

When the first streams of warm water hit my skin, I cried.

I didn't realize how filthy I was until the layers of grime washed away from me. I watched the gray swirls dissolve down the drain. A shower was something I didn't think about when I lived at home, except when Mom yelled to hurry because there was a drought. But she had no problem running the sprinklers four times a week so the grass could look like a green carpet.

But I felt different standing in Pearl's shower/bathtub, feeling the water warm my skin, washing all the filth away. I felt like a human being again.

That was until I opened the curtain to get the towel.

Pearl stood right there. I gasped. Pearl had the same expression when she was ringing up an order. Her tone was also matter of fact.

"Were you circumcised for religious or medical reasons?"

I grasped the corner of the curtain and covered the part of me she was asking about.

"I was just picking up your clothes." She held up my boxers and studied both sides. "No skid marks or cum stains. I'm impressed."

She bundled up my clothes and tucked them under her arm. She then plucked the towel from the bar and handed it to me.

"You look like you're shivering."

I was, and not because I turned off the water.

. . .

I kept the towel wrapped tightly around me as I stepped out of the bathroom. If I didn't feel vulnerable before, I did then. Pearl had my clothes. And she saw me without them. I hoped I didn't run into her mother.

I turned the corner where an open door led to a room. Curiosity got the best of me, so I stepped inside. It reminded me of Muriel's room. Lots of sports trophies and plaques. A bookcase filled with books. A desk by the corner window with an old MacBook Pro. And a twin bed that I assumed was Pearl's. Some clothes were folded on the bed. I was relieved there was no BDSM gear or some weird shit like that. I'd hate to think she'd brought me here to be her sex slave.

"You can put those on. We're about the same size."

I stared at Pearl for a moment. Maybe she wouldn't make me be her sex slave, but she was going to dress me in women's clothing.

I picked up the clothes. There was a t-shirt and what looked like men's sweatpants.

"Are these your boyfriend's?"

"Mine. Men's sweatpants have real pockets."

"Oh."

I looked at the clothes. I looked at Pearl. I wasn't sure if she would let me have my privacy, especially when she had already seen everything she could see about me. But I knew the beach trick of slipping my clothes under my beach towel.

Then a voice bellowed down the hall. I assumed it was her mom calling her name, but it sounded like, "Puh! Puh!"

She held up both palms towards me. "Stay here."

She closed the door behind her.

I didn't have to do the beach trick anymore, but I still felt uncomfortable putting on her sweatpants. Especially because I had to freeball it where she kept her private parts. I then put on her t-shirt. It was blue with "Reseda Regents" on the front. I had seen people around the library wearing shirts like that. I guessed this was from the local high school. I also guessed that Pearl had recently graduated or is still in high school. And if she were still in high school, I felt even creepier about freeballing it in her sweatpants.

I was relieved to see a high school diploma. It was from 2015, so she was at least a year older than me. Her diploma had all these gold seals on it, meaning that she graduated with honors. The other plaques and certificates told the same story. Her sports trophies were equally impressive. They were all from basketball and softball. Muriel played softball too, but Pearl's trophies were more impressive. Her tallest said, "Most Valuable Player, Valley Mission League." Pearl would have kicked my sister's ass in softball.

I then came to her biggest certificate. It was from the City of Los Angeles. In beautiful colored calligraphy, it said, "Award of Merit to Pearl Hawthorne for being awarded the Girl Scout Gold Award." It had the city seal with a green, yellow, and red ribbons and was signed by a city council member.

Pearl's awards impressed me, but they also made me confused. If she was so smart and so successful, why was she working full time at Buck & Awesome? Shouldn't she be going to college? Especially a cool one out of state, like Muriel?

The door flung open. Pearl walked in holding a plate with a sandwich and a bottle of water. She backed into the door to close it.

"I brought you something to eat." She handed me the plate. "I don't know what you wanted to drink."

"Water's fine. Thank you."

She quickly backed towards the door, holding her palms up towards me. "I have to go. Stay here."

Again, she closed the door.

I could understand why she wouldn't want her mother to know I was there. But the bedroom isn't the best place to stash a guy. I should've eaten the sandwich, but I wondered if there was a place I could hide if needed. There was a door that I suspected was her closet. I put the sandwich down next to her MacBook Pro and walked over to open it. I hoped it wasn't where she kept the dead bodies.

It was a walk-in closet, but a tiny one. I knew I shouldn't snoop around in her stuff, so I gave it a quick glance. There weren't a lot of clothes. The baggy dresses. Blouses, short skirts, shorts. She seemed to like short things when she wasn't wearing men's sweatpants. She had a couple pairs of jeans and a shirt that looked like a softball jersey in navy blue with white underneath the sleeves. Her old Girl Scout uniform hung in the corner. Leaning against a corner was a bat bag. Next to it on the floor were a couple basketballs and some rope.

I closed her closet door. I really needed to eat, and I didn't know when she'd be back. I didn't want to get kicked out for creeping around in her closet. Especially since she still had my clothes.

. . .

Pearl was gone for a long time. What was wrong with her mom that she needed so much of her help? And why would she leave me alone in her room? She barely knew me! Well, at least she knew I was circumcised.

The sandwich was good, though. Wheat bread with deli mustard, Black Forest ham, lettuce, sprouts, and tomato. And she didn't skimp on the ingredients. Usually, poor people get the broke-ass sandwich, like cheese. Or peanut butter without the jelly because that would be too nice. And it would be on this cheap spongy white bread. That's what they gave the poor people at school for lunch. Yes, Dana Point has poor people. And we made fun of them while our parents brought us Chipotle.

Pearl and her mom may be poor, but not poor enough not to buy decent food. Or maybe Pearl gave me the good food while she had peanut butter.

And she let me, a homeless person, stay in her room. She trusted me to be here alone. I wouldn't have taken any of her things. I'm not that kind of person. But could I trust some homeless person as much as Pearl trusted me?

I looked at her bookcase. You can learn a lot about people by looking at their bookcase. She had the books you'd expect a girl to have. The full set of *Harry Potter*. And *Twilight*. And *The Hunger Games*. And *Nancy Drew*. And *Wonder Woman*. And a whole bunch of that John Green shit. She also had *Fifty Shades of Grey*. I thought only middle-age women got off on that BDSM stuff.

There were some thick books called *The Talisman*. They must have been her high school yearbooks. I only got two of my high school yearbooks. One for freshman year and one for sophomore year. I didn't get one for junior year because I was in the military academy. Dad bought one for me for senior year before I dropped out. I'll probably never get it, and I didn't deserve to have it, anyway.

I was relieved she didn't have *Face Time with Jesus*.

.   .   .

That's when the door flung open. Pearl had folded my clothes in a neat stack and handed it to me.

"I'll drive you home."

.   .   .

She already knew I was homeless, so I figured I'd have her drive me straight to the Explorer.

She stared at it for a moment. I didn't think she'd be the type to pass judgement, but what did she think about this? The guy she worked with, showered in her shower, and freeballed in her sweatpants lived in an SUV.

But she nodded and said, "You found an environmentally sound use for that vehicle."

I couldn't help but smile.

She then turned to me. Her expression turned grave, and the evening shadows made her expression more serious.

"Are you going to be OK?"

"I've been OK so far."

She then stared at the dashboard and exhaled hard. "I can't keep my mom waiting."

"Then don't." I opened the car door and stepped out. "You've done more than enough for me, Pearl. Thank you."

For the first time, Pearl seemed speechless.

I smiled and closed her car door. "See you tomorrow."

"See you." Her voice seemed tight. Regretful, perhaps?

But as I watched the taillights of her Kia disappear, I knew she had nothing to regret. Thanks to Pearl, I felt like a human being. At least for a little while.

And she silenced the hateful voices in my head.

⬧ ⬧ ⬧

I didn't realize how much better being clean made me feel. As soon as I climbed inside the sleeping bag in the Explorer, I started getting sleepy. But I still reached over and made sure I locked the doors. I guess I cared enough about myself that night to make sure I was safe. I then drifted off into a deep sleep, probably the first I had since I was thrown out.

Until I heard something like pouring water.

I pulled out my iPhone and checked the time. It was 11:33 p.m. Could it be raining? Nobody talked about rain. We weren't supposed to get moisture in Southern California until the next El Niño or when we're covered up by rising seas.

It had to be something else. Or *someone* else.

I reached under a pile of clothes and pulled out my folding knife. I bought one when I was dealing and kept it stowed in my Explorer. I thought about buying a gun, but they cost too much. And I sucked at shooting in military school. There was no way I could take out somebody with a gun, but I could stab him like a motherfucker if I had to defend myself. Even if it meant looking at blood.

And I had to defend myself.

The rear passenger door was the quietest in the Explorer. Much quieter than trying to open the lift gate with my DIY latch. I slowly unlocked and opened it. I sprung out of the vehicle with my knife open and drawn.

And some dude was zipping up his pants.

We shouted over each other. "What the fuck!? Are you fucking crazy!? Who the fuck are you anyway!? Holy fuck!"

We stopped shouting "fuck" at each other when the dude said, "You live here?"

"Yeah!" I shouted. "So, what the fuck are you doing here?"

The dude looked away and rubbed the back of his neck. "I was just hanging out, you know. I just wanted to go for a walk, you know. Just unwind. You know what I'm saying?"

"I know."

The guy raised his head and stared at me. I could see his eyes in the faint parking lot light. He was nervous. And when someone nervous is standing behind an abandoned theater late at night, he usually reached for a gun. That's when I was sorry I didn't have one. Or learned to shoot better.

Instead, I softened my voice. "I know because I used to too."

He lowered his shoulders. His face seemed to relax. I folded the knife and put it in my pocket.

The dude gave a small smile. "So, you want something?"

I did. I even had the money for it. But I exhaled hard. "No, I'm good."

"You sure?"

I nodded. "But I'll make a deal with you."

He stared at me for a moment. Then I spoke.

"You stay out of my shit, I'll stay out of yours. Deal?"

He nodded.

"And don't piss on my ride again, OK?" I gave him a small smile.

"OK." He smiled back. "But if you ever want anything..."

"I'm good. Really."

He nodded. I nodded back. He turned and walked away. I turned and walked back to my Explorer.

I figured it was better we didn't shake hands or say each other's names. Not just because we didn't trust each other. If I knew him or touched his hand, it would take me back to a life I didn't want a part of anymore. I was clean now, inside and out.

I went back to the Explorer and made doubly sure that all the doors were locked. I glanced at my iPhone. The charge was 64%. I hoped there was enough for the alarm clock to go off in the morning. I had to be at my job on time. A job where using drugs would get me fired.

But I really wished I could have gotten something from him.

CHAPTER FIFTEEN

Lake Forest

One 145-milligram tablet of fenofibrate. One 50-milligram tablet of losartan. One 81-milligram tablet of low-dosage aspirin. One 5-milligram tablet of Cialis. And no Rachel. I figured whatever delivery she was called away on must have been a doozy.

I had gotten good at filling in for her with her sons. David had a game that night. I was surprised to see that Moshe got into watching it. Usually, he'd rather play on the iPad or run up and down the slopes. David did really well. He went 2 for 3 with an RBI double and turned a 6-4-3 double play. His team won. The strange thing about watching your kids play sports is you care more about how they did than whether the team won or lost. That was the way I felt watching Muriel and Dylan. I was glad that I was feeling the same way about David and Moshe.

I took them to In-N-Out after the game. We had the burgers the way Rachel insisted, protein style with the meat and fixings wrapped in lettuce instead of a bun. I let them have fries. When we got home, I made sure they did their homework and showered, and I sent them off to bed with a goodnight kiss.

"Good night, Dr. Glass," David said.

"Good night, Dad—er, Dr. Glass," Moshe said.

"Good night, kids." I let myself smile a little wider.

So, there was more to my relationship with Rachel than "banging an obstetrician," especially when the obstetrician wasn't there to bang.

The *Orange County Register* from this morning was still on the kitchen table. I usually go to the entertainment section. *Pearls Before*

Swine would still be as funny in the evening as it was in the morning. But as I took the paper out of the plastic bag, something caught my attention. It took up a chunk of the front page and had a large photograph. It was too big to ignore.

Then I heard the key turn in the lock. I tossed the paper back on the table.

Rachel stepped through the door. She looked even more exhausted than she did in the afternoon.

"We had to do a C-section." She chucked her purse and keys on a side table by the door.

She seemed too exhausted to walk. And with two difficult deliveries in one shift, I could understand. I moved towards her.

"You need anything?" I closed the door behind her and locked it.

"Just get me to bed."

I put my arm around her to steady her. As we headed down the hallway, she started shedding her clothes. She kicked off her black tennis shoes and left them in the hall. Normally, she would get cross with her kids if they did that. I couldn't fault her after she had been standing in them all day. She loosened the drawstring of her pants and let them fall down her legs. She stepped out of them and kept walking.

When we got to the bedroom, she started tugging on her shirt. I pulled up from the bottom hem and lifted it over her head and arms. Its musty reek was worse than after a long run in the heat. I waited until we were in the bedroom, and I tossed it by the dresser. She reached behind her back for her bra.

"I got it." I unfastened the hooks, and she let her bra fall off her body. She bared her firm, full breasts only for a moment, then she collapsed face down on the bed. Her face leaned off the edge of her pillow. She laid crossways. I reached across her chest and thighs, lifted her gently, and set her lengthwise across the bed. She didn't even stir. She fell fast asleep, naked except for her panties and anklet socks.

I softly closed the bedroom door and turned off the light. I walked around to my side of the bed. With Rachel pressing on top of the covers, I couldn't flip up my end and get under them. So, I lied down next to her.

The faint light that crept in from the parted drapes cast a pale blue glow on her skin. Her body was still except for her back, rising and falling with each breath. Her face was obscured by shadows from her tight overhanging curls and distorted as she leaned off the edge of her pillow. Her lower lip quivered with each exhale.

I rested on my back and stared at the ceiling. I thought about Mr. Shelton lying motionless on the table. And Dad swaying from the rafters. They too were exhausted—exhausted of living. How many times did I feel that way? And if I didn't have Rachel, would I be? Those were the moments when I was afraid of sleeping. If I did, would I wake up?

But I had to go to sleep. I knew Avicii was going to kick me out of bed at four thirty tomorrow morning.

•   •   •

And when four thirty came, Avicii did kick me out of bed. "Wake Me Up" blared out of my iPhone. I reached over and slapped on anything until the music stopped. When I opened my eyes, I expected the lights to be on and a dressed Rachel exhorting me to hurry and get ready for our workout. But the room was still dark. I turned to my side. Rachel was still asleep. I figured she would be asleep the rest of the morning. I would have to get the kids ready and drive them to school. After two tough and long deliveries the day before, she deserved her rest.

Without her, I felt disoriented. Do I run without her? Although I ran the trails behind her housing complex dozens of times, I didn't completely know the way without her. Besides, she was my motivation to run. Before we started dating, I couldn't be bothered to walk to the supermarket a couple of blocks away.

I could be motivated to pick up the newspaper in the driveway. I tucked it under my arm and carried it into the house. Instead of tossing it on the kitchen table, I kept it with me as I went into the study. I tossed it on the sofa and went to my MacBook Pro. I tapped the trackpad to wake it up.

My inbox was full of the usual junk. I scanned through the list, hoping Dylan would finally write back. I found an email from Muriel.

Hey, Dad.

Sorry I haven't written recently. I've been busy with studying for midterms and softball. I pinch hit in our game against Purdue. I got a single and drove in a run. Coach says that if I keep working hard, I can start next season.

I smiled. I was happy to see her doing well. I really needed to make plans to fly out to Minnesota and see her.

But as I kept reading, I stopped smiling.

BTW, do you know what's the deal with Mom? She keeps calling me, saying people are lying about her and Steven. And is it true they kicked Dylan out of their house? Have you heard from him?

I clicked Reply. I had to let her know.

89

CHAPTER SIXTEEN

Reseda

"You look different." Magdalena handed me the bag of pan dulces.

"I took a shower."

"At the Rescue Mission?"

"At a friend's."

She gave me a broad, crooked smile. "You have a good friend."

I smiled back. "Have a good day, Magdalena."

"You too, Dylan."

.   .   .

Truth was, I still didn't know what to make of Pearl. Or how I would act when I saw her at work. Or how she would act. I knew not to make a big deal about it on the job. But what about afterwards? Should I see her again? If I needed to shower again, would she ask me to come?

.   .   .

All those questions went away the moment I put on my apron. I found Quang, Pearl, Fatima, and Kishana staring at the refrigerator case in the back of the store. The lights were out. I knew this was bad.

Veins popped on the side of Quang's face. He shook his head and uttered something in Vietnamese. Probably "Holy fucking shit!" He exhaled and turned to me.

"The refrigerator case went bad last night. Throw everything away."

He turned and continued muttering "motherfucking cock and shit balls" in Vietnamese.

I didn't blame him. The closing crew stocked the unit completely. Milk, butter, cartons of eggs, deli meats, cheese. All generic brands. They probably didn't taste good. Except for the milk because milk is milk. But sitting overnight in a busted refrigerator, they were dangerously inedible. Quang had to throw several hundred dollars in the trash.

Even remainders can be so bad, they're worthless.

I rolled out one of the trash cans from the back and dumped armful after armful of food into it. I then rolled it outside and tossed the food in the dumpster in the back.

When I returned, Kishana handed me a paper sign and a roll of duct tape. "Tape the refrigerator door shut and put this sign on it. Corporate says they'll have a new unit out here tomorrow."

I looked at the sign. "Sorry. Temporarily Out Of Service./Lo Siento. Temporalmente Fuera De Servicio."

I tore off a short piece of duct tape to attach the sign to the door. Then, I had to tape the door shut. I peeled off a length and tucked it between the refrigerator unit and the freezer. It was a good thing the freezer didn't fail, because that food would have been damp and stinky as well as spoiled. I tucked in the end and pressed it tight. I then pulled the strip across the door. As the tape peeled away from the roll, it made a long, sustained scraping sound. The grating noise made me tighten my shoulders and grind my teeth. I was grateful when I reached the other side of the door. I peeled off some more tape and tore the end. I pressed it against the side of the refrigerator.

I peeled off another piece of duct tape and discovered why we were able to sell it for a dollar. It didn't look like there was enough tape to go across again. I figured I better ask Kishana for another roll.

When I turned around, Pearl was there. She wore another button-down short-sleeve blouse and short skirt.

"Looks like fun."

I was surprised that she wasn't sarcastic.

"Want to join me?" I smiled.

She pushed her brownish blond hair back over her shoulder. "I'd like to, but I can't."

I blinked for a second. I couldn't figure out why her reply sounded odd. Especially when she looked down at her wrists.

"I have to take Mom to the doctor after work." She put her hands together in front of her. She rubbed the top of her left hand with her right thumb.

I stepped closer to her. "Is your mom OK?"

She glanced back at the register and then stepped back. "I have a customer."

"No pro..." She was halfway down the aisle before I could even finish.

I looked down at the floor at the bottom of the refrigerator case. Quang didn't mention the water on the concrete floor. Perhaps it dripped from the food as I threw it away. I knew I had to mop it up.

. . .

I didn't think about Pearl the rest of the shift. I couldn't. There was too much to do. After mopping up by the refrigerator case, I had to restock the paper towels and toilet paper, clean up the toy aisle because some mother let her kids run crazy there, clean the bathrooms, clean up the toy aisle again because another mother let her kids run crazy there, spent about ten minutes helping this man look for plastic anchors for putting screws in drywall only to find that they weren't the right size. Then this one girl asked for a pregnancy test. It made me think about Zoey, which started bringing up hateful thoughts for me.

Then Mrs. Cimino came in and asked, "How's your day?"

"Great." I hoped she didn't know how big of a lie that was.

"And how's the book?"

"Good." I hoped she didn't know that this was a lie too.

But the way she stared at me, she must have known. I thought she'd get pissed off at me. But she spoke in her gentle voice.

"I had a hard time the first time I read it. It said so many things I didn't want to hear, but I stuck with it. So should you."

"Dylan?"

I turned around. Kishana stood behind me.

"Can you dump the trash in the back?"

"Sure." I then turned to Mrs. Cimino. "Excuse me."

She nodded. "Of course."

I was nervous that Kishana caught me chatting with Mrs. Cimino, but I was relieved that I didn't have to talk about that fucking book anymore. Steven said so many things I didn't want to hear because they were all total bullshit. Stupid war stories, Biblical passages seemingly picked out at random, long-winded sermons, and, of course, "Wealth is the sign of God's favor." Why would Mrs. Cimino find such a steaming pile of tree pulp so profound that it saved her life? And what happened in her life that she had to read Steven's garbage to save it?

It didn't matter because I had some actual garbage to get out. I headed to the back of the store where I had put the big-wheeled trash can. I dragged it around the store and dumped the smaller trash cans into it. Then I wheeled it outside.

And when I got to the dumpster, I froze.

I thought I closed both lids, but one of them was open. I took a step closer. Something seemed to be shuffling around inside. I wished I had that folding knife with me. I took one step closer, then another. The shuffling got louder.

Then a blur. I bolted back. From behind the dumpster, soft footsteps.

"Hey!" I shouted.

A figure froze. Her back was towards me. At least she looked like a woman with long black stringy hair. The baggy, ratty coat she wore made it hard to tell.

"What are you doing?"

The figure turned around. It was a woman, and she looked fairly young. She wore stained, faded jeans with the bottoms torn up and fringed around her feet. If she wore shoes, I couldn't tell.

And clutched in her hands were the refrigerated items I threw away that morning.

I pointed to them. "You can't take those! They're spoiled!"

Her voice cracked and strained. "My children are starving."

"If they eat that, they'll get sick!"

"If they don't eat, they'll die!"

"Lady!" I stepped towards her. She turned quickly and ran. One of items fell out of her arms and landed on the asphalt. But she turned back, picked it up, and kept running.

I knew I should chase after her, but what would I do if I caught her? Make her throw the food away? When I left, she'd come back and get it. And if she didn't take spoiled food from our dumpster, she'd take it from somewhere else. And if I were that desperate, I'd steal spoiled food from a dumpster too.

I thought I hit rock bottom. I didn't think anyone could fall further than me.

CHAPTER SEVENTEEN

Lake Forest

"You'll be hearing from my lawyer, Dr. Glass!" The voice of Leo Shelton's widow blasted from the other end of the line.

I replied calmly, "Mrs. Shelton, I know how upset you are, and I am deeply sorry for your loss…"

"Sorry? If you were sorry, you would have done more to save him!"

I remained calm, "The paramedics did all they could…"

"Then why didn't they use those paddle things!? Those things can restart a heart, right?"

No. Defibrillators can correct an arrhythmic heartbeat. They can't restart a heart that had stopped. But I couldn't tell Mrs. Shelton that.

"And why didn't you prescribe him medicine to save him? Medicines are supposed to cure everything, right?"

No, especially when the patient won't take them. All the things I prescribed and recommended to Mr. Shelton could have prevented his early death, but only if he used them. I couldn't tell Mrs. Shelton that either. The only thing I could do is listen to a frightened and heartbroken woman rant about a painful situation she couldn't control.

"I'll sue you, Dr. Glass! I'll sue the hospital! I'll sue the paramedics! I'll sue the County of Orange! And if I could sue God, I'd sue Him too!"

She became silent, waiting for me to respond.

"Mrs. Shelton, all I can say is that I am deeply saddened for your…"

She hung up on me.

I couldn't be mad at Mrs. Shelton. I understood the rage she felt. I had seen it before.

. . .

It was a mistake to put Grandma Dinah in the back seat with Mom. It was a mistake to have her in my car at all. I was driving. Teresa was seven months pregnant with Muriel, so she had to sit in the passenger seat next to me. Grandma Dinah and Mom sat as far apart as the back seat of my 1993 Ford Escort would allow.

I didn't expect Grandma Dinah to be there. We had a falling out since I married Teresa. She didn't like her, she didn't like that she's Christian, and she didn't like that I married her because I got her pregnant. Mom wasn't completely happy with the arrangement either, but she tried to get along with Teresa and treat her like part of the family. Mom helped us plan the quick wedding and gave us a beautiful toast. Grandma Dinah and her side of the family didn't come.

And they didn't come that day, even though it was Maury's funeral. Grandma Dinah did. I was relieved that she was on her best behavior. She didn't say a word through the whole service, but I could imagine all the horrible things she could say. Her silence was more damning than her words.

We drove back to Mom's house. We pulled into her driveway and kept the engine running.

"Wouldn't you like to come in?" Mom's voice was both sweet and strained.

"Of course." I turned off the ignition. Teresa turned sharply towards me and scowled. I was breaking an agreement we made to leave as soon as we dropped off Mom and Grandma Dinah. How I could I say no to Mom, especially at a time like that?

The click of the power door locks broke the silence. Each of us opened our door. I stepped around to Teresa's side.

"Do you need…"

She shook her head angrily in reply.

Mom came around to Grandma Dinah's side. Grandma Dinah had her cane out and put one leg after the other out of the car.

"Let me help you." Mom held out her hands.

"I'm fine," Grandma Dinah grumbled. "Why does Oliver's car have to be so damn small?"

Teresa's scowl tightened more, even though she confronted me with the same question many times.

Grandma Dinah wobbled as she tried to come to her feet. Mom reached out again, but Grandma Dinah shook her off. I waited as Grandma Dinah made her way out of the car. Teresa stood impatiently at the other end of the driveway. Mom followed close behind as Grandma Dinah trudged slowly up the walkway. It seemed strange to see this once physically intimidating and brutal woman act so feeble. I went over to the door Grandma Dinah left open and closed it. I then went back over to the driver's side door, stuck the key in the lock, and turned it. All the power door locks clicked.

Teresa and I had to wait until Mom got Grandma Dinah to the door and unlocked it. We waited until they were through the doorway and past the tile entryway before we followed them in. The house didn't seem the same as I remembered. Dust particles glowed in the shafts of light that snuck in through the shades. Everything seemed old and dingy. The beige carpet had worn spots. I noticed a stain in the family room. That was when Grandma Dinah hit Maury so hard, he bled.

Mom walked over to me. "You gave a wonderful eulogy."

I nodded. "Thank you."

We continued to the family room. Teresa took a seat at the sofa.

Grandma Dinah grimaced at her. "We're still sitting shiva."

Mom narrowed her eyes at Grandma Dinah. "She doesn't have to. She's pregnant."

"And she doesn't know our traditions." Grandma Dinah sat down on the love seat and looked away.

Teresa scowled at me again, but she opened her eyes wide, as if to beg me to hurry up and leave. I turned to Mom. She tightened her lips. She shifted her eyes towards Grandma Dinah, who was staring silently off into the distance. I didn't know what to do. I started formulating excuses for leaving, but I tossed each one out when I thought about leaving Mom alone with Grandma Dinah.

Mom cleared her throat and forced a smile. She knelt in front of Teresa. "So, how have things been coming along with the nursery?"

"Fine." The word came out with a nasal snark. Teresa exhaled before speaking again. The snark went away. "We ordered the crib and dresser. We're still trying to decide on a theme. We're looking at either *The Little Mermaid*, *Beauty and the Beast*, or that new one, *The Hunchback of Notre Dame*."

I glanced at Grandma Dinah. She still stared off into the distance in silent anger.

Mom kept her focus on Teresa. "You must be excited you're having a girl."

Teresa finally smiled. "We are. I can't wait to go clothes shopping with her. It's so much fun to dress up a girl."

We didn't know it then, but Muriel would prefer jeans and t-shirts to frilly dresses, and a new glove and softball bat over a Barbie Dream House. It didn't stop Teresa from driving me to near bankruptcy from shopping at the Disney Store, The Children's Place, and Baby Gap for clothes Muriel would outgrow in a month.

Mom smiled. "So, have you and Oliver picked out a name?"

"Well..."

We hadn't talked about a name. I was surprised that she was going to answer.

"I was thinking," Teresa said, "I know there's a tradition in Judaism to name children after a loved one who passed away. So, I was thinking we would name our daughter after Oliver's brother Maury."

I was surprised. Pleasantly surprised. Mom blinked her eyes to hold back tears. She reached over towards Teresa and clasped her hands.

"Oh, Teresa. That is a wonderful thing for you to do."

"It's a stupid thing, if you ask me."

All faces turned towards Grandma Dinah. She didn't turn her head as she kept grumbling.

"Do you really think after what happened..."

Mom let go of Teresa's hands and stood up. "Mother, this is not the time..."

Grandma Dinah finally turned towards us. "Then when? Are we supposed to keep wringing our hands and saying 'What a tragedy' and 'It's a shame he passed away so young' when we know full well..."

Teresa and I looked at each other. She kept her eyes fully open and shook her head rapidly, silently begging me to leave. I couldn't. I found myself frozen in place, like I always did when things like this happened. Especially when Mom raised her voice.

"How can you talk about this?" Her voice started to tremble. "Right after his funeral?"

Grandma Dinah shook her cane. "Come on, Josephine! Don't pretend no one knows that happened to Maury. No one will say it, but we all know…"

Mom's anger turned to tears. "For the love of God, Mother! How could you…"

"Could I what? Tell the truth! Your son was an addict, Josephine! When they found him in that motel in Costa Mesa, he had overdosed on—what is that crystal stuff again?"

"We did everything we could to help him!"

"Well, you didn't do enough. Did you, Josephine?"

Teresa looked at me. She then put her hands on her belly and spoke softly to Mom. "This talk, it—it really isn't good for the baby."

I had to say something. "Perhaps we should…"

"Go." Grandma Dinah snapped a curt wave. "Just go. It's not like you're a part of the family anymore anyway."

Once again, Mom had to defend me. "Oliver has his own life. He has his career. He has a wife and a baby on the way…"

Grandma Dinah's curtness grew. "And how they going to raise this baby? Jewish? Christian? Are they going to have her baptized? I hope that priest doesn't drown the little…"

Mom stepped over to Grandma Dinah and planted his fists on her hips. "You're the most hateful, bitter, spiteful, miserable human being who ever walked the face of the earth!"

"And you're a terrible mother! You raised one son to knock up a shiksa and the other to die of an overdose!"

"And you drove your son to commit suicide!"

WHACK!

Even at her age, Grandma Dinah's hand moved so fast I didn't even see it. Mom seemed unfazed. She snapped her face forward and narrowed her eyelids.

"Get out of my house!"

"What did you say, Josephine?"

"GET OUT OF MY HOUSE!!"

After Mom's shout, silence. We remained fixed in place. I was too afraid to turn my head. Then Grandma Dinah leaned forward and put her weight on her cane to raise herself from the love seat. Her shoulders remained slumped as she stood. She shuffled a few steps forward and stopped. She turned her head slowly towards us and gave us a hateful glare.

"You will never see me again."

She continued shuffling out of the family room and past the bloodstain on the worn beige carpet.

She made good on her word. She died not too long after that. Jews have the ability to die out of spite. Anything to make someone feel guilty. No amount of guilt would make me go to her funeral. She had some money, but she wrote us all out of her will. She gave her entire estate to charities supporting Israel. So, in a way, Rachel wound up with her inheritance.

•   •   •

DING.

The sound startled me back to reality. It was from my iPhone. There was a new email. I put my thumb on the Home button to unlock the phone and tapped on the Mail app. The message was from Muriel. I cradled the phone in my palm as I slowly scrolled through her message. I knew she would be upset, but I didn't expect how distraught she would be.

Then Alison stuck her head in the door. "Dr. Glass, Mr. Sembello is here for your two thirty."

"Thank you, Alison. Um…" I glanced down at my phone for a moment. "Have Joy take his vitals. I'll be there in a few minutes."

"OK, doctor." She closed the door behind her.

I should write Muriel back, but more importantly, I needed to write to Dylan. I tapped the icon for a new message. This couldn't wait.

CHAPTER EIGHTEEN

Reseda

"You haven't clocked out yet?"

Quang stood over me. I was kneeling in the toy aisle stacking jump ropes and bags of toy soldiers in the bottom rack. Another mother let her kids run wild.

I stood up. "Shouldn't I finish up here?"

Quang shook his head. "Closing crew will do it. You can't work overtime."

I nodded. Quang hated paying overtime. As I headed towards the front of the store, he followed close behind me.

I glanced at the clock above the front door. I went into overtime, but only by 15 minutes. I could have checked the time on my iPhone, but I never took it out of my pocket while at work. I don't know what Quang and the others would think about me sleeping in my SUV when I had a fairly new iPhone.

Quang followed me into the office. "You're off tomorrow." He made it sound like a reminder and an order.

"I know." I hung up my apron and clocked out.

"See you Saturday." It also sounded like a greeting and an order.

"See you."

•　•　•

In a way, I was glad I didn't see Pearl after work. I had to charge my iPhone. I figured I'd go to the library. Maybe check my Facebook and email, even though it would make me depressed.

First, I had to eat. And Thursday was when Magdalena served her special tacos.

She served authentic Mexican tacos, soft-shelled with handmade corn tortillas. No cheese, though. Kosher food doesn't mix meat and dairy. But her ground beef had the most amazing flavors, and she filled it with lettuce, diced tomatoes and onions, cilantro, and the best salsa I ever had. Others must have loved her tacos too because the place was always packed on Thursday night. People waited outside to get in. But I knew the quickest way to get a seat.

I came in through the back door into the kitchen. And Magdalena was waiting for me with a hug and a kiss.

"How many?"

"Two, please." But I knew Magdalena would make it three.

"¡Tres!," she called out to her cooks. I was right.

The kitchen echoed with clanking spatulas, clinking plates, and someone singing in the corner. Murmured voices came in from the front of the restaurant. It was noisy, but noisy with a positive vibe. It was a noise that could drive away all those hateful voices in my head.

Magdalena handed me a plate. Three tacos, just as I thought. I reached into my pocket.

She shook her head. "You enjoy."

I set the plate on a side table and smiled. "Why are you so good to me?"

I realized that was a corny question, something that was usually said as a compliment and didn't require an answer.

But Magdalena gave one anyway. "Why shouldn't I be good to you?"

She was indeed Jewish, answering a question with a question. But I wanted an answer.

"But really. I'm just some guy off the streets. Why would you be so good to me?"

"Because of Mamá. Her name was Frieda Barchevsky. I named the restaurant after her, you know. She survived Auschwitz. She saw the worst in humanity, but she never lost faith and never stopped loving. She told me, 'Magdalena, the world will crush you if you let it. Your only defense is kindness. Always be kind.'"

I nodded.

Magdalena gave her crooked smile. "Your friend seems to feel the same way."

"My friend?"

"Your friend who let you use her shower."

Her? How did she know? What do I say?

"¿Señora Magdalena?" A cook at the other end of the kitchen saved me from having to answer.

Magdalena looked at the food on the side table and patted me on the cheek. "Enjoy."

I picked up a taco from the plate. The plate she gave me because she was kind.

• • • •

But staring at my Facebook page, I didn't see a whole lot of kindness.

I didn't know why I even bothered looking. The library was about to close. Why was I wasting time making myself miserable knowing that people I thought cared about me have gone on and forgotten me?

I wondered if Pearl had a Facebook. But she's probably too busy taking care of her mom. And what is wrong with her mom anyway?

I decided to check my email. I figured there would be another email from Dad. And there was.

> *Son,*
>
> *I told Muriel all about what happened to you. She's anxious and upset.*

Muriel? Upset? Since when did she ever give a fuck about me? At home, we'd go for days saying nothing more than "Morning" and "Did you use my toothbrush again!?" She was always busy with school, sports, music, and her boyfriend. Actually, boy*friends*. There was her official boyfriend Kevin. Steven and his dad fixed him up with her at church. But Kevin was gay and super in the closet because his parents would have literally killed him if they found out. So, she kept up appearances to save his ass. Muriel's real boyfriend was Raúl. And they fucked like crazy. She asked me to buy her condoms because God knew what a shitstorm Mom and Steven would unleash if they found their perfectly perfect girl was getting it, especially from a Latino.

Muriel told me all this stuff. And made me swear on my life not to tell anyone. And I didn't. But I never told her any of my shit because I knew she'd run to Mom and Steven if I did the slightest thing wrong. Like when she caught me watching porn on my computer. I thought spanking a kid with a belt was illegal.

But I continued with Dad's email.

We're both very upset that Mom and Steven would toss you out like this and not care about you.

Was this what his emails were really about? Making himself look good while making Mom and Steven look like shit? They were shit, but so was Dad. There were so many times I wanted to talk to him, especially when things were bad in school and home. But there was always a reason we couldn't meet. He got a last-minute appointment, or someone needed an emergency appendectomy. And when we did get together, it was just small talk like, "Did you see the Angels game last night?" or "What do you think about that new Captain America movie?" I just wanted to break down, bawl like a baby, tell him how fucked up my life was, and if I could live with him, things would be better.

But I just wound up saying, "Yeah" and "Fine."

I don't know why I couldn't be open with him. Was it because I was a man, and a man can't be open with other men? As I sat there thinking about it, I wondered if I was really open with my friends. I thought I could talk to them about everything. Mostly, we talked about weed and pussy.

Please, Dylan, if you get this message, email or call me right away. We pray every day that you're OK. Please, Dylan. Please contact me.
Love,
Dad

I moved the mouse pointer over the Reply button and clicked. A new email message opened. Dad's email address was in the To box. The Message box had a bunch of blank space with his email below it. I started typing.

Dear Dad,

I stopped. Now, what do I say? I kept typing.

I'm OK.

I stopped again. What do I tell him? What would he think? And if I told him I was OK, would he stop emailing me? Was that all he really wants to know? Did he just want to stop feeling guilty? Or did he want something he could wag in front of Mom and say, "Dylan wrote to me and not you, you sawed-off bitch!"

But I kept typing.

I'm OK. I'm in LA.

No. Don't say "LA." Reza warned me the first time I said it. "Don't say 'LA.' Say 'the Valley.' People in the Valley hate when you call it 'LA.'"

So, I backspaced it.

I'm OK. I'm in the Valley. Don't worry about me.
Love,

What the fuck did I mean "Love"? He didn't love me! Or did he? If he didn't really love me, why would he care what happened to me? Or was it because of guilt or to show up Mom? I backspaced again.

I'm OK. I'm in the Valley. Don't worry about me.
—Dylan

That looked wrong. That made me look like a dick. He is my dad. I complain about him not caring about me. But do I really care about him? Aren't I the one in the wrong? I mean, he lives in a nice home and has a nice girlfriend. I sleep in a Ford Explorer *he gave me*. I depend on others for food and to get clean. I work in a minimum-wage job that's the only thing that keeps me from dumpster diving for spoiled food. Who's the one who doesn't have his shit together?

And didn't Magdalena say I should always be kind? Why can't I be kind to my own dad?

"The library will be closing in fifteen minutes. The computers will be shutting down in five minutes. Please bring your books to check out. Thank you for visiting the West Valley Regional Branch Library."

I logged off the computer without sending the email.

CHAPTER NINETEEN

Lake Forest

Moshe had a horrible day. Some kid at school called him a "dirty raghead." He thought "Mo" was short for Muhammad. He got a C- on a test. I would have been happy with Dylan getting a grade like that, but anything less than a B was unacceptable to Rachel. I don't know what she said to him, but he looked shaken by the time I saw him at the game. Baseball was rough too. He struck out every time at bat. When his coach put him in at second, he let a ball go past him down the middle. He immediately moved Moshe to right. I thought that was a humiliating thing to do to a kid, but I said nothing. Teresa would have wound up getting ejected for the things she would have said.

He left the dugout dejected with his head hung low.

"Stop dragging your bat bag," Rachel scolded.

Moshe adjusted his bag higher.

I looked over at David. He walked quietly, his body tense. I thought I would try to break the tension.

"In-N-Out?"

"I have dinner ready at home." Rachel didn't turn her head.

Her Yukon and my Lexus were parked side-by-side. Sometimes, I offered to let one or both of her kids ride home with me. I figured it was better not to ask.

Rachel opened her lift gate. Moshe put in his bat bag. As he turned towards the side of her car, I glanced at his face. I could see a tear.

I knelt in front of him and put my hand on his shoulder.

"Don't take it so hard, Moshe." I said with a smile, "You did your best."

"How would you know? You looked at your phone the whole time." He pulled sharply away from me.

• • •

After dinner, I was still staring at a screen. This time, my MacBook Pro.

"No answer?" Rachel held a saucepan she was wiping dry with a towel.

"No."

For a moment, I thought she was going to whack me over the head with that saucepan, especially with Moshe complaining I didn't pay attention to him during the game. Instead, she set it on the sofa and put the towel inside it. She walked over to the desk and leaned against it.

"Do you think he read your email?"

"I don't know." I sighed.

"So, what are you going to do?"

"Wait. What else can I do?"

"You can file a missing person report."

"But what if he doesn't want..."

Rachel grimaced at me. "You have to find out. It's upsetting your daughter, and it's upsetting you."

I glanced at my iPhone at the corner of the desk and exhaled hard. I looked back at Rachel.

"I'm also upset I hurt Moshe's feelings. I feel awful that I kept checking my phone..."

"He has to accept it." Her voice turned firm. "Children around here feel like they're the center of the universe, and we parents have to lavish them with our undivided attention all the time. We're doctors. We get important messages from time to time. We have to check our phones. We have things to do. He has to deal with it."

If she were trying to absolve me for checking my phone for Dylan's response, it didn't work. It made me feel even more guilty and uncomfortable. Especially with what she said next.

"But don't tell Moshe or David they did their best when they haven't. 'I did my best' is an excuse. It's meaningless. You either did something, or you didn't."

I never realized how hard Rachel was on her children. It seemed to work on David. He was a top athlete and an A student. But what about Moshe? Was she being too hard on him and expecting more from him than he could do? I couldn't say anything to Rachel about this. They were her children. I had my own children to worry about.

"I'll give Dylan a few days. If I don't hear from him, I'll submit a missing person report."

Rachel nodded. "I better check on the kids and finish the dishes."

I nodded. She stepped away from the desk and went to the door. As I watched her leave, I noticed something on the sofa.

"Wait! You forgot something."

Rachel turned around. She saw the saucepan and towel on the sofa.

"I wondered why I hadn't seen it."

I thought she was referring to the saucepan. But she picked up the *Orange County Register* from this morning. I forgot that I left it there.

"Sorry. I forgot all about the paper," I said.

She took the newspaper out of its plastic bag and unfolded it. As she stared at the front page, her eyes grew bigger.

"You better look at this." She handed me the paper.

As soon as I saw the large-type headline below the masthead, I gasped.

CHAPTER TWENTY

Reseda

I hated days off. I had nothing to do. Nothing but lay in the Explorer. That's what I did the first days after I arrived in Reseda. I'd lay in the back all day, hoping that if it got hot enough, I'd get fried to death. It worked on dogs and toddlers strapped into car seats, but it didn't work on me. The minute it got too uncomfortable, I got out. I just sat against the shady side of the SUV until it cooled off enough for me to go back inside and dream about dying of heatstroke.

But on this day off, I wanted to go out. I wanted to see Reseda, or at least the parts I hadn't seen. I took some cash out of the center console to buy some lunch, locked up the Explorer, and just started walking. It wasn't like I had anywhere to go or had to be back by a certain time.

I noticed things walking around that most people don't see just driving by. Like the smell of flowers from the flower shop. All those fragrances blending together. Or the people working out in the fitness studio, shouting and squatting in their tight spandex. There was an art supply store with murals on the front and sides of the building, all of them beautifully painted.

They had a lot of auto shops. One had a Dodge with its front-end caved in. Obviously, someone wasn't paying attention while driving. Or someone was drunk. That's what happened to Doug. He drove home buzzed from a party and totaled his new BMW M3. His dad was really pissed. He grounded Doug for two weeks and bought him another one. I still don't know how Doug beat that manslaughter charge.

I finally came to that park, the one that was supposed to have showers. But I didn't see any buildings that looked like they had showers. It was just a grassy area with picnic tables and lots of trees. But it looked like there was another part of the park on the other side of the wash. Maybe the showers were there. Or maybe they were at the buildings just past the park. My mission became to find those showers. I needed some way to get clean. I couldn't keep asking Pearl. I didn't want to impose, and I didn't want her to keep looking at where I was circumcised.

I followed along this street called Kittridge towards those buildings. But they weren't a part of the park. It was a high school, the one Pearl went to. It was like everything else in Reseda. It looked old, but they painted it to make it look nice. The school colors were almost like the ones at Dana Hills, shades of blue.

I wondered how much better things would have been for me if I stayed in high school and got good grades. Muriel did great in school, and she wound up going to a university. Most of all, she got away from our family. I still believed she didn't give a fuck about me. Why would she when she had a great life in Minnesota?

But Pearl did all the things Muriel did and then some. Why was Muriel able to go to college, and Pearl had to work at Buck & Awesome?

． ． ．

I finally found the showers. I walked down this street next to the high school, crossed a bridge that went over the wash, and found some buildings by the softball field. The showers were part of changing rooms by the pool. The building didn't have good hours on weekdays. They would be closed by the time I got off from work, and they were closed on Sunday. I could go on my days off. I guess I could handle showering only once or twice a week. I had gone without showering for a month.

But as I left the building, I felt sad. It wasn't the usual feeling that made me want to step in front of cars, jump off buildings, or slit my wrists. It felt heavy. It made every step difficult. I could only walk across to the softball field and plant myself on the metal bleachers.

I started thinking of something Steven used to say in his speeches, "God takes us where we need to go and teaches us the lessons we need to learn." So, why did He take me to Reseda? And what was I supposed to learn here?

I stared out on the flat dirt of the softball field. I hated being dragged to Muriel's softball games, but I admit that I was excited to see her play. I wondered what would have happened if I had stuck with the sports I played. Would my family root for me like they rooted for Muriel?

I wondered what Pearl was like as a softball player. And I remembered that Pearl didn't live far away.

.   .   .

The heaviness and sadness started to lift as I walked towards her house. But when I got to her street, Amigo Avenue, I froze. What the fuck was I doing here? Was I just creeping on her? What if she saw me? How could she? She would be at work. She had just started, so Quang wouldn't give her a day off so soon.

And if I went to her house, what would I do? Just stare at it? And what would she or her neighbors do if they see some random homeless guy stare at her house? They'd call the cops, that's what. OC sheriff's deputies can be dicks, but there's no way I'd fuck with the LAPD.

I turned around and started walking back. That heavy sadness started weighing on me again, but I had to shrug that shit off. I knew it would be a long walk back. And I hoped my Explorer was still there when I returned.

Then something blue whizzed past me. Was that Pearl's car?

I turned around and headed up Amigo. It was Pearl's car. It pulled into the driveway in front of her house. Her red taillights flashed brightly.

And I found myself walking towards those lights. I had no idea why. I had no reason to be there. I *shouldn't* be there.

Until I discovered why.

Pearl opened the trunk and took out a wheelchair. She seemed strong. That wheelchair must have weighed twenty pounds, and she pulled it out and opened it like it was no big thing. She opened the passenger side door.

I continued walking up Amigo. Pearl didn't seem to know I was there, which was a relief to me. But she seemed to be arguing with the person in the passenger seat.

"C'mon, Mom. I have to get back to work."

"But, Pearl, I'm so tired."

"Mom, please!"

I cut across the front lawn of the house next to Pearl's and hid behind some bushes along her front yard. That was super sketchy and stupid. Especially because that street had a Neighborhood Watch sign posted on it. I expected the LAPD to show up any minute and give me a serious ass-whooping. In LA, cops whoop white people's asses, not just Blacks and Hispanics.

"Please, Mom! I just started there! If I come back from lunch too late, they'll fire me!"

"But I have to gather my strength..."

I got out from behind those bushes and started walking, then striding, then running. I slowed down when I stepped onto their driveway and approached Pearl.

She looked at me with shock and anger. She didn't speak. I couldn't speak until I caught my breath.

"Let me help."

I looked inside the car. Pearl's mom looked thin and pale, and she had a pink floral bandana around her head. My Grandma Josephine, Dad's mom, looked like that after a chemo session. And she looked that thin and acted that tired the month before she died. And my heart sank for her and Pearl.

As I looked at Pearl's mom, it was hard to tell how old she was. She looked old from how frail she was. But at the same time, her face looked young.

But Pearl needed to get back to work. So, I held out my hands to her mom. And her mom reached out to me. She started to lift herself out of the car.

"Watch your head," I whispered.

Slowly, she raised herself out of the car. Pearl held the wheelchair steady as I held her mom's hands. She pivoted and lowered herself into the wheelchair. I moved the footrests into place and put her feet on them. I moved out of the way as Pearl started backing up her mom and taking her to the front door. I closed the passenger door of Pearl's car.

Pearl unlocked the front door of her house and then glared back at me.

"Wait there."

•   •   •   •   •

After about ten minutes, Pearl got out of the house and locked the door. She glared at me again.

"Get in."

I complied. I assumed she was driving me back to Sherman Way. Unless she was driving me into the mountains to die.

She didn't say a word as she stepped into the car and turned the key. She remained silent as she backed out of the driveway. She went down the entire length of Amigo Avenue, turned left onto Victory Boulevard, and stopped at the signal at Reseda Boulevard before she spoke.

"I won't ask why you were here."

"Why not?" I said, "I would."

The green light came on. There wasn't a green left turn arrow like the traffic lights in Orange County. She had to creep forward into the intersection and wait until the way was clear before turning. At that point, the signal had turned yellow. She turned onto Reseda Boulevard. And spoke again.

"If you want to have sex with me, you can't."

There were so many ways I could have responded. Only one sounded right.

"What's her prognosis?"

"Depends on who you ask. Six weeks. A year. One says she can still make a full recovery."

"What do you think?"

We stopped at a traffic light. She stared ahead at the cars in front of us.

"I don't have a say in it."

The light changed.

I fell silent. I remember how awful Dad felt about his mom. Even though he was a doctor and could bring other people back to health, he couldn't save his own mom.

We turned onto Sherman Way. We went past the abandoned movie theater. Buck & Awesome appeared on our left. I exhaled softly.

"If there's anything I can do…"

"Help me tell Quang why I'm late."

* * *

Quang was a lot more understanding than either Pearl or I expected. He still tightened his face and wagged his finger.

First to Pearl, "If you need extra time to help your mother, let me know in advance."

"Yes, Quang."

Then to me, "And you, Dylan, you get out of the store. Don't come back until work tomorrow."

"Yes, Quang."

I knew I couldn't hang around. I turned and headed towards the exit. When I stepped out the door, Pearl had returned to her register. I didn't expect her to stop and say thank you. She had a job to do.

CHAPTER TWENTY-ONE

Lake Forest

Two o'clock, and my schedule for the rest of Friday afternoon was clear. I had some follow-up calls and claim forms to sign. Then, I would be out the door by four.

Rachel wasn't as big on Shabbat as I expected someone from Israel to be. She and her ex belonged to a synagogue in Aliso Viejo. She hadn't been a member of a synagogue since her divorce, but she goes on High Holy Days. Rachel didn't do the bit where you can't turn on the oven, so you had to eat cold cuts and gefilte fish. Grandma Dinah wasn't like that either. She made sure we went to shul and were miserable from sundown to sundown.

With Rachel, we had the candles, challah, and wine. We also kept the mitzvah of having sex.

I checked in with Alison at the front.

"Dr. Glass, Mr. Marchenko called. He set up an appointment for two thirty."

"Why?"

"He's still concerned about his visit to the ER."

"Didn't the doctors say he's fine?"

"He wants a follow-up, and he says he needs to have his cholesterol checked again."

"We did a blood panel two months ago."

"He says he just wants to make sure."

I suppose I shouldn't complain. He was helping me make my car payments.

Alison leaned forward. "I suppose you saw the news."

"Yes. I'm surprised he has been doing that well in the primaries."

"That's not the news I'm talking about."

I thought for a moment. Then I remembered the front page of the *Register*.

Alison gave a small smile. "It seems like a bit of, uh, shaduh... chayda..."

"Schadenfreude. It means 'happiness at the misfortune of others.'"

"No, I was thinking of that word that means 'what goes around comes around.'"

"You're thinking about karma. However, people can feel schadenfreude over someone's karma."

"Is that what you're feeling, Dr. Glass?"

I thought for a moment more.

"I don't know how I feel about it, Alison."

•   •   •   •

"I had to play that damn *Treasure Planet* DVD again to get Dylan to go to sleep. If I have to hear that whiny-ass song from that Goo Goo Dolls singer one more time..."

Teresa staggered into the bedroom, exhausted. She had a full schedule taking care of the kids, getting them to school, and cleaning up the house. This wasn't the life she expected or wanted from me. It was hard to have luxuries since I started my practice and had to pull extra shifts at the hospital to keep us afloat financially. My student loans were taking longer to pay off than expected, and the practice wasn't earning enough to cover expenses. The bedroom was the only place we could find time to be together and have any happiness.

She opened the middle drawer of our dresser. There, she kept the bustiers, the teddies, and the leather corsets. She had several hundred dollars' worth of negligee in that drawer. She pulled out each item and looked at the size tags with despair. She had a difficult pregnancy with Dylan. She spent three months on bed rest and put on twenty extra pounds she never got off.

"I don't have a damn thing to wear!"

"Then wear that."

"You want me like *this*!?"

She turned around sharply. She wore a red Anaheim Angels 2002 World Series Champions t-shirt and a pair of loose denim mommy shorts.

"Yeah." I spoke with a smile and low, soft voice.

Teresa just slumped her shoulders. "You think I'm fat..."

"Of course not!" I got out of bed. My blood started to swell as I rushed towards her. I still found her physically attractive. When I put my hands on her forearms, the warmth of her skin stirred me more. But she wasn't feeling it. She looked away from me.

"But I'm tired of feeling like some dumpy econowife."

"You're not." I glided my hands down her soft, warm arms and wrapped them gently around her wrists. I gave her a small tug towards the bed.

She looked down at my hands. "Then can you tie me up?"

She still liked things spicy, but it became less like wasabi and more like Taco Bell sauce packets.

I opened the top drawer of my nightstand. The red silk rope was coiled up on the right side next to the matching red satin blindfold. The rest of the drawer was filled with VHS tapes, books, magazines, and assorted accessories, including a butt plug she only used once. She had several hundred dollars' worth of merchandise in that drawer too. The rope itself was $15 plus tax and shipping. I could have bought the same length of rope for $3 at The Home Depot.

Teresa stepped to the edge of the bed. Her bare legs touched the fitted sheet where I had pulled back the covers while getting out. She brought her arms behind her back.

"Last time, you said that was uncomfortable," I said.

"I don't feel tied up unless my hands are behind my back."

Sex had always been a grand performance for Teresa, and she was the star. I had been glad to be her supporting actor. We didn't mesh anywhere else besides the bedroom. She would complain about money. She would complain about having to drive everywhere to take the kids to school, Muriel to softball practice, and Dylan to tee ball. She would talk about how gauche the other mothers were, especially the ones from the nearby megachurch who she called smug and self-righteous. But for

Teresa and me, everything worked out in the bedroom. We settled many arguments with our genitals.

I pulled the rope out of the drawer and walked around behind her. The back of her t-shirt had the roster of the World Series team. She crossed her wrists over Mike Scioscia. The last time I tied her up, she complained that it hurt. So, I looked up the proper way to bind a woman's wrists on a website, something called "Hawthorne." I folded the length of rope in half so one end formed a loop. I slid the rope between her back and wrists and held the looped end between Troy Percival and Darin Erstad. Then, I threaded the two loose ends through the loop until the rope encircled her wrists. I pulled the loose ends. It had to be the right amount of tightness. If it were too tight, it would cut off her circulation. Too loose, and she wouldn't get off.

Bondage didn't completely make sense to me, but it was better than anilingus. It did turn me on. Usually, she wouldn't trust me to do the housework, shop, manage our finances, take care of the kids, or even pick out my clothes for work. Yet, she trusted me enough to make herself vulnerable to me.

I wrapped the rest of the rope around her wrists and tied it in a neat square knot. This was only the first of the ropes she wanted around her. She wanted her ankles bound too. Then around her torso. And if she had been on some Japanese website, I would spend hours doing macrame on her body. I just wanted to get off.

I put my arms around her and pulled her tight against me. Her bound arms did feel good as they pressed against my stomach. Usually, she started squirming, which really got me aroused. She would then reach down and fondle me. But she did neither that night. Her arms and fingers were still.

"Are you going to gag me?"

I turned her around and pressed on her shoulders until she sat down on the edge of the bed.

"How about this?"

I leaned over and pressed my lips hard against her. My weight made her lean back. I reached under her thighs and pulled her onto the bed. Those extra pounds made her harder to move, but I still had enough youth and adrenaline back then. I pulled my lips away from her and rolled her on her stomach. When she was tied up, she liked when I reached around her from behind. I slipped my right hand up her shirt and clasped my left hand over her mouth. I liked it when she tried to struggle against my body, and how warm her breath was on my palm as she moaned. But she felt unusually passive that night. I had to do something to stir her. I rested my chin on her shoulder and whispered into her ear.

"I want you, Teresa."

I reached for her breast. She still had on her bra. I stuck my hand under the cup and rolled her nipple between my thumb and forefinger. Now, she was starting to flex her jaw violently. I thought I finally got her going, but she pulled her face away from my hand.

"My bra," she gasped. "Be careful with it! It's new."

"OK, OK." I pulled my hand quickly out of her cup.

I knew one other way that was sure to stir her. I moved my right hand down from under her shirt and into her shorts and panties. My fingers dipped between her labia. She hadn't gotten moist yet, but I knew the right place to touch.

She let out a soft moan.

I slipped my left arm under her torso and held her tight. She started to squirm and moan, which made me harden. As her moisture touched the fingertips on my right hand, I got fully engorged. I released both my hands and reached for the button and zipper of her shorts. I pulled them and her panties down over her buttocks.

"Wait, wait," she gasped.

"What?"

She turned on her side and looked up at me. "Spank me."

I froze.

She lifted her head towards me. "You heard me?"

"Of course."

"Then spank me!"

I moved away from her and sat up.

"I…"

She turned her head and stared at me.

"I can't," I murmured.

"You what?"

"Teresa, you know how I feel about…"

"Grandma Dinah? Again?"

"I…"

She rolled on her back and sat up straight. "Jesus Christ, Oliver! For fuck's sake!"

"You know that…"

"I didn't say to beat the shit out of me! I just want a love spank."

"Teresa, you know I can't…"

"You can't stop living in the past! That's what you can't do, Oliver! You can't stop talking about your father! And your grandmother! And your brother! You can't even shut up about your fucking high school!"

"Teresa, please! You don't understand…"

"*You* don't understand! We have a life, Oliver! Right here and right now! Maybe you're too damn busy to notice, but you have kids who want your attention. And a wife who's tied up and wants to be fucked! You can still fuck me, can't you, Oliver!?"

I leaned her back on the bed and rolled her on her stomach. Then I untied her wrists. When I got her hands free, she rolled on her back again, swung back her arm, and slapped me hard across the cheek.

"Then, fuck you!"

She pulled up her shorts and panties as she scrambled out of bed. She slammed the bedroom door behind her.

•   •   •

"Everything sounds fine, Mr. Marchenko." I pulled the stethoscope away from his chest. "You can button up now."

I went to the counter and flipped open his chart. "Your last blood panel from February looked good. Your triglycerides were slightly elevated, but manageable. Everything else is normal. So, why do you want another cholesterol test?"

"Do you know how old I am, Dr. Glass?"

I flipped to the front page of his chart. "It says you'll be 55 in July."

"That was the age my father was when he died."

I turned towards him. "How did he die, Mr. Marchenko?"

I expected to hear a clinical cause of death, but he told me something different.

"He died without meeting my wife or going to our wedding. He died without seeing his grandchildren or showing them his medals from Korea. He never got to take my mom to Europe. He wanted to show her the village in Ukraine where his family came from and see the house in Ribeauville where her family hid Jews from the Nazis. He never saw my son play Lucky in his high school production of *Dames at Sea*, or my daughter win a blue ribbon for her photography at the Orange County Fair."

He leaned forward and stared directly into my eyes.

"I don't want to wind up that way. I want to grow old with my wife. I want to walk my daughter down the aisle at her wedding. I want to hold my grandchildren. Life is so short and goes by so fast. I don't want to miss out, Dr. Glass. You understand, don't you?"

I nodded.

"Then, will you please order my cholesterol test?"

CHAPTER TWENTY-TWO

Reseda

God takes us where we need to go and teaches us the lessons we need to learn. Whenever I tell people this in speeches or in ministries, they begin to feel peace about their circumstances. They stop looking for people to blame and stop feeling like victims in their own lives. God is in control at all times and in all situations. When you think He is bringing trials and suffering in your life, He offers His grace to get you through them.

I set *Face Time with Jesus* down on the sleeping bag. It was still daylight, so I parted the black plastic tarp to let in enough light for reading.

I laid back on the sleeping bag and thought about what Steven wrote. So, what was God doing when he brought cancer into the lives of Pearl and her mom? Or Dad and his mom? Where was God's grace when He let Grandma Josephine die? Or a couple weeks later when Dad learned Steven was fucking Mom?

That was why I had such a hard time taking in what Steven wrote. As I tried to read those supposedly uplifting words, the words that Mrs. Cimino said saved her life, I can't erase my image of the man who wrote them. He had sex with my mom while Dad was grieving for his. He made fun of that pastor whose son died. He beat me with a belt, told me how worthless I was, and threw me out of the house. Those were the reasons I had a hard time reading his words. They may be words from the mouth of God, but they were written with the hands of an asshole.

But there was one time I had seen him do something genuinely kind. We were about to leave the mall, and there was a homeless man holding a cardboard sign. I expected Steven to do what he always did, drive past him while muttering, "Wealth is the sign of God's favor." But this time, Steven stopped.

"Randall?"

The homeless man's eyes opened wide. "Steven, is that you?"

"Yes!"

Steven seemed strangely pleased, but I felt increasingly uncomfortable. Especially with all those cars behind us in the driveway. But Steven persisted.

"You've always sung so beautifully. Sing 'Che gelida manina' from *La Bohème*, like you did in the barracks."

I looked away in embarrassment. Not only was Steven holding up traffic, he was humiliating this poor homeless man by making him sing in public.

But the man complied without hesitation. And Steven was right. He sang beautifully. I didn't understand a word he sang, but it was the most beautiful thing I've ever heard. And instead of honking their horns and cursing him out, everyone behind us leaned out their car windows and applauded. Someone even caught it on video and posted it. And this homeless man gave the biggest smile, like he had this beautiful gift that he had to keep locked up for so long, and he finally let it be free.

Steven's smile broadened too. "Get in!"

It seemed ironic as I sat homeless in my SUV, but at the time, I felt unnerved about letting some homeless guy in our car. But Steven was cool with him, and he did sing like an angel. He also didn't seem all smelly and gross like I thought a homeless person would be. Or what I wound up being. Steven let his friend hang out at our house for a bit. He then gave him money and sent him on his way. I thought it was cool that Steven went out of his way for an old friend who needed help.

But why wouldn't he help me when I needed it? Perhaps I should have learned how to sing opera.

·   ·   ·

TAP TAP TAP.

What the fuck was that? My whole body stiffened.

TAP TAP TAP.

I reached under my pile of clothes for the folding knife. But what if it's a cop? If I came out holding anything that looked like a weapon, I'd be dead. But what if it isn't a cop, but that drug dealer I saw the other night? Or a thief?

I parted the black plastic tarp to look. I couldn't see anything, so I parted it further. I slowly opened the rear passenger door and jumped out.

"What are you doing here?"

I must have startled Pearl because she stood there stiff and nervous. Or maybe she was stunned by the funk that came out of the car. She clasped her hands behind her back. It was the same way they made us stand at the military academy when we're about to get our asses chewed out. I didn't notice her outfit earlier, but she wore a short dark blue skirt and a light blue button-down dress blouse.

I relaxed my shoulders, hoping it would put her at ease. She unclasped her arms and let them fall to her sides.

She took a deep breath. "I'm sorry I didn't get a chance to thank you."

I smiled. "That's OK."

She stared at the Explorer. "You really sleep in that?"

I nodded.

"Can I look?"

I nodded again. I already been in her bedroom. Why not show her mine?

I opened the lift gate. She stepped to the bumper and looked around. She didn't seem grossed out or turned off. But something caught her attention.

"So, do you believe in God the Celestial Concierge, who answers all your prayers if you donate generously to the TV ministry of your choice?"

I blinked a few times until I realized she was looking at my copy of *Face Time with Jesus*.

"Oh, that." I felt a lot of things towards Steven, but I never felt as embarrassed as I did then. It felt worse when Pearl turned to me, expecting some sort of answer.

"Mrs. Cimino gave it to me," I replied.

"Mrs. Cimino?"

"You know. Short, thin, curled gray hair. One of our regulars."

"She must think you need saving."

"Isn't it obvious?"

I smiled. Pearl smiled back.

She looked into the Explorer. "May I come in?"

I nodded. How was I going to say no? She crawled in on her hands and knees. Her skirt was rather short. Did I see her panties?

I was getting that vibe from her, a vibe I felt with Zoey and other girls before. If I got too close to her, we were going to start fucking. It was something neither one of us could stop or control. It was just going to happen. And as Pearl turned around and sat on my sleeping bag, that vibe was starting to overpower me.

But I didn't have a condom. And I wasn't going to run to the gas station to get one because Carlos was there, and I didn't trust the condoms they sold there anyway. More than that, I still didn't know how I felt about Pearl. Yes, she had been kind to let me shower at her house, and I felt bad about her and her mother. But she was still someone I worked with. And having sex with someone you work with is super awkward. And she already made it clear that if I wanted to have sex with her, I couldn't. And I wasn't completely sure I even wanted to.

She stared at me from inside my SUV. "Aren't you coming in?"

As I climbed inside the Explorer, I couldn't help but brush against her. Her legs, so soft and smooth. She still had defined muscles from what must have been years of playing sports. I turned to my side, propping myself up with my arm. She settled onto my sleeping bag, resting on her back. She bent her leg. Her hitched-up skirt showed more of her firm, muscular thighs.

I watched her chest rise and fall with each deepening breath. The buttons on her blouse climbed up a neat line across her good-sized breasts, and they seem to puff out a little where she had tucked her blouse into her skirt. Oh, how I wanted to pull out her shirt tails and unbutton every one of those buttons. How I wanted to caress those firm thighs. But I knew her body was a trap. I'd get stuck in those thighs, never to escape.

She turned her head towards me. Even her neck muscles looked sexy as they shifted under her skin.

"Ever feel uncomfortable here?"

I did at that moment. Our breath and body heat made the back of the Explorer warm. I was grateful I left the lift gate open, or we might have suffocated. Or started fucking like crazy.

"Not really." I wiped my forehead. It really was getting warm. "I guess it can get uncomfortable when it gets hotter. It gets hot in the Valley, doesn't it?"

She gave a small nod. She didn't wear any makeup. Working minimum wage, how could she afford it? But Pearl's lips were full and smooth, and hard not to kiss.

Those lips parted. "Why did you come here?"

"I got kicked out of the house."

She gave a small smile. "How'd you fuck up?"

I exhaled hard. My breath felt warmer with her there.

"Come on," she encouraged, "You can tell me everything. I already know you're circumcised."

My voice got caught in my throat. It sounded like a deep, soft gurgle. I realized I had no choice to let it all come out. She already knew I was homeless. What more could I say that would turn her off?

"I partied, you know. Did all that party stuff. Drinking, drugs…"

"Sex?"

I nodded. Why was she so fucking interested in that part of me? If it's because she really wanted to fuck me, why did she say I couldn't?

She turned to her side, facing me. The way her skirt hitched up. The muscles flexing beneath her skin. Then those deep set pale blue eyes locking on to mine. I wanted her so bad, but I knew I couldn't.

She fluttered her eyelids. "Where did you come from?"

"Dana Point. You know where that is?"

"Orange County, right?"

I nodded.

Her eyes narrowed slightly. "So, what are you doing here? You could be living by the beach."

"I've already lived by the beach. I wanted to be somewhere different."

"Behind an old movie theater?"

"It's different."

"So, what's the OC like? Hot blonds in tiny bikinis? Daily trips to Disneyland? Retail therapy at South Coast Plaza?"

"It's nothing like TV."

"Same with Reseda. No one's going to teach you karate by washing his car."

I smiled. They once showed us that movie in the military academy. The instructor talked about karate moves, and muscle memory, and adapting to pain. I didn't think that was all that movie was about.

She shifted closer to me. Her breath warmed the car.

"So, what are you looking for?"

Pearl asked me some tough and embarrassing questions. But this was the first one I couldn't answer.

"I don't know." I turned and rested on my back. At first, the felt headliner seemed the most comfortable thing to look at. But its blankness, the seams, and the small patches of worn cloth made me more uncomfortable.

"It's OK if you don't know," she said. "We don't know what we're looking for until we find it."

I turned my head towards her. "What are you looking for?"

She stared directly into my eyes. "Something I know I can't have."

I didn't know what she meant. Was it for her mom to get well? Probably. My heart broke seeing how sick she was. How it made her look so old, even though—who knows how old she is?

Did she mean that she couldn't go to college? She clearly couldn't afford the time or money to go with her mom being sick.

But what if it's *me* she wanted and couldn't have? If she wanted me, she could. Was something holding her back?

I couldn't come right out and ask her though. I had to prod.

"I'm surprised you don't find me disgusting. Sleeping in an SUV like this."

"Why should I? You fucked up. We all do."

"Not you. I saw your high school diploma. And those trophies."

She looked away.

"I mean, you were a superstar at—what was the name of your high school?"

Pearl sat up quickly. "I got to go."

She got out of the back of the Explorer, straightened out her skirt, and flattened the front of her blouse. I followed her to her Kia, which she had parked next to my car. The taillights flashed as she unlocked the car with her remote. She looked back at me.

"Let me know whenever you need to take a shower." She opened her car door. "And thank you for helping me today."

"You're welcome," I said with a soft smile. "See you tomorrow."

She nodded. "See you."

She was about to enter her car, but she stopped. She leaned against the roof of her car and stared at me. A serious stare.

"It's Reseda High School. And my fuck-up? Trying to be too good."

She got in the car quickly and shut the door.

I stood and watched the reverse lights glow white as she backed out of the parking space. She put the car into drive and pulled away.

That heavy sadness returned as I headed slowly back to the Explorer. I lowered myself on the bumper and stared at the cracked and faded gray asphalt of an abandoned parking lot.

•　•　•

Cold and wet. Something cold and wet on the back of my arm. My eyes flew open. It was still dark outside, and the inside of the Explorer was pitch black. I fumbled for my iPhone. When I could feel the hard rectangle, my thumb poked around for the Home button. My eyes focused on the glowing screen. I unlocked the phone. The time was 2:17 a.m. I turned on the flashlight on my phone. First, I shined it on the back of my arm. It was wet there, but how? Then I shined the light on the black plastic tarps against the windows. They were all dripping wet. It must have been condensation. Was it because both Pearl and I were in the back?

That was when I noticed something damp and sticky somewhere else.

"Shit!"

I scrambled out of the sleeping bag and shined the light on my boxers. I lifted the waistband and looked inside.

"Shit! Shit! Shit!"

Blowing a load in my boxers was bad enough at home. The first time Mom and Steven caught me, I got the belt. They should have gotten a visit from Child Protective Services. Still, I knew better than to spank it. And if it happened by accident, I had to take a shower immediately and throw the boxers away on my way to school. Mom would just figure our maid Lucinda lost them, and she would give her a scolding. It didn't bother Lucinda because Mom would bitch at her in English, and Lucinda only spoke Spanish. I learned the best Spanish swear words listening to Lucinda.

But I had no spare boxers to throw away. Mom and Steven only gave me three. Two of them got so crusty and stunk so badly after several weeks I couldn't wear them anymore. I blew my load in the pair Pearl washed for me. I guess I ruined my perfect "no cum stains" record.

And how was I going to wash myself off? Pearl offered me the use of her shower, but she was the reason I shot my wad in the first place! And how was I going to get to her house before work? Walk down Reseda Boulevard at 2:17 in the morning in my sticky boxers with the stench of cum? I'd attract psychos like flies to shit!

There was only one thing I could do.

•   •   •

Reza lowered his Persian language newspaper. "What are you doing here so..."

"Is it open?"

He nodded.

I ducked in as fast as I could and made sure that door was completely locked. I even jiggled the handle to be sure. I had to get completely naked. Jeans, sticky boxers, t-shirt, everything off my body as fast as I could. I turned on the water. Not too hot, not too cold.

Then, I had to get my dick under the water. The sink was just a little higher than I needed it to be, so I had to get on my tiptoes until I could flop my balls over the edge of the sink.

But I couldn't reach the water. I wasn't *Boogie Nights* material.

I had to cup the streaming water in my palm and splash it on my circumcision. I felt horrible for whoever was going to use this bathroom next. With enough water and soap, I was finally clean. I pulled my dick out of the sink and sighed quietly. I patted it down with paper towels. I then did a quick wash of my face, hands, and the back of my arm where I got wet just so I didn't have to bother Reza again in the morning. Another patting with paper towels, and I threw on my clothes as fast as possible. Not the boxers. I couldn't wear those again. But I couldn't throw them in Reza's trash can. He'd never let me use his bathroom again if he knew what I did. I carefully folded them with the jizz in the middle and stuffed them in my pocket.

I straightened myself up and opened the door. And there were two LAPD police officers right outside the door.

I could have thrown up on myself right there. That would have made a bigger mess, but at least I could have showered in jail. Instead, I smiled.

"Good morning, officers."

I walked by them like I was supposed to be there. The officers just glanced at me and let me go by.

Once I got past the door, I looked back at the gas station. Through the windows, I saw one of the officers go into the bathroom.

I took the long way back to the Explorer. I didn't want the officers to know I slept there.

I stopped by a trash can in front of the abandoned theater. I pulled the stained boxers out of my pocket. I exhaled and continued walking with the boxers still in my hand. I could have thrown my boxers away at home, but I no longer had spare ones to throw away.

•   •   •

And I didn't have any boxers to wear. I couldn't wear the other ones without itching like crazy, and those shitkickers could have smelled them from the donut shop. I could go to the laundromat. There's one across the street from work. I had the money, and I could buy laundry detergent at Buck & Awesome.

Or I could ask Pearl to—No, I spent my whole life having others do things for me. Mom and Steven even paid people to do things for me. It was time for me to do things for myself.

But when I walked across the street, the laundromat was closed. It didn't open until 7:00 a.m. And I didn't know how long it took to wash clothes. They might not even be done by the time I had to get to work.

My last resort was to go commando until I could do my laundry after work.

•

Which turned out to be a horrible idea.

The day before, I had walked all over Reseda in my jeans. They felt gritty and had a nasty, sweaty funk. My balls felt like they were bouncing against sandpaper. My dick would wind up a chaffed raw stump by end of the day. But it would mean I wouldn't have to worry about blowing my load in my boxers anymore.

I glanced at the cars driving past on Sherman Way. But I didn't feel like stepping in front of them, even though it was the only way to stop the discomfort. I thought back to when I freeballed it in Pearl's sweats, how soft and fluffy the insides were. Even that made me think about my discomfort, how I now had to dangle in my nasty jeans, and I how I wished there was something that could distract me from this pain.

"¡Hola, Dylan!"

Thank God for Magdalena. I was surprised to see her working on a Saturday morning. I thought Jews were supposed to take off on Saturdays. Dad told me that, but he worked Saturdays anyway. I was grateful Magdalena worked that morning.

I smiled at her, but she could tell something was wrong.

"Are you OK?"

I couldn't tell her, "No, because my nut sack is getting sanded off layer by layer." I had to change the subject.

"I'm curious. How did you recover from your stroke?"

I wished I hadn't said that. She wasn't mad, though. She let out a small "Hm" and thought for a moment.

"I stopped being angry about it."

"Angry?" I couldn't imagine such a kind woman like Magdalena being angry at anything.

"All my life, I've done things myself. When Mamá died, I ran this restaurant by myself. When my husband left, I raised my children by myself. I worked all day and night. I could cook everything on the menu, clean the dishes, greet the customers, manage the finances, and still be home in time to kiss my children good night."

She looked away for a moment and then stared right at me.

"I had just turned 50. That may seem old to you, but I still felt young. I had more energy than some half my age. My oldest was in college. My youngest was about to graduate high school. How was I going to take care of them? Would they have to give up their lives to take care of me? What will happen to the restaurant? Would it have to close after Mamá and I ran it for 40 years?"

"You must have been scared."

"And angry." Her face tightened in a way I had never seen it before. "What did I do to get sick? I did everything right. I never smoked. I never overate. I worked on my feet all day. Why did I get sick? How could God do this to me?"

"How did you get over it?"

Her face loosened up. "I remembered Mamá. How she suffered so much more than I did. How she suffered in Auschwitz. How hard it was for her to come to America to start a new life. I did everything the doctors and therapists told me. I had to relearn everything. How to speak. How to write. How to walk. How to cook. I couldn't get back everything." She jiggled her cane a little. "But I was able to get back to living."

"And that's what stopped you from being angry?"

She gave me one of her crooked smiles.

"I realized God brought this stroke to me, just as He brought suffering to Mamá's life and mine. I had to learn to appreciate life and remember to be kind, just as Mamá taught me."

She nodded at me. I nodded back. She smiled.

"Now, are you OK?"

I thought for a moment. As I listened to Magdalena, I had forgotten about how uncomfortable my jeans felt. I couldn't complain about anything when I heard what she had been through.

So, I said, "Yes, Magdalena."

"Good." She handed me a bag of pan dulces.

CHAPTER TWENTY-THREE

Lake Forest

Little League dealt us a rough schedule. Moshe's game in Foothill Ranch was the same time as David's at Heroes Park. Rachel and I decided we had to split up. She would go to Moshe's game, and I would go to David's.

David put on his uniform and packed his bat bag the moment he got out of bed. We had gathered around Moshe's bedroom door, waiting for him.

"Come on, Moshe. We're going to be late!" Rachel called.

"I'm coming," he whined from behind his door.

After a moment, his bedroom door opened. Rachel carefully inspected his uniform. Her eyes narrowed. She knew something was wrong.

"Where is your cup?"

"Do I have to wear it?" He whined, "It's uncomfortable, and it hurts!"

"It will hurt more if you get hit there." She pointed towards his room. He slumped his shoulders and walked back in.

•   •   •

David sat quietly on our way to Heroes Park. A glance in the rear-view mirror showed me why. He had his earbuds in, and he bobbed his head to the music. The iPod was a birthday gift from his father. There was no way Rachel would buy her kids their own. An iPhone was out of the question.

I was lucky to find a space in the parking lot, and it wasn't too far from the field. I got out first. As David got out of the car, I took a quick glance at his screen. Rachel couldn't have possibly let him download that song.

I waited until he pulled out his earbuds. "Aren't you a little young to be listening to that?"

"It gets me pumped for the game."

I opened the lift gate and hoped he had the radio edit version of that song. As David pulled out his bat bag, something in the bed caught his attention.

"Is that your glove?"

I forgot about the glove. It was a softball glove I bought when Muriel started playing. We used to play catch in the park. I also used it with Dylan when he played. It wasn't made for baseball, but I had broken it in enough by then so I could grip baseballs with it. I kept it in the back of my Explorer. When I gave the Explorer to Dylan, I moved the glove to my Nissan Pathfinder. When the Pathfinder got totaled, I moved the glove to my new Lexus. I didn't know why I kept a glove with me long after I stopped playing catch with the kids. Or I didn't know until David asked me.

I nodded.

"Can you warm me up?"

"Sure." I smiled and reached into the bed for my glove. It felt stiff from sitting unused for years. I flapped it open and closed to loosen it up. David walked down a slope to an open strip of grass next to the AA field. I followed him down and picked a spot a few yards away from him. I kept flapping the glove open and close, but it still felt stiff.

David already had his bat bag open and his glove on. I called out to him. "Do you have a ball?"

He pulled out a ball and tossed it to me. He had a strong and accurate throw that made the ball pop solidly into my glove. My glove still felt stiff, so I chucked the ball hard into the pocket to loosen it up some more. I did several times until I thought the glove was loose enough. I pulled the ball out of the glove and looked at it. It was an old, yellowed ball that said "Saddleback Little League" in faded blue print. That was the league Mom would have signed me up for if I had the heart to continue playing after Dad died. Or if Grandma Dinah allowed me to play.

I looked down the field. David held up his glove and wiggled it a little. It was how baseball players said, "Throw it to me."

My muscles still remembered the proper mechanics of throwing. I still worried if my throw would be strong and accurate enough. It popped into his glove. He scooped it out of his glove and into his throwing hand. He gave another strong, straight throw that made the ball pop in my glove. I threw it back to him. He threw it back to me. We started getting into a rhythm. Throw and pop. Throw and pop. The ball made a beige arc between us.

"Dr. Glass?" David called out as he started another arc towards me. The ball popped in my glove.

"Yes?" I shouted as I hurled the ball back.

The ball popped in his glove. "How long have you lived with us?"

He threw the ball back. I waited for it to pop in my glove.

"About six months. Why do you ask?" I threw the ball back. It popped in his glove.

"I know nothing about you." He threw the ball.

The ball popped in my glove. "What would you like to know?"

I could tell he was thinking as he watched the ball arc into his glove.

"Why did you become a doctor?"

I stood and thought as the ball arced towards me and popped in my glove.

"I want to help people. I know how hard it is when people get sick. I want to help them get better."

Throw and pop.

"Did any of your patients die?"

Throw and pop.

"Yes, David."

Throw and pop.

"How did that make you feel?"

Throw and pop. I took the ball out of my glove for a second and studied its yellowed skin.

"It's a part of life. It happens to all of us."

I threw the ball. This time, it went off target. But David scooted over and made the catch. He stepped back to where he stood.

"I don't want to be a doctor." He tossed the ball back.

"Why?" The ball popped in my glove. I held it there as I waited for his answer.

"They're always tired and unhappy. And they don't feel anything."

I found myself staring at the grass at the tip of my tennis shoe. I then looked up. David was holding up his glove and wiggling it.

· · ·

"1-2-3, Bruins!"

David's team broke from their huddle and lined up along the third-base line as their opponents, the Hurricanes, lined up along the first-base line. The two teams slowly walked towards home plate. As they passed each other, they held out their arms and gave a sportsmanlike slap on the hand and a murmured "Good game." Each team then rushed to their dugout.

The Bruins won 10-6, but both teams seemed equally enthusiastic about getting out of the dugout and getting snack.

Some parents went down to the field for maintenance duty. I stayed on the bleachers and waited for David.

As I looked out on the field, I wondered if I ever saw Dad happy. I had seen him smile a few times, including when I won that trophy. He could even tell a joke in a quiet, droll sort of way. It made people burst out laughing because no one expected that from him. People especially laughed when he said "goodbye." It seemed random and funny to them, even as it made me cringe and caused Mom to turn away in grief. He stopped telling jokes after that patient died.

If I got that unhappy after any of my patients died, I would have hung myself in the garage too. It was better not to feel.

"Dr. Glass?"

I looked down. David was holding up a red ticket.

"Mrs. Fernandez gave all of us tickets for food at the snack bar!"

I nodded. "You remember what your mom said. Get something healthy."

"Yes, Dr. Glass." He ran to catch up with his teammates.

I realized I gave him useless advice. They never sell anything healthy at a snack bar.

• • •

I followed David. The snack bar was in a brick building at the other end of the park. The kids gathered around the windows to place their orders while I stood with a group of parents chatting nearby.

"I hope they get what they deserve," a woman behind me said.

"Greedy bastards like them give all us Christians a bad name," a man grumbled.

"You got us good today."

The words seemed to be directed to me. I turned to my side. A short, stocky man in a San Diego Padres cap stood next to me. I assumed his son played on the Hurricanes. I could tell from his dour expression he took the loss to David's team personally. Muriel's teams had been on both sides of the scoreboard, so I knew how to respond.

I gave a sportsmanlike smile and held out my hand. "My name's Ollie." Again, I knew better than to introduce myself as Oliver.

"Grant." He gave my hand a firm shake. "Who's your kid?"

"David. He's number 12." I glanced towards the snack bar as he handed the woman his ticket.

"Good player. Turned a mean double play."

I smiled, but not too much. David's play killed their rally in the third.

"Which one's yours?"

"Emmett. Number 47."

I thought for a moment. I didn't recall seeing him on the field.

"What position does he play?"

"Bench." His expression soured. He then reached out and touched my arm. It was a signal to move away from the rest of the group of parents. I followed him to an open spot a couple feet away. He lowered his voice. "His coach. Total daddy ball. His kid and his friends always get the prime positions. That's the problem with sports. Too damn political."

I heard this type of talk before. The parents who thought their kid would be the next Jennie Finch or Derek Jeter if their stupid coach would let them play. There was something in the frustration in Grant's voice that kept me from blowing him off.

"If he wants to play next season, I'll let him play. If he doesn't, I'll let him quit. No point forcing your kid to do something he hates. Sports don't do a damn thing for kids anyway. See him?" Grant turned his head towards a tall man with a Mets cap walking towards the Majors field. He had a large equipment bag slung over his shoulder. I assumed he was a coach. "Fredrickson managed an All-Star Team to a District 55 championship last year. His oldest got a girl pregnant at 15."

Dylan had his problems, but at least he didn't get a girl pregnant.

"So, what would your son do instead of baseball?"

Grant's frown grew deeper. "Why make kids do anything? Doesn't matter how many organized activities you put them in. They're going to be their own people anyway. Let them be who they want to be."

"Dr. Glass?" David held up a hot dog and a can of Coke.

I turned to Grant. "See you later."

"See ya," he replied.

I started walking with David. I patted him on the shoulder. "You better finish that before we get home. We don't want your mom to see that."

David turned his head and gave me a conspiratorial smile.

· · ·

There were no smiles when we came home. I could hear Moshe's cries before I reached his bedroom door.

"He made a fool of himself today!" Rachel's face scrunched into a display of anger I had never seen from her before. But it was too similar to angry faces I had seen in my past.

David must have felt uncomfortable too. He shuddered as he stood beside me. I patted him on the shoulder.

"Why don't you get changed?"

Without a word, he rushed into his bedroom.

I extended my hand a little and waved my fingers to tell Rachel to follow me. We walked into the living room. I turned and faced her. She folded her arms and stiffened her stance.

I spoke calmly, "What happened?"

"There was a fly ball. He ran away from it. It dropped right in front of him."

I saw this happen many times when eight-year-olds play softball and baseball. I've even seen Major League players drop routine fly balls. The anger on Rachel's face showed there was more to the story.

"Then what happened?"

"The coach tried to correct him. But Moshe, he threw his glove down on the ground. The coach had to pull him off the field and made him do pushups behind the bleachers. Now he wants to quit!"

The words "Then let him quit" formed in my mouth, but I couldn't bring myself to say that. Nor did Rachel give me a chance to say it.

"Do you know how expensive it is to have your kid play sports? The registration is expensive enough. Plus, you have to buy the equipment, the cleats, the uniforms. And most parents pay to get professional coaching for their kids. And have them play on travel teams. I don't want to spend all that money and have him quit just like that! And what if it's not just baseball? What if he wants to quit soccer too? What if I can't get him to do anything!?"

I could tell her about what Grant said to me, but I couldn't bring myself to say that either.

Instead, I softly told her, "Do you want me to talk to him?"

She turned away from me. "He's my kid. I'll deal with it myself."

.   .   .

I felt useless in this situation, so I retreated to the study. I tapped the trackpad to wake up my MacBook Pro. I opened Mail to look for a reply from Dylan. No reply.

I could understand why Rachel didn't want me to talk to Moshe. He was her son. But if she asked me to talk to him, what would I say? What advice could I give him? What advice did I give to Muriel and Dylan?

I tried to replay every conversation I had with them. I came up blank. I could remember clearly what happened with Dad 35 years ago, or Grandma Dinah 20 years ago, or Teresa 13 years ago, but I couldn't recall any experiences with my own children. I once talked to Dylan about some Captain America movie, but that was about all I could remember.

What was wrong with me? Was I so focused on my own career and my own pain that I missed out on Muriel and Dylan's childhoods? And if I were more present, could I have helped Dylan? Would things have turned out better? Would he still get kicked out of his house and wind up missing?

In my peripheral vision, I noticed the *Orange County Register* next to the sofa. I picked it up and opened it. That large-type headline, that photo, and that article I couldn't bring myself to read. I folded the newspaper up again and put it into my briefcase. I figured that someday, I could bring myself to read it.

And someday, I would show it to Dylan.

CHAPTER TWENTY-FOUR

Reseda

What Magdalena said helped me feel better. I could get through this workday with my dick flopping in my jeans. I pretty much forgot about it with all the work I had to do.

We got a new shipment of Mother's Day cards. Not Hallmark, of course, but a lot of them were actually nice. I took a package of cards out of the box and carefully tore off the cellophane wrapper.

"Lovely selection this year."

I turned around. Mrs. Cimino stepped gingerly around the boxes I had stacked in front of the card display.

"Yeah, I think so too." I slipped the cards and their envelopes into a rack. I reached into the box for another package. I didn't want to be rude to Mrs. Cimino, but I didn't want to get in trouble for chatting. I tore off the cellophane wrapper for the package.

"I used to love getting Mother's Day cards from my children."

"That's good." I slipped the cards and envelopes into the rack and reached for another box. I had to keep stocking the rack. If Mrs. Cimino really was trying to save me, this was not the time.

"I liked their handmade cards. Especially Bernice's. She was such a wonderful artist."

"That's very nice." I started tearing off the cellophane for another package of cards.

"I'm sure you'll want to pick one out for your mother."

I froze. The wrapper between my fingertips. The package half opened. Mrs. Cimino stared through me as if I were as clear as the cellophane. Then she abruptly stepped back.

143

"I'm sorry." Her voice turned somber. "Did your mother pass away?"

"No, it's..." I couldn't think of a way to describe Mom without saying "bitch." So, I just threw out, "We don't talk."

"I see." Her voice sounded unusually tense.

I'd never seen Mrs. Cimino upset before. Even when we ran out of her favorite brand of generic bar soap. Was she angry that I didn't talk to my mom? She is a mother. She probably has grandkids too. So, she'd be pretty pissed if they forget to send her a Mother's Day card. So, why did she say she *used* to love getting Mother's Day cards from them? Did they stop for some reason? Maybe they died. That would make it even worse!

I was relieved when Mrs. Cimino exhaled softly and let her shoulders relax. But then she said, "Did you read that part of the book about forgiveness?"

I thought when I dropped out of school, I didn't have to take any more pop quizzes. And if Mrs. Cimino was pissed at me, I'd hate to make her more pissed by giving the wrong answer. There was that one thing I read. I hoped it was the right one.

"Was it about a key to freedom? Or something like that?"

"'All of us are broken. All of us are flawed. All of us have sinned against God, each other, and ourselves. Until we see the grace in the brokenness in ourselves and others, we cannot receive God's grace.' That was the hardest thing for me to learn." She stared at me for a moment, then she patted me on the shoulder. "I'll let you get back to work."

I watched her continue down the aisle. She seemed to walk a little stiffer. What happened to Mrs. Cimino in her life? Where was she broken? She didn't seem broken at all. How could she be if she thinks she's trying to save me? Yet, something seemed to set her off when I told her I didn't talk to my mom.

I looked at the cards in my hand. They had a watercolor painting of some roses on them. Printed in some fancy script, it said:

Thinking of you across the miles on Mother's Day.
Although we live so far apart,
You'll always be with me in my heart.

I shook my head and stuck the cards and envelopes in the rack. Then, I reached into the box and took out the next package of cards. I quickly tore off the cellophane and stuck the cards in the rack without reading them. I made short work of that box of Mother's Day cards. Anything to forget about forgiveness and brokenness. And my mom.

· · ·

But the next box of cards was harder for me. Graduation cards. I would have graduated high school this year if I hadn't dropped out. Or gotten kicked out. I thought about Pearl's high school and how things would have been different if…

"It's a long day livin' in Reseda."

I turned around. Pearl stood next to me. She wore one of those short baggy dresses again. I guess she ran out of clothes too.

I stared at her. "What'd you say?"

"It's a long day livin' in Reseda."

"Why'd you say that?"

She looked at my lap. "'Cause you're freeballin'."

I stood up and folded my arms. "You have a thing about dicks."

She smiled. "Many women do."

"I have to do my laundry."

She tugged on the sleeve of her baggy dress. "So do I."

"There's a laundromat across the street."

"I have a washing machine and dryer. Remember?"

· · ·

Hours later, I was standing in what she called a service porch. It was basically her laundry room, but it also had the water heater, a cabinet for her cleaning supplies, and a door that led to her backyard. She let me wear the same Reseda Regents t-shirt and sweatpants as last time. Oh, how good it felt to wear something soft!

She walked in carrying a plastic laundry basket piled high with clothes. I saw mine on the top. She wore a Reseda High School Softball t-shirt and white cotton shorts.

145

Muriel had lots of high school t-shirts too. Every team she played on gave some sort of shirt. She'd go to games for all the other teams, and she'd get those t-shirts too. Along with blue face paint so she could paint D and H for Dana Hills on her cheeks for all the football games. A picture of her with that DH once showed up in the "OC Varsity" section of the *Orange County Register.*

I never got into the whole school spirit thing. Now, I'm sorry I didn't.

Pearl set the laundry basket on top of the dryer and flipped up the lid of the washing machine. She started picking through the pile and tossing in items. There were other items she set aside. She seemed to have some system to decide which items to put in.

"Can I help?"

"I got it under control." She tossed in a pair of socks.

"I'd like to learn."

"I'm doing a dark wash. Look for lightweight dark colored items."

My fingers grabbed something lightweight and dark colored. And soft.

"Like this?"

I plucked the item out of the pile. It was a pair of panties. My cheeks burned. She didn't bat an eye.

"Yeah."

I tossed them in the washing machine. I was glad to get those out of my hands. I don't know what would be worse, if they were hers or her mother's.

As I pulled back my hand, I accidentally brushed against the front of Pearl's shirt. She wasn't wearing a bra. I could tell. Her breast jiggled as I touched it. Her nipples poked up the R and the A of "Reseda."

"Sorry," I said.

"No problem." She seemed like she just caught her breath.

Which made it a problem for me. Looking at her breasts bounce a little as she moved. I wanted to reach underneath that high school softball—No. That was way too creepy. The whole thing was fucked up. Pearl and I were legal adults, yet we dressed like high school kids. I'd still be in high school if I hadn't dropped out. Are we adults or high school kids? Who the fuck are we?

I went back to picking through the pile. I stepped a little further away to avoid touching her again. Although I kind of wanted to.

"Who did your laundry?" She pulled out a t-shirt without looking up at me.

"We had a maid."

She set some white items aside. "Poor little rich kid, huh?"

"Now, just poor." I looked through the pile. "Did we get them all?"

"Wait."

She moved aside some t-shirts and pulled out my boxers, the ones I blew my load into. I gasped. But she just looked at the stain like she was figuring out a math problem.

"When you cum, you cum hard."

She was about to toss them in the washing machine.

"Wait!" I cried.

"The sperm's already dead. It all comes out in the wash anyway."

I still cringed as she tossed my cum-stained boxers in with her clothes.

"Besides." She turned to me and smiled. "My bad, right?"

How did she know? And how could I answer?

But she just looked back at the cabinet. "Can you get me a bottle of laundry detergent?"

•   •   •

Her shower, which gave me such relief last time, now made me unnerved. What did she want from me? Did she want me? And why did she say I couldn't have sex with her? Was she married? I didn't see a wedding ring, and she was living with her mom. Or maybe she had a boyfriend. Maybe he was in the Army overseas.

But even if she were free, did I really want her? Could I really have her? What the hell could I offer her? I was sleeping in a fucking SUV!

The girls I knew in Dana Point wanted to be treated right. They wanted guys to take them out to dinner, and not at Taco Bell. They wanted the Pacific Swordfish at Harbor Grill and Yogurtland for dessert. And the best top shelf nug. They wanted a new Forever 21 dress for their birthday, and you better get the right size. The size she *thinks* she is. If she says she's a size 8, and you know she's a size 10, you still get her the size 8. If you get her the size 10, she'll get pissed because she thought you called her fat, even though she'll exchange it for a size 10 later.

I could tell Pearl wasn't that type of girl, but I would want to treat her right. She *deserved* it. And it pissed me off I couldn't do it. And maybe she knew it, which is why she said...

The door creaked open. I grabbed the edge of the shower curtain and clutched it tight over my circumcision.

But I could tell from the direction of Pearl's voice that she stayed near the bathroom door.

"Mom wants you to join us for dinner."

• • •

I got dressed in her bedroom. My clothes were still in the wash, so I got back in that high school t-shirt and freeballed it in her sweatpants again. She let me charge my iPhone next to her MacBook Pro.

I still didn't know what to think as I walked towards the dining room. I had been in mansions that were four times the size of this house. They had cathedral ceilings, crystal chandeliers, and designer couches that cost as much as a compact car. But Pearl's house was the first place where I felt nervous.

Her house was clean and neat. The dark tan carpet seemed dated and faded, but it was well vacuumed and in good repair. They had a sofa and love seat in tan corduroy. It wasn't fashionable, but it looked comfortable. There was a small crack that ran down one wall. Probably from that big earthquake they had about twenty years ago.

One wall had pictures of Pearl. All ages. Some when she was a baby. A child in her Brownie outfit. Pictures of her in Girl Scout uniforms and sports uniforms. There were some pictures of Pearl and her mother together. One showed her mother with her arm around Pearl's shoulders when she was on a youth softball league. It must have been a Mother's Day picture because she was holding a bouquet of flowers. Pearl's mother looked tall and broad shouldered. I noticed that when I transferred her to her wheelchair. If Pearl wore her mom's dresses, no wonder they were big on her. Pearl's mom had the same length and style of hair, except hers was blonder than Pearl's. I then realized that Pearl's mother looked young. And there was no father in any of the pictures.

"The ones in her high school uniforms are my favorite."

Pearl was wheeling her mom into the hallway. She seemed stronger and more cheerful from the day before. She must have regained her strength after chemo. The strength showed in her smile.

"Navy and Columbia blue, such beautiful shades. My school's colors were red and white. Boring."

Pearl seemed a bit embarrassed. That seemed odd considering the type of things she said to me.

"Go on. Have a seat." Pearl's mom spoke with an accent. I couldn't tell where it was from.

Her mom had deep-set blue eyes like Pearl, and her skin seemed a few shades lighter. She must have come from somewhere in Europe. But Pearl's last name was Hawthorne, an American name. Was that her father's name?

Pearl wheeled her mother towards the table. She stopped to move aside a chair that was at the end. I was about to offer to help, but Pearl had already moved her mother to the table. Pearl turned and headed to the kitchen without a word.

I looked out across the table. Plain stainless-steel flatware on paper napkins, but everything was clean and properly arranged. White plastic tumblers filled with ice water. Mom and Steven had Lucinda do all this work, but Pearl was doing it. On top of her job at Buck & Awesome. And taking care of her mother. No wonder why she couldn't go to college. She had no time!

"Have you ever had zlikrofi?"

I looked up at Pearl's mom. "No."

"It's delicious. I never could make it like my mother, but Pearl does an excellent job." She reached out her hand towards me. "She said your name is Duane..."

"Dylan." I smiled. "And your name is?"

"Hannah."

I reached across and shook her hand.

"You were so kind to help me the other day, Dylan."

"Thank you."

"No, thank you."

"It was so nice that Pearl found...Oh!"

Pearl walked in holding two large plates. She served Hannah's dish first, then mine. She returned to the kitchen.

Back home, this was expected. Lucinda served us, then disappeared. But this felt awkward. Pearl wasn't my servant! I was relieved to see Pearl return with her own plate of food.

It looked delicious. Little dumplings, which looked like gnocchi or mini raviolis, but served with cubes of meat, sliced carrots, and pearl onions in some sort of white cream sauce. It reminded me of beef stroganoff. I couldn't wait to dig into Pearl's creation. But there was something we always did at home, something we couldn't start a meal without doing. I looked around the table. Hannah started eating first. Then Pearl started. So, I followed.

It was just as well. I hated saying grace. It seemed like such bullshit. We'd have a terrible day where Muriel and Mom got into some sort of fight, Steven shouted all sorts of shit at me for one thing or another. But at dinner, we were all supposed to hold hands like we're one happy family, thank God for a dinner Lucinda busted her ass to make, and then we'd go back to the arguments we had before dinner.

But the food Pearl made was delicious. The dumplings were filled with potatoes, bacon, and onions. They were rich by themselves, but with the meat and that cream sauce—Wow! I didn't know what country Hannah was from, but it must be someplace awesome to make such great food.

I turned to Pearl. With a big smile, I said, "This is de..."

But she frowned at me, as if I were about to violate some Old World custom by thanking her.

Hannah tried to break the awkwardness. "I understand you're from Orange County."

"Yes. Dana Point."

"Are you familiar with Garden Grove?"

Now, Pearl turned her glare towards her mother. For a moment, the two of them distorted their faces into taut expressions. They were having some sort of silent argument.

From the service porch, a loud BZZZZZ!

"I better get that." Pearl set down her fork and rushed from the table.

Hannah sighed. "It has not been easy for her."

I nodded. "My grandmother had cancer too." I wasn't going to tell Hannah how her story ended.

Hannah stared into the distance. "I never wanted to be a burden for her. She's such a smart girl. They offered her a scholarship to Oklahoma. Then..." She looked down.

I wanted to say something encouraging. But all I could think of was some bullshit from Dr. Steven Fucking Dimity.

"I once read that God takes us where we need to go and teaches us what we need to learn."

As the words came out of my lips, they seemed trite and condescending. And probably offensive. When she looked up with her eyes open, I thought I must have pissed her off.

"You read the book?" She seemed excited.

I blinked my eyes. "*Face Time with Jesus?*"

She gave a small smile and shook her head. "Oh, I don't read things like that."

She reached for the rims of the wheelchair and rolled herself back. She then moved to a bookcase that was built into the back of a divider between the entryway and dining room.

"I found this book at the library bookstore. They were giving it away for free."

She pulled out an old paperback with a cracked spine and faded print. She set it on her lap and wheeled back to the table.

"This book helped me when I really needed it."

She set it on the table. It definitely wasn't *Face Time with Jesus*. The cover had a faded pastel painting of a mountain stream with a rainbow and a glowing white angel floating over it. Hannah pushed the book towards me. I picked it up and looked at the cover more closely.

The Healing Power of God's Light by Reverend Patricia Williams Story.

I flipped over the book and read the description on the back cover.

As Ernest Holmes wrote in The Science of Mind, *"There is one power in the Universe, and we can all use it." Reverend Patricia Williams Story shows how you can tap into this Infinite Intelligence to heal any situation in your life. You will learn how to use the crises in your life to achieve greater personal growth and strength by overcoming them. Discover* The Healing Power of God's Light *and find your way to a better life.*

Reverend Patricia Williams Story is the senior minister of the Windham Hill Church of Religious Science in Palo Alto, California.

This definitely wasn't *Face Time with Jesus.*

I looked up at Hannah.

"You may borrow it, if you like," she said.

"Thank you."

At the same time, we both turned towards Pearl, who had returned to the table. But she was standing up. She picked up her plate with most of her food uneaten.

"I'll finish it later." She carried the plate to the kitchen.

I stared at the food still left on my plate. The food Pearl worked so hard to make.

"You should eat." Hannah encouraged.

• • • •

I couldn't understand why Pearl was so uncomfortable around her mom. I was uncomfortable around my mom, but that's only because she was a bitch to me. I don't know what Hannah did to make Pearl upset.

And I didn't know why Pearl was uncomfortable with me.

"Your clothes are in my bedroom."

I looked into her deep-set pale blue eyes. "Are you OK?"

She turned away. "I need to get you back."

• • •

Pearl had neatly put my clothes in a single pile. Everything I owned in the way of clothing was a stack about a foot and a half high. Next to it was a large gray Kohl's bag. I assumed I would put anything I didn't wear into that bag. I used to fill up an entire closet with my clothes, but I didn't wear most of them. All I had in that pile was all I really needed. And thanks to Pearl, it was all clean.

I peeled off Pearl's clothes and slipped on my boxers as quickly as I could. I didn't want to be naked in her room for that long. I stared at that Reseda Regents shirt. I was now glad Mom and Steven didn't give me that Dana Hills High School Dolphins sweatshirt. I didn't want to dress like a high school kid. I certainly didn't feel like one. Not anymore, at least.

I grabbed my boxers, a t-shirt, jeans, and socks and slipped them on quickly. I then put on my shoes. I had gotten good at getting dressed in a hurry. I straightened up my pile of clothes. I grabbed both handles of the bag and snapped them hard. The bag opened fully. I slid the opening of the bag underneath the pile and pulled up both ends quickly and firmly. The pile remained neat inside the bag.

I had to get my iPhone and charger, which was plugged in next to Pearl's MacBook Pro. The charger was snug inside the socket. I pulled hard. As the charger came out, my hand accidentally bumped her laptop. And the screen came on.

I found myself drawn to her laptop. She had her web browser open with a bunch of tabs. Didn't she keep her screen locked? I always kept my screen locked, especially with the shit I used to look at. Maybe she recently used her computer, and the lock didn't take effect. Or maybe she just didn't bother. Her mom was the only other person in the house. She wasn't going to look at her computer.

But I was. I couldn't help myself.

I was surprised she didn't have Facebook open. I had Facebook open all the time at home, back when it didn't depress me. I looked through the tabs and none of them were for social media.

But one tab caught my attention. I thought twice about clicking it, but I couldn't resist.

Classic Bondage Hall of Fame

All the best bondage from the 1970s to today!

What the...? Why would Pearl be interested in...?

It got weirder as I scrolled down the page. Was that? No, it couldn't be...

That's when I saw the hands grab the top of the screen. My hands fled from the trackpad as the lid came slamming down.

Pearl's fuming face glared at me.

•   •   •

We didn't say a word that whole drive up Reseda Boulevard. She pulled up behind the Explorer and stopped. She kept the engine running. She didn't even put it in park. She just turned and stared at me. She expected me to get out, and she would drive off.

But I had something to say.

"Pearl, I'm really sorry..."

"It was my mom. Satisfied?"

"But why would you be looking at..."

"It's none of your fucking business."

I grabbed the Kohl's bag with my clothes and reached for the door handle. She exhaled hard.

"Dylan." She exhaled hard again. "I said if you want to have sex with me, you can't."

"Why?"

She gave another hard exhale. There seemed to be some dampness in it, like tears.

"You wouldn't like me if you got too close."

"Pearl, you've seen me. I'm the lowest I've ever been in my life. What could you possibly show me that would make me dislike you?"

"You've already seen it. I'm a freak."

"Pearl, c'mon..."

"Please!" She sniffed. She took one hand off the steering wheel and wiped the corner of her eye. After a deep breath, she said in a soft voice, "Just go. Please."

"Let's talk about it tomorrow after work."

"I'm off."

"Then we can talk about it..."

"We won't. Good night, Dylan."

"Pearl, I…"

"Please." Her voice cracked.

•   •   •

I watched her Kia zip across the parking lot too quickly. When she got to the driveway onto Canby, her taillights glowed bright. The car seemed to jerk, as if she braked too hard.

The heavy sadness came over me again as I trudged back to the Explorer with a Kohl's bag full of clothes.

"Girl problems, huh? Especially on a Saturday night."

I turned around. It was the drug dealer. My irritation burned away the heavy sadness.

"We made a deal," I growled.

"I ain't getting up in your business. Just thought you'd like a little help."

I looked at the baggie he pulled out of his pocket.

"That shit doesn't help. I know."

"At least you won't give a fuck about it anymore."

He was right. I blotted out a lot of rough stuff on that shit. But I wasn't sure blotting it out was what I wanted to do.

I shook my head. "I'm good."

"You sure?"

"Sure."

"All right." He shoved the baggie back in his pocket.

I thought our exchange was over. I headed back to the Explorer. The heaviness came back to me, but I had to keep going.

"I quit once too."

I set down the Kohl's bag and faced him.

"I quit everything. Weed, shrooms, meth, bars, acid, molly. All that shit. Even booze. It ain't because of no probation neither. I wanted to get clean. I wanted to go straight and live a good life. I wanted to make my parents proud of me for once. And when I did, I felt great! Didn't get sick no more. Didn't spend my whole day figuring out how to get my next high. I could think clearly again, you know?" He took a step closer to me. "Then, you know what happened? Life kicked my ass again. You do everything right, and life still fucks you over. So, what do you do? How do you cope?"

He took a few steps away from me. I thought he was finally going to leave, but he stopped.

"You're gonna need me someday. 'Cause life's going to fuck you over too. Life's gonna fuck you in the ass so hard, you just want to die. And when it does..." He turned away. "You know where to find me."

He kept walking until he disappeared into the dark.

CHAPTER TWENTY-FIVE

Lake Forest

One 145-milligram tablet of fenofibrate. One 50-milligram tablet of losartan. One 81-milligram tablet of low-dosage aspirin. One 5-milligram tablet of Cialis I knew I wouldn't use. Rachel kept her arms folded while she sat up stiffly in bed. I knew she was still fuming about Moshe at the baseball game. There had to be more to it than him missing a fly ball and wanting to quit. I also knew I had to do something to calm Rachel down, at least so we could sleep.

First, I had to brush my teeth. Dad knew the connection between dental health and overall physical health long before most other doctors did. He instilled in me the importance of taking care of my teeth. I hoped I passed it on to Muriel and Dylan.

With clean teeth and fresh breath, I was ready to face Rachel. She said nothing as I folded back the covers and got into bed.

"Should I let him quit?" She relaxed her shoulders and set her hands in her lap.

I folded the covers back over me. "What does he want to do?"

She stiffened her shoulders again. "He's eight years old. How would he know what he wants?"

"Even at that age, kids know what they want and don't want."

"If you leave an eight-year-old to decide what he wants, he'd eat ice cream and play video games all day."

I smiled. She frowned. I guessed she wasn't joking.

"But kids know what causes them pain. Does he have problems with his coaches? His teammates?"

I pretty much knew the answers from what I saw at practice. Was Rachel seeing the same things I did?

"It doesn't matter." Her voice rumbled. "You do what you're supposed to do. Coaches and teammates aren't there to make you happy. You're supposed to work hard to make *them* happy. And then they will be good to you."

"But what if you work hard, and they still don't like you? You talked about how parents push to make sure their kids get the best treatment. Kids, coaches, and teachers can be political too. What if Moshe feels he's being screwed over?"

"For starters, I would never allow him to say 'screwed'!" She folded her arms again.

"Sorry…"

"You don't know what a pain Moshe has been. From the moment he was born, he caused problems. He was colicky. He never slept through the night. I tried to follow all the advice I give my patients, and nothing worked!"

"Dylan was like that too. Then we read the book by Dr. Lipschitz…"

"You read that garbage! That man's a fraud! I don't even think he's a real doctor! His books are why almost every child born after 1991 is an entitled, self-important brat!"

"Then what did you do? How did you help him?"

"I had stay up all night with him, even when I was on call. Avraham did nothing. He said he needed his sleep so he could be alert in court. And he wasn't even a lead attorney. He just prepared briefs. And whenever anything came up with Moshe, if he got sick and threw up all over the car, or if he got in trouble at school, I was the one who had to take care of it. Avraham didn't even want to deal with it. 'It's the woman's job,' he'd say. I was sick of it, so…"

"Are you blaming Moshe for your divorce?"

Rachel froze and swung her head toward me. "I never said that!"

"But you're implying it."

"Are you a doctor, or am I sleeping with another lawyer?"

I held my hands in front of me with my palms facing forward. "I'm not playing lawyer, and I'm not accusing you of anything, Rachel. I'm just saying if that's the way you feel about Moshe, that's a hell of a thing to put on an eight-year-old kid."

"You think all children are perfect and cute? They can be rotten little monsters! They can come out like that from the womb. I've seen more than my share!"

"So, are we supposed to be like the Spartans and kick them off a cliff?"

"You do what a parent is supposed to do and discipline them! No one disciplines their kids anymore! They treat them like little angels and cater to their every whim. That only makes them bigger monsters than they already are!"

"How would you define discipline?" I grumbled.

"I'm not surprised you don't know what discipline means."

I folded my arms. "What's that supposed to mean?"

"You tell me you did such a good job with Dylan? He got kicked out of the house…"

"He got kicked out of Teresa and Steven's house."

"What difference does that make? How did you raise him when you were married to Teresa? What kind of discipline did you give him? What did you do for him after your divorce besides paying child support and his military school? What did you do to straighten him out after he got arrested? What are you even doing to look for him now that he's missing?"

My jaw loosened and fell slack. I couldn't answer any of her questions. She knew it. She tightened her posture even more.

"If you don't know how to raise your own kids, don't tell me how I should raise Moshe!" She kicked off the covers and bolted out of bed.

• • •

I lost my mood to sleep. I retreated to the study. Rachel would be on the family room sofa, her preferred spot to sleep when she didn't want to sleep with me. I figured I would be alone in the study.

I tapped the trackpad on my MacBook Pro. No point letting it sleep when I couldn't.

There was a new email from Muriel.

Muriel Glass
Dad: Please read

It sounded urgent. I opened the message.

Dear Dad,
I just heard the news about Mom and Steven. I can't believe that this happened!

I glanced back at my briefcase, which still contained the front-page section of the *Orange County Register* with that large-type headline.

But I'm really worried about Dylan. Did he ever write back? Do you know if he's OK?

I exhaled. I couldn't answer her questions any more than I could answer Rachel's.

I've talked to my roommates about this. They said we should file a missing person report. Dylan can be in real trouble. Something might have happened to him! I can't believe you or Mom have done nothing to look for him!

Now Muriel was accusing me too.

Was I wrong not to file a missing person report earlier? What if he really didn't want to be found? If I looked for him, would I be undermining Teresa's and Steven's discipline? But from what I read about them...

What would I have done if Dylan was living with me? Would I have kicked him out too? How could I ask that? I didn't even know what he did! I knew he had problems, but what did he do that was so horrible that they tossed him out on the street to fend for himself? Would I have given up on him like Teresa did? But perhaps being out on his own would be good for him. He would have to straighten out to survive. Or he might...

I continued reading Muriel's letter.

I'm not blaming you or Mom. I know you tried. I haven't been a good sister. I could have done more for him. I wish I had.

I could feel Muriel's heartbreak because I felt that way about Maury. How many times did I stand frozen with fear while Grandma Dinah beat him? How many times did I tell on him because if I didn't, she would do worse to me? How many times did I take some perverse satisfaction from watching her tear him down because it was closest thing I got to praise? I should have stood up for Maury, protected him, and told him I love him. Instead, I just watched him crumble away.

If you want me to come home and help you look for him, I will. I have midterms and softball, but Dylan is more important. He's made me upset so many times, just as I know he's upset you and Mom, but I love him so much. I can't bear seeing anything bad happen to him. I hope he's OK, and I hope he gets straightened out. I love you very much, Dad.
Love,
M

I couldn't let her come home and ruin her school. Yet, I thought of all the times when I buried myself in my homework so I didn't have to hear Maury be beaten.

What should I do? Talk to Teresa? No, especially with the situation she was in. Should I file that missing person report? Should I call his friends? I didn't know any of his friends!

I knew I should write to Muriel. But the clock on the computer screen said 10:39 pm. It would be 12:39 am in Minnesota, too late to call or text.

What do I do?

．　　．　　．

POUND POUND POUND.

I looked up from my Macintosh SE. I was in my second year of pre-med at UC Irvine. I rented a room in an apartment near campus. Although UC Irvine was a short drive from our house in Lake Forest, I couldn't study there living with Grandma Dinah.

POUND POUND POUND.

The clock on my desk said 10:39 pm. A pounding on my door that late at night meant something bad happened. Perhaps Kent, one of my roommates, got in trouble again. I knew I had to answer that door before the pounding woke up Joey. The lease was in his name, and he went to bed at 9:00 pm so he could get up at 4:00 am to go to work. He would be ticked off if someone woke him up. I rushed to the door. I gasped when I opened it.

"Maury?"

He stood trembling. He only wore an El Toro High School t-shirt, a pair of jogging shorts, and sandals. Blood caked around his nose and lips.

"Oh my God, Maury!"

I put my arm around his shoulders and led him into the apartment. I could feel his scapulas and clavicles through his shirt. Was Grandma Dinah starving him? Or was this from the drugs? I let go of him and closed and locked the door. I then took a closer look at his face. He showed signs of epistaxis and contusions on both cheeks. There was a small laceration on his upper lip and abrasions on the side of his face.

"She's never done this to you before."

"It's been bad, bad…" A tear ran down his cheek.

I looked nervously at Joey's door. I then turned to Maury and patted him on the shoulder.

"Let's get you cleaned up."

．　　．　　．

"He can't stay here." Joey was still in his Ralphs uniform, complete with apron, dress shirt, and slacks.

"He's my brother!" I begged him.

Maury sat in the corner of the room with his arms clutched around his knees.

"The landlord has rules," Joey spoke firmly. "I can't have another person living here."

"Then don't tell him." Kent was sprawled out on the sofa, half-drunk again.

Joey jerked his head towards him. "I should have told him what you did to the bathroom!"

"Cleaned it up, didn't I?"

I stood up and gestured to Joey. "You don't understand what's going on with my brother. He's facing serious abuse at home."

"It's not my problem..."

I heard a gasp and whimper from Maury.

"You know I'm a good roommate, Joey. I'll take care of everything, Joey. I won't get you or Kent in any trouble..."

.   .   .

I realized this was not what happened.

.   .   .

"I don't make the rules, Ollie. Even the landlord doesn't make the rules. The Irvine Company says you can't have more than three people living in this size apartment."

"I'll pay for us to get a bigger place!"

"We have a six-month lease, Ollie! Look, I don't want any trouble."

POUND POUND POUND.

I went to the door and opened it.

Mom was standing on the other side.

And behind her was Grandma Dinah.

· · ·

Definitely, this was not what happened.

· · ·

"Maury," Mom's voice quivered. She was clearly doing this under duress. "It's time to come home."

I stared back at Maury, who was clutched into a ball and crying in the corner.

"Please don't let them take me, Oliver! Please don't let them take me!"

Mom started trembling too. "I'm sorry, Maury. You really need to come..."

Grandma Dinah shoved past Mom and stepped through the door. "Maury is coming with us. Now!"

Maury burst into frightened sobs. "No, Oliver! For the love of God, no! Don't let them take me! Please! Don't let them take me!"

I stepped in front of Grandma Dinah. "He's not going."

She stood still and stared at me. I stared back at her and stood rigidly. Her wrinkled lips tightened before speaking.

"So, you're fantasizing that the thing in the middle of your back is a spine." She wagged her finger at me. "But this wasn't how it happened, was it, Oliver?"

Grandma Dinah stepped slowly around me. She kept her eyes fixed on me as she moved.

"I don't remember exactly when you caved in, Oliver. You're better at remembering things than I am. Was it when I threatened to stop paying for your college, or was it when your roommate said no?"

"You refused to pay for college! I paid for it myself with hundreds of thousands in student loans that took me years to repay. And we wound up getting kicked out anyway because of this dirtbag here." I stuck out my arm towards the Kent-shaped lump on the couch. "After he drank up an El Torito Grill at happy hour, he caused $500 damage to the kitchen!"

"I did?" He mumbled.

Grandma Dinah took another step towards me. "So, you know your history. You just don't learn from it."

"I learned one thing, Grandma Dinah. I'm not afraid of you anymore."

"Yes, you are..."

"You're dead. You died a lonely, bitter woman!"

"But you still fear me."

"No, I don't! And I'll prove it! Hit me!"

She stared blankly at me.

"Go on. Hit me!"

She remained still.

"Hit me, damnit! HIT ME!"

She cocked back her hand. My eyes closed. I waited for the WHACK! The sting. The beating she delivered to Maury so many times. But I felt nothing. I opened my eyes. Grandma Dinah's hands hung relaxed by her sides.

"I never had to hit you to make you fear me." She let out a small grin.

•   •   •

"Oliver?"

Rachel was leaning against the doorway. I had to blink my eyes a few times to make sure I still wasn't dreaming.

She stood up and walked into the room. "Were you talking to yourself?"

"Uh..." I looked around the desk until my eyes fixed on my MacBook Pro with Muriel's email. "Muriel wrote to me. I was, well, just thinking about what to write back."

She nodded. "I'm going back to bed. You want to go too?"

"Yes, but I should write back to Muriel first. I should write to Dylan again too."

"Don't be up too late. We have a lot of errands to do."

I nodded. I forgot Sunday was our errand day.

"I may be asleep by the time you get in," she said. "So, good night."

"Good night, Rachel." I turned to my MacBook Pro.

"Wait." She walked towards me and gave me a kiss on the lips. It was quick and close-mouthed. Nothing passionate, but enough of a sign to let me know it was safe to come back to bed. "Good night, Oliver."

"Good night."

I watched her leave the study and then turned back to my screen. I should reply to Muriel, but I needed to write to Dylan first. I started a new email.

> *Son,*
> *We are wondering where you are.*

No. Not strong enough. I wasn't good at expressing myself, but I had to let Dylan know how urgent this was.

> *Son,*
> *We've become frantic wondering where you are.*

I also had to let him know how important it was to Muriel.

> *Muriel is very upset. She wants to come home from Minnesota to look for you, even though she has midterms next week.*

Would this be enough to convince him? I had to tell him more.

> *We're considering calling the sheriff and filing a missing person report.*

Good. If he wanted to us to find him, he would tell us instead us getting sheriff's deputies involved. If he didn't want us to find him, he would write back anyway to tell us not to file the report.

166

That was if he could write back at all.

Grandma Dinah was right. I didn't stand up for Maury that night at the apartment. When I told him to go back to her and Mom, it was the last time I saw him alive. After that, he ran away from home for good, and he didn't finish high school. I didn't see him again until I had to identify his body after he overdosed.

Was this what would happen to Dylan? Would I ever see him again?

My eyes started to burn. I bit my lip to keep from crying out loud. Everything I felt flowed from my fingers to the keyboard.

Dylan, I know I haven't been as close to you as I should have been. There are so many times I wanted to hold you and tell you how much I love you. I know things haven't been easy for you, and I should have been there to help you. I wish I had asked more about how you're doing. And when you told me, I wish I would have listened. I wish I could have done more to help you. I would hate to think anything bad happened to you. It would destroy me to lose you. So, please, Dylan. Call me, write me, just let me know that you're OK. If you don't want me to be in your life, I can accept that. I just want to know that you're safe. Please know that I love you, and Muriel loves you. Write as soon as you can.

Love,
Dad

I clicked Send, exhaled hard, and gave a silent prayer to hope he gets it and replies.

CHAPTER TWENTY-SIX

Reseda

I woke up early. Nothing that happened the night before made sense. In a way, it was good I didn't see Pearl at work for a day. I didn't know how things would be if I had to face her.

Since I took a shower at Pearl's, I didn't have to wash up at the gas station. After sticking my dick in his sink the other night, I'm sure Reza wouldn't be happy to see me. I had some spare time, so I decided to look at the book Hannah let me borrow. I opened the lift gate and sat at the edge of the bed. It had become light enough to read.

I stared at that pastel cover with the mountain stream, rainbow, and glowing angel. I then tried to place it with the pictures of Hannah on that website. I didn't take that close of a look at them. They were just pictures of her with ropes wrapped around her. And she was fully dressed. She wore short dresses, miniskirts, and partially open blouses, but they weren't that much different from what Pearl wore to work.

Then I remembered. Pearl wore one of her mom's dresses. The one that was baggy on her. The one she wore the first time I met her.

But why would Pearl be so upset about that? Yeah, having your mom pose for a bondage site is pretty creepy. But she wasn't doing anything you wouldn't see in some action movie or TV show where there was some damsel in distress. Grandma Pauline was in a bunch of those. I'm sure guys jerk off to that too.

And if it bothered Pearl, why did she have it up on her computer? And why was her computer unlocked? Did she *want* me to see it? And why would Pearl dress like her mom did in those pictures?

It was creeping me out, so I went back to the book Hannah loaned me. Perhaps this Reverend Patricia Williams Story had something to say about all this.

Hannah had stuck a lot of Post-It notes on the pages, the same way people at our church tag a Bible. I started flipping through the pages. She had marked up passages in yellow highlighter, also like the people at our church.

One of Reverend Story's passages caught my eye.

God takes us where we need to go and teaches us the lessons we need to learn. When we understand this truth, we can feel at peace about our circumstances. We can stop looking for people to blame and stop feeling like victims in our own lives. God is present at all times and in all situations. Amid the trials and suffering in our lives, we can connect to His Infinite Intelligence to help us get through them.

I stared at that passage for a long time. Something seemed oddly familiar about it.

I set the book aside and reached for *Face Time with Jesus*. Once again, Steven's self-satisfied face stared back at me. No mountain streams and glowing angels for him. As I thought of all the times he lectured at churches or lectured me about one thing or another, I remembered where the passage is. I saw it the other day. It was right after he talked about getting his medals directly from President George W. Bush. And that's where I found it.

God takes us where we need to go and teaches us the lessons we need to learn. Whenever I tell people this in speeches or in ministries, they begin to feel peace about their circumstances. They stop looking for people to blame and stop feeling like victims in their own lives. God is in control at all times and in all situations. When you think He is bringing trials and suffering in your life, He offers His grace to get you through them.

The words were a little different, but they said about the same thing.

I know nothing about writing books, but I know you can't copy something someone else wrote and not give that person credit. I did that once on a paper at school. I copied and pasted some stuff from Wikipedia and changed a few words here and there. Not only did I get an F, I got suspended for three days for an "ethics violation."

But who jacked whose book? They usually put the year they published the book right after the title page. So, I turned to that page in Steven's book.

© 2010 by Dr. Steven H. Dimity.

And then I looked at the page in Reverend Story's book.

Copyright © 1988 by Reverend Patricia Williams Story.

Why would Steven rip off a New Age book from the eighties? Didn't that shit go out with the Jheri curl? Yet, Steven always complained in his speeches about "hippie liberals with their crystals and meditation." He might as well complain about parachute pants and Milli Vanilli.

So, why would he rip off this Reverend Story? And what else did he rip off?

• • •

The morning continued to get weirder. When I got to Magdalena's restaurant, she wasn't there.

I stopped by the door and looked around. Perhaps she was busy, or she wasn't ready to come out just yet. I didn't expect her to do anything for me, but a morning wasn't the same without her smile and kind words. Or her pan dulce.

I couldn't be late for work, so I kept going.

"Hey, amigo!"

A guy was holding the bag of pan dulces. I recognized him as one of the cooks. I stopped and walked towards him.

He held up the bag. "Magdalena said to give you this."

"Where is she?"

"Magdalena, she's not feeling too good."

"Will you tell her I hope she feels better?"

"Sure thing." He smiled, but that smile quickly faded. He handed me the bag.

"Thanks."

He started to turn away. I called out to him.

"It's nothing serious, is it?"

He forced a smile. "Have a good day."

I watched him walk back into the restaurant with his shoulders slumped. I knew this wasn't good news.

•　　　•　　　•

Things got worse when I reached the store's parking lot. That black lifted pickup truck was there. I kept walking. If I just ignored them...

"Yo, faggot!"

It wasn't going to work.

The fat guy with the Need Beer cap was the one who called me out. He was sitting in the bed of that lifted pickup truck with a bunch of his equally fat t-shirt and baggy jean wearing redneck friends. One guy had a stained and stretched out white t-shirt with a faded picture of a Confederate flag with a skull and crossbones. The other guy had a yellow-and-black Cobra Kai t-shirt.

I knew that you couldn't show those dicks that you're afraid of them. They get off on that shit and just fuck with you some more. I walked over to them. They looked up. They seemed surprised, not thinking I'd step up to them. Probably planned out how they'd fuck with me if I ignored them.

The guy in the Need Beer cap jumped off the bed and stepped up to me.

"You know, you got some balls, like a white boy should." He stared down at me. "So, why you take orders from a gook?"

I stared back at him. "'Cause he's my boss. You do what your boss says. You'd know that if you had a real job."

I couldn't help but smile. I soon realized that was a mistake, especially when I noticed the rifle rack with the big-ass shotguns in the back window of their truck. Then, Need Beer thrust out his hands and pushed me hard on my shoulders. He stepped up to me again and stuck his face into mine. He reeked of stale chewing tobacco.

"You think you're fuckin' funny, don't you?"

My mouth took over. "At least I can think. What do you keep in your skull anyway?"

He shoved me back again. Now, his buddies were getting off the truck bed.

"Listen, you little cocksucker! I can beat the livin' shit out of you!"

He couldn't. I knew he couldn't. If he could, he wouldn't need his squad of fellow inbreds with him. I bet he couldn't even throw a decent punch. And we were right in front of the donut shop and other stores with customers around. If Need Beer started shit, someone would call the cops. I might be in the hospital, but he and his boys would be in jail. And getting food from an IV for a week or two is better than spending a year licking jelly out of someone's ass crack.

And they knew it too. None of them made a move. Except for the guy in the white t-shirt with the Confederate flag and the skull and crossbones. He was the only one who terrified me, because he had those crazy eyes that were wide open with pupils that darted from one side to another. He wasn't a tweaker. He looked too fat to be a tweaker. He was just fucking nuts. And he looked like he was ready to jump me right then. But the guy in the Cobra Kai shirt grabbed his arm. They all turned to the end of the parking lot. A black-and-white pulled in.

Need Beer stepped away from me. "You're lucky, motherfucker!"

I stood up straight. "I have work to do."

I turned away from them.

Need Beer shouted from behind me. "This ain't over, motherfucker! Not for you or your terrorist friends!"

I could have glanced back and said something witty, like a hero in an action movie. But I wasn't in an action movie. I had a minimum-wage job to go to, and those trailer-park assholes already made me late.

• • •

It was a day when I was grateful to work. I restocked housewares and soft drinks, straightened up the toy aisle after another mother let her kids run wild, and cleaned the bathrooms. All with a smile on my face. Anything to take my mind off everything that happened.

"Dylan, will you restock hardware?"

"Of course, Kishana."

Anything to take my mind off...

A box of rope.

Each coil of rope was neatly packaged in a clear plastic bag with red, white, and blue printing.

Nylon Rope - 10 feet (3.05 meters)
Proudly made in the USA!
Hundreds of household uses!

I knew about uses that proud American manufacturer couldn't have imagined.

I figured the sooner I got this rope on the rack, the sooner I didn't have to think about those uses. The plastic bag had a hole on the top. I stuck the metal peg through the pole.

"Where is Pearl?"

Mrs. Cimino stood there with her pleasant smile. I had to give a pleasant smile back in return.

"She's off today, Mrs. Cimino." I reached into the box for another package of rope.

"I think she's quite smitten with you."

I stared at the rope in my hand and then turned to Mrs. Cimino.

"No need to feel embarrassed about it," she said. "I met my husband Hugh at our first job. We worked at the drive-in. You remember me telling you about the drive-in, don't you?"

"Yes, Mrs. Cimino."

"We worked at the snack bar. He worked the grill and fryer, and I worked at the cash register. We hit it off well. After our shift, we'd go to his Studebaker in the parking lot. His father owned a liquor store, so we always had something fun to drink. We'd share a couple bottles of Schlitz or Brew 102. Or a nip or two of Cutty Sark. Then later, well..."

She let out a mischievous grin. "Let's say we fogged up the windows of that old Studebaker, if you know what I mean."

I did. I couldn't imagine kindly Mrs. Cimino getting buck wild, but hell, she was young once too.

"Those were wonderful times." Her grin faded. She sighed.

I glanced at the rope and then looked at Mrs. Cimino. I knew I had to get back to stocking the rack before Quang caught me, but her face deepened into a sadness I hadn't seen before. A sadness I couldn't turn away from.

"What happened, Mrs. Cimino?"

She looked down at the floor. I had never seen her that silent before.

"Mrs. Cimino? Are you OK?"

She looked directly at me with a strange intensity.

"We don't always appreciate the people we love until one day, they're gone. That's when you realize how much they meant to you. How much you miss them."

"Is that what happened to…"

Mrs. Cimino held up her hand to silence me. "Just take my advice, Dylan. You'll know how much you love someone by how much you miss them when they're gone."

• • •

I thought about what Mrs. Cimino said on my walk to the library after work. Since it was a long walk, I had a lot of time to think. What happened to her? And what happened to her husband? And her daughter Bernice? And why did she have to tell me about all that? Was she really trying to save me? If so, from what?

What she said about love made sense. She said you know you love someone by how much miss them when they're gone. Did I feel that way about Pearl?

I didn't feel that way about any of the other girls I had been with. Most of them were just randoms, anyway. And Zoey, who wanted to run away with me so we can have our child, I wasn't so broken up after it was over. She made it clear I couldn't be with her. It was what it was.

But Pearl, whenever she would leave, I felt a heavy sadness afterwards. A sadness I haven't felt about anything or anyone. And even the sadness kept me from thinking about my usual hateful thoughts about myself. I didn't think about jumping off buildings or stepping into traffic. She was kind to me. She let a homeless guy like me into her home to shower. And washed my clothes and served me dinner. No sane woman would do that. Yet, she did that for me.

And I felt bad about her mom and her cancer. And how Pearl had to give up her dreams and become practically a servant to her, knowing that she might still die in months despite all her care.

But there were also things about Pearl that put me off. All those awkward questions. All the times she focused on my dick. And yet, she told me I can't have sex with her. Was she just being a tease? Or was there something holding her back? She seems ashamed of her mom's past. And yet she looks at her pictures. And what was the deal with her bookcase? Didn't she have *Fifty Shades of Grey*? And *Nancy Drew*. Didn't some girl get tied up a lot in those books too?

I still didn't know how I felt about Pearl. If I could know her better, I could find out. Or if I really missed her if I didn't see her anymore.

⋅ ⋅ ⋅

That was why I started looking for room rentals on Craigslist. I didn't want to feel dependent on Pearl for a shower and laundry. I wouldn't know if I really loved her as long as I depended on her for things I should do myself. I also didn't want her to get resentful or feel like she's my slave. The way she seems to feel taking care of her mom.

I also knew how sketchy my situation was with my Explorer. I had parked behind the abandoned movie theater for over a month. I didn't want to go back there one day and find it was stolen or towed. I was lucky it hadn't been already.

But what I found on Craigslist discouraged me. Most of the listings in Reseda were in Spanish. Now, I wished I knew more Spanish than swear words and conjugations of "ser." But I didn't need to translate how much they charged for rent. They were more than I could afford.

Then I saw this ad for a roommate in Encino.

Kind elderly man (age 74) seeks live-in help. Male preferred 18-24 in good shape. Perform odd jobs for room and board.

I didn't want to guess what kind of jobs he had in mind. At least, it would put a roof over my head.

I still had one other option. I checked my email. Dad's previous emails were still there, including the one I started to reply to. The email was still saved as a draft. I could still edit and send it. But I saw a new one from him.

Son,
We've become frantic wondering where you are.

Again with the "we." Who the fuck did he mean by that?

Muriel is very upset. She wants to come home from Minnesota to look for you, even though she has midterms next week.

Fuck Muriel. If she was so upset, why didn't she write me herself? Even though she couldn't reach me by text, she still had my email address. And she was trying to guilt me by saying she'll ditch midterms to look for me. Doesn't this passive-aggressive bullshit come from the Jewish side of our family?

We're considering calling the sheriff and filing a missing person report.

Then why haven't you? Most parents who give a shit file a missing person report the second they know their child is missing. Even if they murdered the child themselves and just wanted to use it as cover.

But what was I doing, having such rude thoughts about Dad and Muriel? Didn't Magdalena say to always be kind? And didn't Mrs. Cimino say you know you love someone by how much miss him? Obviously, Dad loves me enough to keep writing to me. So why haven't I written back to him? Did I miss him? Did I love him?

Mom told me that Dad didn't get custody of me because he didn't care enough to try. I believed her at first, and so I hated him for not caring about me. When I found out what really happened, I still hated him for not standing up for himself and trying harder to keep me.

In church, they tell you to honor your mother and father. What if they don't honor you? Do you have to love someone only because they used their sperm and egg to make you? Doesn't love have to be earned? That's what Steven seemed to say. But something in that Reverend Patricia Williams Story book said something different. I felt so confused.

That's when both sadnesses hit me at once. The heavy sadness of feeling alone and the hateful sadness of deserving that loneliness. Of crying out for someone to love me and wanting to step in front of a bus to silence that cry.

I logged off the computer without reading another word of Dad's email.

CHAPTER TWENTY-SEVEN

Lake Forest

"Help bring in the bags." Rachel opened the lift gate of the Yukon. David dutifully dashed to the rear of the vehicle and picked up a couple of plastic bags. Moshe slowly got down from the booster seat and slumped his shoulders on the way to the back.

The Yukon had the biggest cargo bed I had ever seen in an SUV. It was bigger than my old Explorer. But Rachel covered the entire floor of it with grocery and retail store bags in a range of whites, beiges, and grays. She tackled shopping with the aggressiveness she gained in the Israeli army. I had never seen anyone argue so vigorously to get a store to accept a coupon, which I suspect was expired.

I scooped up a couple bags. David came back for his second load. Moshe straggled behind.

I couldn't blame Moshe for being exhausted. Rachel drove us all over South County to find the best deals, from Kohl's in Laguna Niguel to a Persian market in Costa Mesa. She probably spent more on gas than she saved on merchandise.

Moshe finally made his way to the back of the Yukon. Rachel handed him a bag.

"Be careful, this has glass."

I set my bags on the kitchen counter. I took my iPhone out of my pocket. No reply from Dylan. I got a reply from Muriel.

Dear Dad,
Thank you for writing back to me. I'm glad you sent Dylan another email, but we really need to file a missing person report. I know you

don't want me to miss my midterms and hurt my softball, but it's getting hard for me to...

CRACK!

I put my iPhone on the counter and rushed to the front door. Moshe stood trembling in the entryway. He had a beige plastic bag from Ralphs clutched in his arms. By his feet was a shattered glass pickle jar. Pickles and shards of glass scattered in front of him. The pickle brine spread out around his feet, across the entryway, and into the carpet.

I could hear Rachel's gasp before she appeared in the doorway.

She instantly scolded him in Hebrew. He replied with cries and pleas. To my right, David froze in place. His posture seemed uncomfortably familiar.

I walked over to Rachel and Moshe. I kept my voice soft and calm. "Look, it's just an accident..."

She snapped at me, "I told him to be careful!"

Moshe whined back, "I was careful!"

Rachel shot back with angry Hebrew.

I looked down at the pickles, brine, and glass. "We should clean this up..."

She shouted at Moshe. "Moshe, you broke it! You clean it up!"

He cried, "Ima!"

"A kid his age shouldn't handle broken glass."

"When I was his age, I was learning how to respond to air raid sirens and what to do when terrorists attack. Don't tell me that Moshe is too young to clean up broken glass!"

I held out both palms and started backing away. "OK. OK..."

As I headed back to the kitchen, I felt foolish. She was right. Moshe was her son. Who was I to tell her how to raise him, especially when my kids had problems of their own? I picked up my iPhone to read the rest of Muriel's email.

I had to stop reading. Rachel's shouting at Moshe became too hard to ignore.

I never imagined Hebrew could sound so angry. The guttural *kh*, the hissed out *sh* and *tz*, the *ah* and *ai* that sound like howls. I only knew of Hebrew from the Torah, prayer, and the uplifting verses of "Hatikvah."

I didn't think of Hebrew as a language parents could use to chew out their kids. And Rachel's Hebrew was growing especially harsh.

"IMA, BEVAKASHA!" Moshe's urgent cry shot up my spinal cord.

I stuffed the phone in my pocket and rushed out of the kitchen. As I turned the corner, I saw that Rachel had closed the front door. Her face became reddened and contorted. David stood stiff and frozen in place.

Rachel clutched Moshe's right shoulder. Her face red and trembling. His pale, quivering, and tear streaked.

"Rachel, what are you doing?"

She turned her enraged face toward me. She said nothing.

My run turned into a stomp. "What *are* you doing?"

Rachel's jaw shook.

"Ima?" Moshe cried.

"David." The firmness and calm of my voice surprised me. "Take Moshe to his room."

David remained planted and rigid, just like I used to be.

"Go on." My voice remained firm.

David hesitated. He then took a few stiff steps towards Moshe. Rachel whipped her head around. David stopped again. He couldn't even look at his mother. I dreaded what might happen next, especially since I caused it.

But Rachel relaxed her grip on Moshe's shoulder. She finally let go.

In a small, shaking voice, David whispered, "C'mon."

Moshe walked slowly, haltingly towards the hallway. David passed by his mother without looking at her. I waited until they went to their rooms and closed their doors. I didn't want them to hear what I had to say. Or what she might say to me.

Rachel and I faced each other. Her face still red and trembling.

She raged, "How dare you! How dare you interfere with how I discipline my son!"

"You were going to hit him!"

"Hit him?" She stammered. "You think I would hit my own son?"

"Then what the hell were you doing?"

"I was disciplining him!"

"Discipline? That was abuse!"

"Is that what you think? Any form of discipline is abuse?"

"You were screaming at him and grabbing his shoulder! That's abuse!"

"Do you even know what abuse is?"

"Do you know what proportionate is? You screamed at Moshe over a stupid jar of pickles!"

"It's not just a jar of pickles, Oliver! It's about responsibility! It's about facing consequences for your actions!"

"So, the consequence for breaking a four-dollar jar of pickles is getting verbally assaulted by your mother?"

"Verbal assault? Is that what you think discipline is? How did *you* discipline your children, Oliver? Give them timeouts? Tell them to use their words, their indoor voices, honor each other's feelings, or some useless garbage like that? No, I know how you disciplined your children, Oliver. You didn't discipline them at all!"

"I never abused them!"

"You abused them by not teaching them. Not setting rules. Not preparing them for life! My parents were tough on me, and I'm glad they were!"

"By what? Turning you into some Krav Maga drill sergeant?"

"You don't get it, do you, Oliver? I had to be tough. I grew up surrounded by people who hate me!"

"You blame the Palestinians?"

"You arrogant American ass! You don't know what life's like outside a suburb, do you?"

"I know you don't scream at your kids, Rachel!"

"You try growing up half-Black around white kids! You try being told you're not a real Jew because you're not Orthodox! You try doing twice as much and get half the credit because you're a girl! That's why I'm glad my parents disciplined me! It made me strong!"

"It made you a brute!"

"Is that what you think of me!?"

"I don't know what the hell to think of you!"

"Do you know what I think of you, ben-zona!?"

"Hey! You curse me out, you do it in English!"

We stopped talking. We just screamed over each other. It didn't matter to us that her children could hear us down the hall and through their doors. We shut ourselves into a ball of noise and hate that neither of us could escape.

Finally, I screamed, "If that's how you feel about it, I'll leave!"

She screamed back, "Fine! Go!"

I wasn't bluffing. I assumed she wasn't either. I stormed down the hallway towards the bedroom and into the closet. I pulled down my suits, shirts, and slacks and draped them over my arm. I knew how to leave a home. I had done it before.

Behind me, Rachel screamed, "That's it! Leave! That's been your answer for everything, hasn't it, Oliver? Run away! Don't deal with anything!"

I grabbed some dress shoes from the floor and placed them on top of the clothes. I stormed down the hall again towards the garage.

Rachel followed behind me screaming, "You coward! You spineless worm! You came off so worried about the kids a few minutes ago! Now, you leave them?"

I opened the lift gate of my Lexus and tossed the clothes into the cargo bed.

I headed out of the garage and back to the bathroom. I swiped my Sonicare, toothpaste, mouthwash, and prescription bottles off the counter and rushed back to the garage to dump them in my Lexus. I rushed back to the bedroom.

"If that's what you want, Oliver, get out! Get out of here! Get out, you worthless piece of slime!"

I went to the dresser and scooped my underwear and socks out of the drawer.

"You're not a real man! You're not a real father! You're not a real human being!" She spat out a bunch of Hebrew obscenities. I stopped listening. All her screaming became just noise to me.

I went into the study and threw the underwear and socks on the sofa. I tossed my MacBook Pro, power supply, and Lightning cable into my briefcase, along with that copy of the *Orange County Register*. I bundled my clothes under my arm, picked up my briefcase, and stormed into the hallway.

"I knew you can leave anytime."

I turned to my left. Moshe's red and tear-streaked face stared up at me. I turned to my right. A frightened David stared at me. I looked back over my shoulder. Rachel's red and hate-filled face glared at me. I turned my face forward and headed to my Lexus. Screams and sobs followed me.

CHAPTER TWENTY-EIGHT

Reseda

I trudged through the streets with sadness hanging on my shoulders. It hung on me all the way back to the parking lot behind the abandoned theater. That was when I stopped. And saw the blue Kia Rio.

I took slow steps towards the Explorer.

"Pearl?"

She emerged from behind the Explorer. She walked differently. With a strut. Sultry. Suggestive. And she didn't say a word.

Her outfit even looked a little different. Her skirt seemed a little shorter. She unbuttoned the top buttons of her short-sleeve blouse. That was the first time I had seen her cleavage. She looked like she teased her hair.

It should have aroused me. But the vibe I usually felt around her wasn't there. The whole thing seemed off. Especially since she sort of looked like her mom in those pictures.

"Pearl?"

She continued to strut over to me until we found ourselves face to face.

I didn't know what to say. My gut wanted to ask her, "What are you doing here?" But I was afraid I would hurt her if I said that. I waited for her to speak.

Instead, she thrust a wadded-up bunch into my hand. I held it up towards the light.

It was a bundle of rope, a folded-up bandana, and a condom.

I looked up at her. Pearl stared right into my eyes.

I clutched the bundle in my hand. I understood what she wanted me to do, but I didn't know if I should do it. This didn't make sense to me. *She* didn't make sense to me. I opened my mouth to try to speak to her. She didn't wait for the words to come out.

"I knew it!" She turned her back to me. "You think I'm a freak!"

"Wait!" I grabbed her forearm. Her skin warm and soft to the touch. Her bicep firm in my grasp. She let her hand drift behind her back. I moved close until I was right behind her. Her arm brushed against my chest and stomach.

"C'mon, Pearl. Talk to me."

Her breathing deepened. Her breasts bobbed with each breath. She swallowed hard. "Grab my other arm and put it behind my back."

But as I looked around the open parking lot, I started getting nervous. What if someone passed by and thought I was kidnapping her? What if they called the cops? All of this seemed super sketchy.

I let go and stepped away from her. "Let's get in the car."

I shoved the rope, bandana, and condom in my left pocket and reached into my right pocket for my keys. Her breathing grew heavier as I opened the lift gate. This must have been a fantasy of hers, getting tossed in the back of an SUV and getting bound and gagged by some kidnapper. And I'm supposed to be her kidnapper. But this wasn't a role I asked to play.

She climbed into the back. I definitely saw her panties this time. She really wanted this.

And how many times did I want her? How I wanted her the last time we were in the back of the Explorer. And in the laundry room. I should have wanted her at that moment. But something felt wrong.

But I closed the lift gate anyway.

The back of the Explorer felt more cramped, more heated. I had to turn on the flash on my iPhone so I could see her.

"Pearl, what's going on?"

"I want you."

"You said I can't."

"I can't help myself."

She put her hands behind her back and pressed her ankles close together. It was like she was showing me how she wanted to be tied up.

I could picture the ropes around her, just like in the pictures of her mom. But that just made me feel more uncomfortable. And Pearl seemed to know it.

"What's wrong, Dylan? I thought you want me. I could tell."

I wanted her. She knew I did. But not this way. I've had girls throw themselves at me. But that wasn't who Pearl was.

I slid myself closer to her. I put my arm around her. She kept her arms tightly behind her. They trembled at my touch.

"Pearl, you know how much I like you..."

"Then what are you waiting for?"

"I..."

I looked down at her thighs. Her skirt hitched up higher as she sat. She started rubbing her knees together slowly, raising one and then the other. Either she was fantasizing herself trying to wriggle free or urging me to pull those knees apart and climb in between.

The vibe started coming back to me. But even that vibe frightened me. I looked back up at her.

"Did something happen? Was it about last night?"

Her voice was unsteady. "What makes you think anything happened?"

Her breathing got heavier. So did mine. It was getting hot in the car. Water beads popped onto the black plastic tarp.

She spoke quickly and urgently. "I told you my fuck-up was trying to be too good. I'm tired of it, Dylan. I don't want to be good anymore. I want to be free. I want to feel safe. I want to be myself."

My hand drifted down her arm to her wrists. I wrapped my fingers around them. I rested my other hand on her right thigh. My thumb and forefinger drifted beneath the hem of her skirt. She closed her eyes. Her lips parted. She breathed hard. I didn't have to tie her up to make love to her. Touching her bare skin, feeling the warmth of her body and breath, seeing her so wild with passion. Sweat beaded on her skin. In the faint light of my iPhone's flashlight, she looked like she was glistening. The vibe came back. Blood rushed inside me.

But I was feeling suffocated. The black plastic tarps were drenched with water beads. Sweat dripped off my face. I felt like I was drowning.

"Please, Dylan. You don't know how bad I need this. Tie me up. Tie me up now! You can do anything you want to me."

I couldn't breathe. I had to get air. I let her go, grabbed the latch, and flung the lift gate open. The night air turned the sweat and humid heat into bitter cold. I sat at the edge of the bed, dangled my legs over the bumper, and leaned forward. I sucked in all the air I could, even if it made my nose and lungs hurt.

Behind me, Pearl cried, "What are you doing!?"

I turned around. She still had her hands behind her back and ankles crossed. But I couldn't answer her until I could breathe normally again. Then I heard a whoosh of a car on the other side of the parking lot. I turned my head. A black-and-white headed down Canby. The cops probably didn't see me. The police car disappeared behind the building on the corner.

I looked back at Pearl. Her wrists and ankles waiting for the ropes that bulged in my pocket. A rush of something came over me. I jumped off the bumper and stood outside the Explorer.

"What are *you* doing!?" My anger shocked me.

"I just want you to love me!"

"Really?"

Pearl trembled. "What do you mean? What are you saying?"

"Are you going to tell me what you're really doing!?"

She set her hands free and waved them in front of her. "I want to make love to you! Why are you being…"

"Do you expect me to believe…"

"You're being ridiculous!"

"I don't know what the hell…"

We shouted over each other until I blurted out, "You're setting me up!"

She recoiled until she pressed against the back of the driver's seat.

"Dylan, no!" A tear glistened on her cheek. "I'd never think of…"

"Bullshit!" I snorted in anger and disbelief. "You think I'm fucking stupid, Pearl? You don't think I know what's going on? What you've been doing to me this whole time? I do what you want me to do to you. I tie you up. I gag you. I fuck you like I'm some psycho pervert. And that's when the cops show up and bust me! I get convicted of kidnapping and rape and get locked up for 20 years or more. And you! I don't know what the fuck you get out of this! Maybe you're helping the good people of Reseda get some homeless piece of shit off the streets!"

"Dylan! That's not true! I need you! I—I lo..." Pearl clutched her knees to her chest and sobbed hard and loud.

Maybe she was telling the truth. Maybe she just wanted me to make love to her. Maybe getting bound and gagged like her mom on that website was the only way she could feel loved, free, and safe.

But *I* wasn't feeling safe. Loving her made me feel vulnerable. The way I blew my load in my only clean pair of boxers. The way I almost suffocated being with her in my Explorer. The way the cops could have stopped by at any moment and busted me. I lived on the edge where the slightest misstep meant sleeping in a doorway. Or trying to live on spoiled food from dumpsters. Or going to prison.

She may have loved me, but I was too vulnerable to love her. Especially the way she wanted to be loved.

I reached towards her. She scrunched further away and clutched her knees tighter.

"Pearl, I'm sorry I didn't trust you, I..."

She probably couldn't hear me through her sobs. I realized how much I humiliated her. How much I hurt her. And it made me feel worse.

"You're not a freak, Pearl. You're..."

I felt something wet streaming down my face. I don't cry, not usually. But that heavy sadness bore down on me hard. I pulled the rope, bandana, and condom out of my pocket. I placed them by her feet and moved away from her.

"You're better off without me."

* * *

I couldn't bear to watch Pearl leave. I just sat on the bumper and listened to her wheels against the rough, worn asphalt.

Mrs. Cimino was right. I missed Pearl the second I heard her car fade from the end of the parking lot. I must have really loved her. Now she was gone. And there was no way she would ever come back. She might even have to leave Buck & Awesome if she couldn't bear to work with me. Or I should leave. She needed the job more than I did.

I hung down my head and stared at the asphalt.

"I knew you're gonna need me someday."

I looked up. He pulled a baggie out of his pocket. I climbed into the Explorer and opened the center console.

CHAPTER TWENTY-NINE

Lake Forest

One 145-milligram tablet of fenofibrate. One 50-milligram tablet of losartan. One 81-milligram tablet of low-dosage aspirin. One 5-milligram tablet of Cialis. All sat in their bottles. That night, I didn't care if I had a flaccid penis, plaque in my blood vessels, or a diseased heart. In fact, the sooner I got off this wretched planet, the better. To help things along, I drove to the nearest fast-food place.

"Welcome. Can I take your order, please?"

"Yes, I want something that has at least 2,000 calories, 500% of my daily recommended intake of sodium, and enough cholesterol to clog my aorta like the 405 at rush hour."

After a pause, the man on the speaker came back. "I'm sorry, could you please repeat that?"

I sighed. "Hell, give me a double bacon cheeseburger, a large fries, and a large Diet Coke."

"That'll be $8.45 at the second window."

I edged my car around the curving driveway until I stopped behind an even larger Chevrolet Suburban.

I still hadn't sorted out what happened. Perhaps there existed a parallel universe where I would still be at home with Rachel, David, and Moshe. We would eat a kale and wild greens salad with braised tofu and a cilantro lime vinaigrette. Then, I would cuddle up with Rachel in a warm bed. Instead, I sat alone and homeless in my Lexus SUV as I watched some young man at the window hand bag after bag of food to the man in the Chevrolet in front of me.

Finally, his taillights dimmed, and his vehicle moved forward. I rolled up to the window.

"$8.45 please." The young man looked about Dylan's age.

I pulled out my wallet from my back pocket and took out my Bank of America Angels MasterCard. I handed it to the young man.

"Thank you." He swiped the card on his register and handed the card back to me.

I still had money and a job. I didn't need a mailing address because I got my credit card statements online and paid them with an iPhone app. I didn't combine bank accounts with Rachel, and we didn't buy anything together. I didn't have to worry about her taking anything besides whatever I left at her house. I could function without a home and anyone in my life. I was free, because freedom meant I could ingest the contents of the bag and cup the young man handed to me without judgement.

"Have a good evening."

"Same to you." I put the cup in the cup holder and the bag on top of the console. I rested my foot on the accelerator and drove off.

Freedom also meant I didn't know where to go.

I could check into one of the residence hotels on Lake Forest Drive. Or I could ask other doctors I knew if I could sleep on their couch for a couple days. I didn't have anyone I could call a friend. After I stopped taking those medications, many of the doctors I thought were friends, like Yvette, just fell out of touch.

Freedom also meant being completely alone.

I stopped in a parking lot to eat my food. It was an office building across from the fast-food place. The parking lot was mostly empty. I parked at a far corner of the lot under a light. It must have been one of those energy-saving lights because it was dim and had a slight blue tint. It gave me enough light to eat without having to see what I was eating.

I reached into the bag, pulled out the double bacon cheeseburger, and opened the wrapper. The burger had some heft to it. It was thick, and the grease on the bacon glistened as the melted cheese draped over the textured patties. I understood how someone like Leo Shelton was seduced by fast food to the point it killed him. Fast food is the perfect lover. It is sensual. It offers instant pleasure with little effort. It always satisfies, always comforts, and is always there when you need it. It never argues, never disappoints you, and never breaks your heart.

I opened my mouth and prepared to take my first bite.

"You shouldn't eat that."

My hand froze. The burger remained suspended a few inches from my lips. I slowly turned my head.

Grandma Dinah was sitting in the passenger seat. I lowered my arm. "You again?"

"Who else is going to stop you from shoving that trayf mound of grease into your mouth?"

I shook the burger at her. "Do you think I give a damn this isn't kosher?"

"Do you really want to wipe out a whole week of workouts?"

My imagination was messing with me. She wasn't really there. She had been dead for 20 years. I was going to eat my damn bacon double cheeseburger. Once again, I raised the burger to my mouth. I turned my head slightly.

Grandma Dinah was still in the passenger seat.

I shoved the cheeseburger back into the bag. "Why do you still haunt me?"

"What, you think I'm a ghost?"

Ghost or not, she was definitely Grandma Dinah. Answering questions with questions.

"Then who the hell are you?"

"I'm the voice in your head that keeps you from taking this stylish and powerful Lexus RX 450h in Eminent Pearl White with parchment leather interior, Lexus Enform App Suite with navigation and Bluetooth connectivity, and 15-speaker, 835-watt Mark Levinson Premium Surround Sound Audio System and driving it straight off a cliff."

"You? Save me?" I huffed bitterly. "You drove Dad to end his life!"

"I tried to save him for as long as I could."

"By berating him? Belittling him? Treating him like garbage?"

"Your father was a sick man."

"Sick!? He had depression! His neurotransmitters were..."

"Spare me your med school talk! His sickness was he knew something was wrong with him, and he did nothing about it. He could cure other people, but he didn't see the illness in himself."

She leaned towards me.

"Your father couldn't find a way to silence those voices in his head. But I could." She wagged her finger. "You know what it was."

I thought about it for a moment. I quickly went through everything I experienced with her.

"Fear?"

She nodded. "Fear. That kept the voices in line."

"But that's the worst thing you could do to a…"

"Listen, Oliver. We're not driven by what we love, but what we fear. Since your father couldn't bring himself to love life, I made him fear death. I made him fear offending God and bringing shame to himself and his family. I made him fear leaving his wife and children, especially when he knew he would leave them with me. I even used the Holocaust. I'd tell him, 'Six million of our people were murdered, and now you should kill yourself?'"

"That's disgusting!"

"It worked."

"No, it didn't! He still wound up hanging himself!"

"If it weren't for me, he would have killed himself a long time ago. You wouldn't have even been born."

I looked down at my fast-food bag, which was getting stained with grease.

"Besides," she said, "It worked on you."

My head bolted up and turned towards her. She let out a small, vindicated smile.

"You have the sickness too. So did your brother. But Maury didn't have the fear. He tried to silence the voices with alcohol and drugs. You know what happened."

"What about Dylan? Does he have depression? Does he have suicidal thoughts?"

"If you don't know the answers to those questions, you haven't been a good father."

I stammered. "It's been hard with Teresa, and the divorce…"

"I didn't raise you to make excuses, Oliver! He's your son!"

"He's an adult!"

"That's when he needs you the most!"

I lowered my head.

"Don't cower to me, Oliver! Stop fantasizing about having a spine and grow one!"

"What am I going to do, Grandma Dinah? I don't know where he is. He could be anywhere…"

"Or dead."

My body shuddered.

"You better find him, Oliver." She wagged her index finger again. "Before it's too late."

CHAPTER THIRTY

Reseda

Cold hardness pressed against my back. I turned to my side and put down my hand. My palm pressed against gritty roughness. I struggled to open my eyes, batting my eyelids against the light. When my eyes could focus, I looked around. I had slept on the asphalt of the theater parking lot.

"No. Oh, no!"

I scrambled to my feet and ran to where I had parked the Explorer. The Explorer was gone.

I collapsed to my knees and grabbed my hair at the roots.

"Shit! Holy fucking shit!"

I patted my front pockets. I still felt keys in my right pocket. In my left, nothing but the crunch of paper. I reached inside and pulled out some wads of paper. All I had were a few one-dollar bills.

I breathed hard and rough. Those bills were all I had. My iPhone was gone. I must have left it in the Explorer. And my money! What happened to it!? And that's when I remembered. I must have spent nearly all of it on drugs and God knows what else.

And the book Hannah lent me was in the Explorer. It was gone too. So was Steven's book, which Mrs. Cimino gave me.

I curled up in a ball and pounded my fist against the hard asphalt.

"Gone! It's fucking gone! Everything! It's all fucking gone!"

That was when I looked up and saw the gas station. I shoved the bills—the only thing I had left in the world—back into my pocket. I ran across the parking lot to the gas station.

. . .

When I got there, Reza was mopping up the men's bathroom. A handwritten sign on the door said, "Out of Order/Fuera de Servicio."

And Reza shot me a furious frown.

"You don't remember what you did?"

I didn't remember. But I could tell it was something awful.

Reza leaned the mop handle against the door and rushed towards me. "I was damn lucky Carlos didn't fire me, but he docked me a whole week's salary to pay for the damage you caused!"

I was too stunned to even speak.

"And Carlos had your vehicle towed. You can pick it up at the impound lot after you pay your fine and towing fees."

I stiffened. The Explorer wasn't stolen, but it might as well have been. There was no way I could afford whatever it cost to get it back.

Reza turned away from me and walked back to the mop.

"And when you get it back, drive it far, far away." He turned and glared at me. "I never want to see your face again."

I couldn't say a word. I turned and walked out of the gas station. When I was outside, I took one last look. That's when I noticed the digital clock with the large digits over the register. I was late for work!

. . .

I raced down the sidewalk along Sherman Way, weaving around people on the way. I even hurried past Magdalena's restaurant, forgetting to find out if she was OK.

The signal at Etiwanda turned red, but I ran through it.

HONK!

"What the hell are you doing!?"

A car's bumper was a foot away from me.

I kept running. I cut across the parking lot.

SCREECH!

The back bumper of a car was a few inches from me. Red and white taillights glowed.

I was out of breath by the time I got to the front door of Buck & Awesome. I hadn't even caught my breath when I opened the door.

.   .   .

Quang stood just inside. He folded his arms. Kishana stood right behind him.

"You know what time you were supposed to be here," he uttered firmly.

I was still too out of breath to answer. But I already knew I was fucked.

"You know what time it is now." Quang pointed at the clock.

I slumped my shoulders.

"You've been a good worker up to now, Dylan. But we can't allow this type of behavior." He took a deep breath. "Step into the office."

.   .   .

I stared at the paperwork in my hands. My final paycheck. "Change of Status" and "Disciplinary Action" forms that were corporate-speak ways of saying, "You fucked up, so get the fuck out."

"Dylan."

I raised my head but couldn't bear to look at Quang.

"I had great hopes for you. You let me down." Quang's calm words stung me harder than any yelling. "Now go."

As I stepped outside the office, Fatima's usual smile faded. Pearl spun away from me and lowered her head. And Mrs. Cimino turned to me.

"One mistake. One foolish mistake can ruin your whole life. That's how I lost my family." Mrs. Cimino started to quiver.

It was too much for me. I turned away from her and headed towards the front door. The glare of sunlight made everything glow white. I folded my paperwork and final paycheck into a square and shoved it in my pocket. I then entered the whiteness.

· · ·

When my eyes adjusted to the light, I knew what I had to do.

I crossed the parking lot to the sidewalk along Sherman Way. I glanced at the cars rushing by me. I kept walking, going in the same direction as if I were walking back to the Explorer.

I stopped at Magdalena's restaurant and glanced inside. There were a couple customers, but the servers and cooks seemed busy getting ready for lunch. No Magdalena. No kind words. I kept walking.

I shoved my hands into my pockets. My left hand brushed against the hard square of paperwork and the wadded-up dollar bills. With my final paycheck and what little money I had left, maybe I could get by. Maybe I had enough to get the Explorer out of impound. Maybe I can find a homeless shelter. Maybe I can find a new job. Maybe I can start over. Maybe.

I walked past the abandoned movie theater that was my home. Past the gas station where Reza said I was no longer welcome.

Ahead of me was the intersection of Reseda and Sherman Way. It seemed busy. Cars and trucks rushed by on Sherman Way. I glanced at the cars stopped on the other side of Reseda Boulevard. One of them was a Metro bus. I stood at the corner. The light for crossing Reseda Boulevard had turned on the red hand and countdown timer. I exhaled hard as the traffic light turned yellow. Then red.

And I stepped off the curb.

SCREECH! HONK!

The bumper was nowhere near me.

The driver rolled down the window and screamed at me, "Hey, what the fuck's the matter with you? Are you fucking high?"

I retreated to the curb.

"Fucking idiot!" The shout trailed off as he rushed up Reseda Boulevard.

I lowered my head. I even failed at ending myself.

I found myself at the library somehow. I assumed that I didn't try to step into traffic again. But I didn't hear those hateful words. Or feel that heavy sadness. I just felt numb.

I sat in front of a computer and logged in. I went straight to email. There were no new messages from Dad. But there was an email in the draft folder. I opened it.

Dear Dad.
I'm OK. I'm in the Valley. Don't worry about me.
—Dylan

It was no longer true. I wasn't OK. I was still in the Valley, but the Valley no longer wanted me. I was going to delete the draft, but I just started backspacing. The only thing left was

Dear Dad.

I stared at those words for a moment. I started to type.

Dear Dad.
I'm sorry I haven't written.

I lifted my hands from the keyboard and opened and closed them several times. My whole body trembled. I sniffed. I exhaled and set my fingers back on the keys again. I let the words come out.

Dear Dad.
I'm sorry I haven't written. Since I was kicked out of Mom and Steven's, I just drove. I know you would have wanted me to live with you, but I needed to find some place of my own. I wanted a fresh start. I wound up in Reseda. It's in the Valley. I lived in the Explorer you gave me, but I had a job, and I met some nice people who helped me. I even met a girl.

199

I backspaced those words out. I didn't have Pearl anymore. I blew it with her. Why even mention her?

Dear Dad.

I'm sorry I haven't written. Since I was kicked out of Mom and Steven's, I just started to drive. I know you would have wanted me to live with you, but I needed to find some place of my own. I wanted a fresh start. I wound up in Reseda. It's in the Valley. I lived in the Explorer you gave me, but I had a job, and I met some nice people who helped me. And things were really going well for a while.

I sniffed hard. The next words were hard to write.

But I messed up, Dad. Real bad.

I exhaled. And exhaled again. I didn't want to cry. I just wanted to type the email and get it over with.

I want you to come and get me. There's an abandoned movie theater near the corner of Reseda and Sherman Way. It has a big blue Reseda sign in front. I'll be in the parking lot behind it. If I'm not there, wait, and I'll be right there.

I'm sorry, Dad. I should have come to you first when Mom and Steven kicked me out. I know you and Muriel care about me. I wish I could have been a better son and brother.

Love,
Dylan

I clicked Send immediately. I didn't want to give myself a chance to change my mind.

CHAPTER THIRTY-ONE

Lake Forest

TAP TAP TAP.

I bolted up in my seat. The light stung my eyes.

TAP TAP TAP.

I could finally see. I was still in my Lexus. I must have slept in it overnight.

"Hey, mister?"

I pressed the Start button and rolled down the window. It was a young woman with long blond hair. She wore a navy suit jacket and a short blue-and-white striped dress. She must have worked there.

"Are you OK, sir?"

"Um, yes. I'm fine, fine." I held up my left hand and gave a weak wave.

She stared at me with concern. "Should I call a doctor?"

"No, no." I didn't tell her I was a doctor. I certainly didn't feel like one at that moment.

She glanced further into my cabin. "Your phone's ringing."

I looked past the grease-stained bag filled with a now cold bacon double cheeseburger and soggy fries and a condensation-coated cup filled with watery Diet Coke. My office phone number appeared on the screen. As I picked up the phone, the young woman stepped away from my car.

I tapped the button to answer. Alison's frantic voice was on the other end.

"Dr. Glass, where are you? I've been trying to call you for hours. You have patients waiting!"

I looked on the clock at the dashboard. I couldn't believe it had gotten so late. I pulled the iPhone away from the side of my face and looked at the Ring/Silent switch on the side. I had put the phone on silent. That's why I didn't hear Avicii at four thirty in the morning.

"Dr. Glass?"

I brought the phone to the side of my face again.

"Yes, Alison?"

"Are you OK, Dr. Glass? Is something wrong?"

"No, nothing's wrong. I'll be right in…"

"Something is wrong! Do you need help? Should I reschedule your appointments for today?"

"No. That's fine. Tell the patients I'm sorry. I'll be right in."

"Dr. Glass?"

I ended the call. I was about to put the iPhone back on the passenger seat when I noticed I had an email notification. I tapped the Mail app.

There was an email from Dylan.

As I scrolled through his message, a multitude of feelings rushed through me. Happiness, relief, sadness, and urgency. Wherever Reseda was, I had to get there as quickly as possible.

I dialed Alison.

"Dr. Glass?"

I called our direct line. She knew it was me.

"Alison, cancel my appointments for today. Tell them there's an important family matter…"

"Dr. Glass, what's really going on? I need to know!"

"I found my son."

CHAPTER THIRTY-TWO

Reseda

I knew it would be some time before Dad got the message. And I forgot how long it took me to drive to Reseda, but I knew it would take Dad a while to get here. I had time to take care of a few things before I left. And perhaps make things right.

I stopped at a check cashing place and cashed my final paycheck. I'd pay Reza back for the damage I caused. I then continued down Reseda Boulevard. I had another stop I had to make.

.   .   .

"Dylan?"

Hannah had regained enough strength to stand with a cane.

"May I come in?"

She nodded and stepped away from the door. I glanced at the driveway behind me. Pearl's car wasn't there. I stepped inside and closed the door.

Hannah gestured to the sofa in the living room. I took a seat. She lowered herself onto the adjacent love seat. She set her cane against the armrest and looked at me.

"Is something wrong?"

I nodded and told her everything. I held back on some things at first, the things parents wouldn't want to know about their kids. But I gave in and told her those things about Pearl too. She didn't seem upset. She listened patiently. When I was finished, she reached across and put her hand on mine.

"Don't be mad at yourself." She lowered her head. "I'm responsible for all this."

"Was it because of those pictures?"

"It started long before the pictures." She took a deep breath and looked directly at me. "My family came here from Slovenia when I was young. We left because of the war. We lived in Orange County."

"That's why you asked about Garden Grove."

She nodded. "That's where we lived."

She let go of my hand and leaned back against the cushions.

"I loved being in America. Americans are so free. They can be whoever they want and say whatever they please. And so many different types of people, all living together. When I was in high school, I met this boy." She smiled broadly. "He called me Hannah. He couldn't say my real name, Zana, but I hated that old country name. I loved being called Hannah. I loved being with him."

She withdrew her smile and lowered her eyelids. I leaned forward.

"When I got pregnant, he offered to pay for an abortion. I—I couldn't do that." She sighed and lowered her head. "When my parents found out, they threw me out of the house."

"How old were you?"

"Fifteen."

"They can't do that! You were a minor."

"They didn't care. They were traditional. I disgraced them. To them, it would be better if I died in a gutter."

I watched Hannah as she brushed the corner of her eye with her finger. Looking at her, I saw Zoey. And what would have happened to her if she kept our child. And I saw myself.

I sat up straight. "How did you get here?"

"I found this ad. They were looking for models..."

"You realize how sketchy that was. You could have wound up a prostitute. Or worse."

"I had no choice. I was going to have a baby. I had no job, no money."

"Then how did you get here?"

"I was living with a friend from school. Her parents weren't all that happy with me being there. So, they gave me bus money."

"Even though you could have wound up…"

"They didn't care what happened to me as long as I wasn't their problem."

I sighed. I knew plenty of people in Orange County who were like that. Including Steven and my own mom.

"Then what happened?"

She smiled and had a faraway look. Her eyes seemed to shine as if she recalled something wonderful. "I met Hawthorne. He was the kindest man."

"The guy who placed the ad?"

She nodded.

"And made bondage porn?"

"He had a website, Hawthorne's Bondage Village. This was during the early days of the World Wide Web, back when most people had dial-up. His was one of the first of its kind."

"And you knew about this?"

"Of course. He was completely up front about it. And I told him my situation. He took me right into his home. He found me an ob/gyn and paid my medical expenses. And when Pearl was born, I gave her his last name. He suggested her first name, Pearl. It's from Scripture."

"Was he religious?"

"Spiritual. He believed in God, but not religion. He said there's too much self-righteousness and hypocrisy."

I nodded. I saw enough of it myself.

"So, you modeled for him?"

"Not until I was 18. That's the law. Besides, he insisted that I finish my education. He also taught me how to maintain his website. I learned HTML, CSS, JavaScript, SSL, paywalls. This was when that technology was in its infancy. I was so excited to learn."

"And who watched Pearl when you went to school and work?"

"The girls did."

"The girls?"

"His other models." Her grin widened. "I was like their kid sister. Loretta was the oldest. She modeled back in the seventies. She called herself our 'den mother.' She adored Pearl. And Consuela, her family were refugees like mine. She came from El Salvador. Ginny called herself a 'chocolate goddess.' She was beautiful. Santana was a lesbian. We never judged. Angie had a rough life. She was sexually and physically abused by her parents. She said being with Hawthorne was the first place she felt safe."

"Safe?"

"It sounds strange, I know. But we all had complete trust in each other. Because we trusted each other, we loved each other. When you think about it, love is a form of bondage. You trade a bit of your freedom for companionship, caring, and support." She smiled for a moment. Then her expression turned sad.

"So, what happened?"

"Hawthorne died a few years ago."

"I'm sorry." I reached out and held Hannah's hand. She put her other hand on top of mine.

"We tried to keep the website going, but it wasn't the same." She exhaled hard. "I started a new site, one with pictures we took over the years. But since I got sick..."

"Is that the one Pearl saw? Something about a hall of fame?"

"'Classic Bondage Hall of Fame,' yes. I asked her to watch the site for me, make sure it stayed up and didn't get hacked."

"When did she know about your pictures?"

"I think she always suspected. I knew she had an interest in it too."

I nodded slowly. I regretted not understanding that part of Pearl.

"Still, I wanted to wait until she was old enough before I told her. But in middle school, she had a crush on this boy. She was so in love with him. Then, he found my pictures." She let go of my hands and looked away. "Kids that age could be so cruel, especially on social media. It got so bad, we had to move so Pearl could go to another school. That's why she went to Reseda High School. But she wasn't the same after that. There were many boys she liked, but she didn't date them. She didn't even go to her prom. She was afraid that if someone found out about me, she would get hurt again."

I hung down my head. "Like I hurt her."

Hannah put her hand on my shoulder. "You didn't know."

"And I was scared."

"Of what?"

"Of what the cops would do if they saw us. I mean, think about it. A pretty woman like Pearl getting tied up by some homeless scum..."

Hannah's forehead furrowed. "You aren't homeless scum. Not to Pearl."

I jolted back in shock.

Her blue eyes became more intense. "She trusts you."

"How?"

"She's seen you at your worst. So many people conceal themselves and try to look better than they really are. When you're at the bottom, there's no pretense, no masks. When you find yourself rejected for who you are, you can't afford to act like you're something you're not. And Pearl," Hannah gave a small smile. "She has her way of finding out who people really are."

I thought about all those awkward questions she asked me. I thought she was being rude, but she really was searching for the truth. For someone she could trust.

I looked down at the dark tan carpet in front of me. I realized how much I avoided the truth. Everything that happened in my life felt like a lie. I wanted to pretend that I didn't care about my parents and their divorce. That I didn't care about failing at school. That I didn't care about losing Zoey. And our baby. That I didn't care about Mom and Steven throwing me out of the house. But I did. Maybe that was why I had such hateful thoughts towards myself. And why I tried to drug them away. Or end myself to stop those thoughts and didn't have to lie anymore.

But in Reseda, I found people who honestly cared about me, even though they had no reason to. And all I did was hurt them. And I couldn't pretend that I didn't care, especially the way I hurt Pearl. I could still see her balled up against the back of the driver's seat sobbing. It brought back that heavy sadness, a sadness that bore down on me too hard to pretend.

I looked at Hannah. I had to clear my throat before I could ask a question harder than any one Pearl asked me.

"Did Pearl really love me?"

"Why don't you ask her and find out?"

I exhaled and shook my head. "It's too late."

"It's only too late when you give up."

"But Hannah, I already told my dad to pick me up. He's coming from Orange County."

"Then tell him not to come."

"He's probably on his way now."

"If you go back to Orange County, you'll go back to being the person you were. Dylan, you're here for a reason."

I found myself muttering, "God takes us where we need to go and teaches us the lessons we need to learn."

"You can turn your back on that. You can turn your back on Pearl. Or you can try to save your relationship and yourself."

.   .   .

I rushed up Reseda Boulevard. I hurried past the wash and the old car dealerships at a nearly breathless pace. Hannah said, "It's only too late when you give up." But what if it really was too late? What if Pearl was already gone? What if my Dad was already here?

I was relieved when I saw the signal for Sherman Way ahead of me. Just a few more blocks!

And that's where I stopped.

I saw her again. Long black stringy hair. Baggy, ratty coat. Stained, faded jeans with the bottoms torn up and fringed around her bare feet. She was the same woman who pulled spoiled food out of our dumpster. Now, she was picking through a trash can by a bus stop, looking for crumbs in empty fast-food containers.

I spoke calmly. "Excuse me."

She looked up and gasped. She backed away from the trash can and looked over her shoulder.

"Wait!" I held up both of my palms towards her. She stopped, but she looked jittery. Scared. Ready to bolt at any second.

I reached into my pocket. I pulled out the entire wad of bills. The crumpled one-dollar bills. My cashed paycheck. Everything I had. And I held it out towards her.

"Please. Buy your children some decent food."

She stared at the money for a moment. Slowly, she inched her hand towards it. I nodded. She reached out and touched the cash. The side of my finger brushed against hers. Her fingers felt rough, but they had some spots of softness to them. When I knew the bills were in her grasp, I let go.

She brought the money close to her chest and flipped the edges to count it. That was when her eyes opened wide.

"God bless you, sir!"

"God bless…"

She tucked the money into her jeans pocket and fled around the corner.

I smiled. I felt a lightness that drove away all the heavy sadness and self-hatred I ever had.

But as I stepped towards the corner of Reseda and Sherman Way, I saw Reza's gas station. I trembled for a moment. I gave that woman the money I was going to use to pay back Reza! I calmed myself down. Reza still had a job. This woman had nothing except kids she couldn't feed.

And I had one more thing left to do.

•　•　•

I first stopped behind the abandoned theater. Dad wasn't there. I would recognize his car. He posted pictures of it on Facebook. He got a new white hybrid Lexus SUV. I guess his financial situation did improve. But there was no Lexus parked behind the theater. I still had time for what I needed to do.

I took the back way to the store. I'm sure Quang wouldn't let me in if I cut in from the front parking lot. The stores on Sherman Way were connected by a series of parking lots behind the buildings. When I got to Magdalena's restaurant, I glanced at the screen door to the kitchen. The smells of spicy beef and tortillas floated out, but there was no sign of Magdalena. I had to keep going.

When I got to the store's back parking lot, I gave a deep sigh. Pearl's blue Kia Rio was still there! I had to go around to the front. I went behind the large supermarket and through the alley between the

shopping center and the church. Then past the storefronts to Buck &
Awesome.

But when I got there, I stopped.

The black lifted pickup truck was parked in front of the store.

.　　.　　.

I hadn't even reached the front of the store when I heard the shouting.
And when I looked through the window, Need Beer and his goons were
harassing Fatima. Quang, Pearl, and Kishana tried to get between them.
The guy in the white t-shirt grabbed at Fatima's headscarf. Pearl tried to
stop him, and he shoved her away. Quang jumped in to fight him, and
the guy in the Cobra Kai shirt tossed him to the floor.

I rushed in the door.

"Hey," I shouted, "Leave them alone!"

I was surprised I didn't say, "Leave them the fuck alone!" I guess I
had gotten used to not swearing in the store.

Quang and Pearl looked up. Everyone's eyes turned towards me. But
no one said anything. Except Need Beer.

"Whatcha gonna do about it, faggot?"

I walked up to Need Beer and gave him a military school punch in
his face. He staggered back hard. He tried to punch back. He swung
wildly over my head. Just as I thought. That big fat wimp couldn't fight!

But Cobra Kai could. He punched me in the gut. But when I learned
boxing, I knew how to take that kind of blow. I gave him an uppercut
to his jaw. As he reeled back, I used that one move I saw in that movie
and kicked him in the face.

Kishana shouted, "Dylan! You can't fight in here! We'd be liable..."

"I don't work here anymore, remember!?"

I didn't have time to argue with her, not when I turned and saw
Need Beer barreling down on me. I ducked under him and threw him
over my back. He landed on a display of ceramic figurines. Hundreds of
dollars shattered in a ghastly crash and crackle. But it was worth it to
take out Need Beer.

Then shouts erupted around me. I turned around. The guy with the stained and stretched-out white t-shirt with the Confederate flag stood in front of me. He pulled something out of the back of his belt. Was it a gun? If so, I had to stop him. I rushed towards him...

BANG!

CHAPTER THIRTY-THREE

Reseda

I had been sitting in my Lexus behind the abandoned theater for about an hour, and I started to get angry.

I had never been to this part of LA before, and I decided I would never go here again. Traffic crawled everywhere. Cars were parked on the side of the street, and you never knew when they would pull out. Everything looked old. The squat and small stucco ranch houses on ridiculously large lots with dead and unkept grass. The tired strip malls with payday loans, vape shops, and medical marijuana dispensaries. It certainly wasn't a safe place. There were a bunch of police cars and an ambulance in front of some dollar store I passed by. There are parts of Lake Forest that aren't safe, but nothing could be as awful as this part of LA. I couldn't believe Dylan would intentionally go to someplace like this. I started to think this was some practical joke. Or maybe he was setting me up to get robbed or killed.

That was what I thought as an old blue Kia sedan pulled up behind me. I glanced at the rear-view mirror. My heart pounded as my mind flooded with all sorts of stereotypes I was ashamed to have. But there was only one person in the car, and she was a young woman. Her head slumped over the steering wheel.

My instinct as a doctor said I should check on her. My instinct as a nervous white guy said I should drive back to Orange County as fast as I could.

My instinct as a doctor hadn't vanished.

I got out of my car and walked slowly to the Kia. As I got closer, I could tell the young woman was distraught. I could hear her sobs from outside the car.

I tapped on the window. Startled, she bolted upright. She fumbled for the ignition key, turned it until her dashboard lit up. She rolled down the power window.

"Miss, are you all right?"

She turned her red and tear-streaked face towards me.

"It was all my fault! If only I hadn't…" She heaved out some hard sobs. "Now, I'll never see him again!"

My whole body shuddered.

"Miss, do you know a Dylan Glass?"

CHAPTER THIRTY-FOUR

Reseda

"Dylan?"

Was I dead?

No, I could feel my eyelids flutter. The cotton sheet against my leg. A needle in my arm. Did someone stick a tube up my dick?

"Dylan?"

I felt a warm touch on my hand. I turned towards that touch and opened my eyes. It took me a moment to focus until I saw deep-set pale blue eyes.

"Pearl?"

That's what I thought I said, but it sounded more like "Puh?"

She offered a wide smile, but her lower lip quivered. A tear rolled down her cheek.

"Are you all right?"

That Vietnamese accent. Quang was standing there. So were Kishana and Fatima. And Mrs. Cimino.

"Thank God you're OK."

I turned to the other side and saw Reza standing there.

"And Magdalena asked me to tell you she's fine. She had a fall, but she's doing better."

I turned my head forward and looked at the tiles on the ceiling. All the people I hurt. And yet, they were all there for me. I wanted to tell them how sorry I was. But all I could do is cry. The tears streamed down my cheeks. My mouth only formed sorrowful moans. The moans and tears seemed to go forever. And when my eyes had stopped stinging enough to see, I could look at their expressions, the tears they wiped

214

from the eyes and faces. It was as if I already told them. And they already accepted.

"Son?"

I looked at the front of the bed. Dad was standing there.

•   •   •

Dylan looked much different from the last time I saw him. He looked thinner but more muscular. He shaved off that scraggly goatee he tried to grow when he got back from military school. I was glad that he still took good care of his teeth.

I looked at the people who surrounded his bed. They weren't the type of people I usually hung around. It wasn't just because they were of different ethnicities. I hung around people of different ethnicities in Orange County too, but they were basically the same type of person. They upgraded their smartphones every year, leased new cars every few years, complained about the yields on their portfolios, and vacationed in either Costa Rica or Tahiti. I felt out-of-place with them because I couldn't keep up financially.

Dylan's friends didn't seem like that. They seemed like humble people with humble jobs. They were humble enough to reach out to him when he was homeless and sleeping in his car. The people I knew wouldn't do that. I don't think I would.

And this young woman, the one he called "Puh?" The one in the short skirt and form-fitting blouse? The one I saw in the old blue Kia? Were she and Dylan in love? They must have been, judging by the way she wept in her car and the wide smile when he opened his eyes. If Dylan had a relationship with a girl, I didn't know about it. He never told me. Teresa would sharply insist that he was straight, as if I were supposed to be ashamed if he were gay.

A heavy sadness settled onto my shoulders. I realized how much I didn't know about my own son. He might as well have been in Reseda the whole time, even when we were sitting in the same room in Orange County.

But here we were, in a hospital room 75 miles away from home, looking at each other face-to-face. I had a second chance to reconnect with my son, to be the father I should have been. A second chance a bullet almost took away.

I should say something more, but I had so much to say and didn't know where to start. Dylan was still coming out of anesthesia. He wouldn't hear me anyway.

The African American woman in a dress shirt, slacks, and a name badge sensed my awkwardness. She patted me on the shoulder.

"We should let him rest. I'm sure you'll be able to talk to him tomorrow."

The Middle Eastern man by the side of Dylan's bed smiled. "You look like you could use something to eat."

· · ·

We went to this Mexican restaurant called Mamá Frieda, which was close to the abandoned theater. I had Mexican food plenty of times, but it was nothing like Mamá Frieda. It was kosher Mexican food. I didn't think such a thing existed. It was the best Mexican food I ever had.

I got to know the people who surrounded Dylan's hospital bed. Most of them came from the store where Dylan worked. Pearl, which was the name of that young woman, she worked there too. I didn't recall Dylan having a job before. I listened to their interlocking stories about Dylan's time in Reseda. They spent a month with him, but they knew more about him than I did in 18 years.

"You must be Dylan's father." A female voice with a heavily accented slur came from behind me.

I turned my head. A woman in her fifties supported herself with a cane. She had a cast on her wrist and an abrasion on her right cheek.

"Magdalena?" I assumed she was the woman who had a fall. I could tell from her face that she had a stroke. She made an exceptional recovery just by being able to speak and walk.

She smiled and patted me on the shoulder. "Your son is a good boy."

I blinked with shock. Of all the things Teresa and I ever said to or about Dylan, the word "good" never came up. "Troubled," "difficult," "struggling," and a few Teresa said that no parent should ever say about their own child. These people in Reseda knew things about Dylan I didn't know and saw things in him I didn't see.

"Tha—thanks." I stumbled as I choked back a tear.

The faces around the table fixed their eyes on me, encouraging me to let my feelings out. How could I? How could pour out my soul to people I just met? If I could, what would I say? Where would I start?

Pearl turned to Quang and whispered something. He took a cell phone, which looked like an old flip phone, and handed it to her. She opened it and then turned to me. "Do you have a place to stay?"

• • •

I followed Pearl's blue Kia down Reseda Boulevard, one of the main streets. It was like the other streets I had seen so far in this part of LA, with old buildings that had been repainted and repurposed. Yet this part of Reseda seemed different. Maybe it was the way the streetlights lit up the boulevard. Or maybe the way I was seeing it was different.

I thought about my office building back in Lake Forest. It was probably considered chic when it was built in the seventies, but it became dated and rundown to the point that some said it was hurting my practice. I couldn't afford to move elsewhere, so I stuck it out in that building until they put on a new coat of paint and changed the carpet. It seemed that way in Reseda. People were too proud to move or unable to go elsewhere, so they made the most of what they had. They didn't go on a pointless chase for the new, only to discover that it too someday will become worn out and out-of-style.

I had so many questions I had to ask Dylan. So many things I didn't know about him. But I had questions I had to ask myself too. How do I connect with him after all the years we hadn't? What kind of relationship could we have? I was given a second chance with him. I can't waste it like all the other chances I had before.

Pearl turned right on a street called Victory. I turned right as well. We went past a small strip mall on the corner and then turned into another street called Amigo.

We entered a neighborhood that reminded me of the one in Lake Forest where I spent my teenage years. Ranch-style houses with stucco walls and wood trim. Green lawns and tall, mature trees. Concrete driveways with basketball hoops over the garage door. The houses were further apart, had lower rooflines, and older styling, but it felt, in a way, familiar.

She pulled into a driveway of a house on the right. I parked on the street next to it. At first, I felt a little out-of-place because I thought I was the only one with a new luxury car. I then noticed the Mercedes Benz across the street, and I didn't feel I stuck out too much.

Pearl parked her car and walked over to mine. She looked it over and then looked at me.

"You're homeless too, aren't you?"

I had forgotten about the pile of clothing in the back. I should have put the tonneau cover over it. But in Reseda, I couldn't have any secrets.

I exhaled softly. "I just broke up with my girlfriend."

Pearl continued looking at me. "So, women scare you too."

"Just a few."

She nodded. "You can get your things later. Please come with me."

I followed Pearl into her house. We stepped into the entryway, which was a small space between the door and a partition separating the dining room. A walkway with dark tan carpet led to the kitchen on one end and the living room and a door to other rooms on the other. The house looked smaller than Rachel's house, but not much smaller than the one where I grew up in Lake Forest.

"Mom, he's here."

The door at the end of the walkway opened. I shuddered as a woman walked through. She wore a pink floral bandana around her head, just like the one Mom wore. She walked with a cane, but at a good stride. I felt relieved. At that point of Mom's chemotherapy, she had to use a wheelchair.

Pearl met her mom halfway. I walked over to them.

Pearl introduced us. "Mom, this is Dylan's dad. This is my mother, Hannah."

She reached out for my hand to shake. She gave a complete grip, but not a strong one. I could tell the chemotherapy still weakened her. As I looked at her face, she seemed somewhat familiar, like I had seen her somewhere before.

"It's a pleasure to meet you, Mister…"

"Oliver. Please call me Oliver."

She smiled. "Oliver."

Hannah spoke with an accent. It was hard to place it, but it sounded Eastern European. She definitely looked like someone I had seen before.

"We can sit down, if you like." I knew she was having some trouble standing.

She nodded. I walked around the tan corduroy love seat. She nodded to Pearl. Pearl stepped to her side and supported her as she walked to the sofa across from the love seat.

I started feeling uneasy again. Mom needed help to do the smallest things towards the end. I thought about moving back to help her. Things weren't going well between Teresa and me at the time, so I wouldn't have minded helping Mom just to get away from her. But I worried about what it would mean for our marriage if I did. In the end, I wound up losing both Mom and my marriage.

But I couldn't think about my past as I was watched Pearl help Hannah onto the sofa. What was Pearl thinking? How was she coping? Especially if she had feelings for Dylan.

She was about to sit down too. But Hannah held up her hand.

"We can set up a bed for Oliver in the den. Could you please get it ready?"

Pearl nodded. She seemed to stiffen as stepped away from the sofa.

"This must be hard for her," I said.

Hannah nodded. "I hated to put her in this situation."

"I know. I know how hard cancer is on the whole family."

"Did you…"

"My mother did. I lost her to pancreatic cancer."

"I'm sorry."

I nodded.

"I have Hodgkin's Lymphoma," she said. "My prognosis was unclear for a while, but the doctors are feeling more optimistic."

"I'm glad."

She looked away for a moment. "You haven't seen your son in a while, have you?"

"No."

She turned back to me and studied me with her blue eyes.

"You regret that. I can tell."

My lips parted, but I couldn't speak. I was afraid I was going to break down. She seemed to notice because she leaned closer to me.

I took a deep breath. "His mother took custody after..." I cleared my throat. "I didn't know he was—I mean, if I had known he was—I would have..."

"It's all right, Oliver. You don't have to be ashamed."

I exhaled hard. I could hear a quiver. I exhaled hard again to make it go away.

She leaned closer to me and looked into my eyes. "Your son is a good person, Oliver. But good people can lose their way."

I looked away and nodded.

Hannah reached over and put her hand on my shoulder. "I imagine this has been a rough day for you. You should get some rest."

· · ·

Except I couldn't sleep. I just stared at the popcorn ceiling. The shadows were deepened by the faint light from the slightly parted drapes. The air mattress that Pearl provided was comfortable enough. It was more comfortable than sleeping in my Lexus. The hard part was sleeping alone.

I never slept alone. When I wasn't with Teresa or Rachel, I had thoughts of Grandma Dinah and Dad. Or Mom and Maury. There was always some dark memory, some horrible thing that happened, some argument with words that could never be taken back, someone dying.

That night, only silence.

All the times I tried to forget. All the times I tried to drive away those horrible memories. But in the silence, I *wanted* them to come. I wanted to feel something, hear something. Even those hateful voices that have pricked at me since childhood. I needed their company.

But there was silence. Only silence.

What was it about Reseda that kept the voices and memories away? Was it because it was far from home, far removed from the reminders I saw every day while driving to work? Away from the house where we lived in fear of Grandma Dinah. Away from El Toro High School where

I felt isolated and alone, and no amount of straight As and awards were ever enough. There was that one time in the eleventh grade...

But I could remember nothing. There was only silence.

What was it about this strange place, a place familiar and unfamiliar, that blocked my memories?

These people took Dylan into their arms when Teresa and Steven cast him out. They connected with him when I failed to do so. They forgave him no matter what he did. They saw the good in him we failed to see. They loved him...

The silence was broken. Broken by my sobs.

I couldn't make myself stop. And I didn't want to. I cried about everything. I cried the tears I didn't cry at Dad's funeral. And Maury's. And Mom's. I cried all those tears I had been afraid to shed for years. I cried because I lost my shame about crying. Somehow, Reseda made it OK for me to cry, just as they allowed Dylan to cry. I wasn't going to stop until all those decades of pain gushed out my tear ducts.

• • •

KNOCK KNOCK.

I sat up with a start. The light that came through the windows seemed brighter. I rushed to a small table where I set my iPhone. It was 8:30 in the morning.

KNOCK KNOCK.

I slipped on my jeans and a t-shirt I'd been wearing since I left Rachel's house. I opened the door. Pearl stood on the other side.

"The hospital called. Dylan's awake."

I nodded. "I'll get ready."

"Your clothes are still in your car. Do you want me to get them?"

"Thanks, but I'll get them."

I was about to step out the door, but Pearl stood in place.

"Did your crying heal you?"

She asked the most interesting questions. I had to think about that one for a moment.

"It's a start."

CHAPTER THIRTY-FIVE

Reseda

I had to do some things before leaving. I brought my clothes in from the SUV. Pearl let me shower in a bathroom near her room. She said the water heats faster there.

I also had to take care of some calls. First, I had to let Alison know I would be gone for a while. I never had a patient of mine get shot, but major surgery could take a week or more in the hospital. Next, I called Muriel. She was horrified about what happened to Dylan, but she was overjoyed that he was OK. I had to let Teresa know. She seemed surprisingly sympathetic, but she also seemed a bit frazzled and distracted. I could understand with the situation she was in. I asked her to come, but she declined.

I thought about calling Rachel. I even had tapped her name on my contact list. Would she take my call? Would she even care?

"We're ready when you are." Hannah stepped gingerly with her cane.

"I'm ready." I slipped the iPhone into my pocket.

• • •

I offered to take Pearl and Hannah to the hospital, but my SUV was too high for Hannah to climb up. I followed them up Reseda Boulevard to the hospital.

It was just as well because I needed some time alone. What would I say to Dylan when I saw him? What would we do after he recovered?

. . .

WHHHSK. The nurse drew the curtain around the bed.

ERRRRFFFF. The blood pressure cuff tightened around my forearm.

I had gotten used to the routine. The nurse would wave something in front of my forehead to take my temperature, change one bag that was attached to my arm, drain another bag that was attached to my dick, and shine a flashlight in front of my eyes and my open my mouth so she could shine the light in there.

PFFFFFFT. The cuff loosened.

The nurse glanced at some machine and tapped numbers into an iPad. "110 over 65. Pulse 67."

I wished Dad were here so he could tell me what that meant. He wasn't, so I asked the nurse.

"Is that good?"

"Yes." She closed the cover on her iPad and tucked it under her arm. "The doctor will be in to see you soon."

WHHHSK. She pulled back the curtain.

"Excuse me." I wasn't sure she heard me as she stepped from where the curtain bunched at the end. But she stopped and turned towards me.

"Is my dad coming?"

"I believe so." She smiled and headed out of the room.

I sunk my head into the pillow. What would I say to Dad when I see him? Would it be another bullshit talk about the Angels and superhero movies? No. Not this time.

. . .

Pearl, Hannah, and I huddled in the corner of the elevator. Most of the elevator was taken up by an elderly woman in a wheelchair and a middle-age man who I assumed was her son, and a teenage girl who was probably her granddaughter. I visited Mom in the hospital a few times towards the end. Not as many as I wanted.

Pearl glanced at the newspaper tucked under my arm. I would tell her and Hannah about it later. But this was something I had to show Dylan first.

The elevator stopped at our floor.

"Excuse us, please," Pearl whispered.

The man pulled the wheelchair back, and the girl moved close enough to him to let us pass through.

We stepped into the corridor and looked for the sign to the patient rooms.

Hannah patted my shoulder. "Do you want to spend some time alone with your son?"

• • •

The doctor explained what happened to me. The guy with the stained and stretched-out white t-shirt shot me in the stomach. He then freaked out and ran. The cops caught him a half an hour later. Fortunately, the guy's bullet missed my spine and a major artery. But the doctors still needed hours of surgery and several pints of blood to fix me up.

I glanced at Dad. He deals with this stuff all the time at his job. It must not have been a big deal to him.

• • •

Normally, I could listen to a diagnosis, even the cause of death, with clinical detachment. But this was my son! He was almost killed! I could have lost him!

• • •

"What's his prognosis?"

The concern in Dad's voice surprised me.

The doctor smiled. "Good. We will monitor his vitals and make sure the sutures continue to hold. Starting today, we will gradually increase his activity. He should be able to make a full recovery, but it will take time."

I looked at Dad. He had his practice. He had his girlfriend and her kids. There was no way he could stay here until I get better.

· · ·

I knew Dylan's doctor couldn't tell us how long his recovery would be. I didn't commit to timetables either. It depended on several things, most of which a doctor can't control. If I couldn't stay the entire time Dylan recovered, I could make trips. I wasn't going to abandon him. Not anymore.

The doctor said, "If you have any questions, feel free to ask. The nurses can contact me at the station."

I nodded. "Thank you, doctor."

"Thanks." Dylan's voice sounded different from the last time I saw him. A bit deeper, perhaps. It couldn't have been just from his injuries.

I glanced at the doctor as he left the room.

I then looked at Dylan. In that hospital bed, he seemed like a completely different person. Someone I didn't really know. Someone I never knew at all.

I looked up at Dad, waiting for him to say something. Anything. But he sat silently. It was as if he knew we had to be real with each other, and he didn't know how.

So, I had to speak first.

· · ·

"Do they know?" Dylan said.

"I told Muriel. She said she's coming from Minnesota to see you."

"She's not going to ditch midterms, is she?"

"No. I said you were recovering. She'll come during break."

"What about Mom? Does she know?"

"I told her."

"Then, why isn't she here?"

"You know your mom and I can't be together in the same room."

"Even for this?"

"I'm afraid your mom has problems of her own."

. . . .

Dad reached over to the tray next to my bed. He picked up a newspaper and handed it to me. It was the *Orange County Register* from a few days ago. The front page had a picture of a glum-looking Mom and Steven standing in front of their house. The house they threw me out of.

FACE TIME EMPIRE CRUMBLES
DIMITY PROBE MAY LEAD TO CRIMINAL CHARGES

I looked up at Dad. He tightened his lip. I looked back at the article.

DANA POINT - In addition to mounting accusations of plagiarism and falsifying information, Christian motivational speaker and Face Time with Jesus *author Steven Howard Dimity now faces allegations of fraud related to his non-profit organization, Face Time for Healing. According to Assistant DA Francine Jacoby, Dimity and his wife Teresa "used the organization like a personal bank account. Money that should have gone to charitable work was instead used to furnish Dimity's office in Newport Beach and his private residence in Dana Point."*

I was glad I didn't take all my stuff. It would have been seized as evidence.

I looked up at Dad again. He glanced down at the paper, encouraging me to read on.

Steven did plagiarize from Reverend Patricia Williams Story. And several other authors, including the pastor he made fun of because his son died by suicide. Everything Steven said was a lie. Growing up the only white kid in a bad part of Cleveland? More like an affluent white suburb. That firefight in Iraq? He wasn't even in Iraq. He enlisted, but he got injured in a touch football game in basic training and got discharged. He never earned a Purple Heart and Bronze Star. He never had anything personally presented to him by President Bush, but he did meet him at a Republican fundraiser. And that time when he took in his homeless opera-singing buddy? All staged. He hired an opera singer, actors to drive in the cars behind us and applaud, and a professional film crew to make a video to promote his so-called non-profit. He even staged the visit with the cancer patient at the hospital where he met Mom. It was true that Steven's father went to prison, but for fraud and tax evasion, not armed robbery.

I looked up at Dad once more. Again, his glance urged me to continue. I had to turn to another page.

Teresa Dimity said, "These lies were perpetuated by my husband's jealous rivals, his ex-wife, and godless liberals who want to persecute decent Christian people and destroy traditional American values. We will beat these charges. I stand behind my husband 100 percent."

I lowered the paper and looked directly at Dad. Mom would stand behind a cheating pathological liar but not a husband who loved her. And I could tell it broke his heart.

•   •   •

"How do you feel about this?" Dylan said.

"I don't know. She is your mom. She hurt me, but I loved her."

"But you have a new girl..."

I shook my head. "We broke up."

"Sorry. She looked pretty."

"Pretty is only on the outside, son. It doesn't show you what's underneath."

"What are you going to do, Dad?"

"I don't know. I'm more concerned about what you're going to do."

Dylan looked away. "I don't know either. I lost everything. The Explorer got towed."

"I can pay to get it out of impound."

"But I lost my job."

"I spoke to your boss, what is his name?"

"Quang."

"Yes, sorry. I forgot. He said last night that he's willing to take you back."

Dylan looked up and smiled. "That's great."

•   •

Dad smiled back. "So, do you still want to leave?"

I blinked and stared at him at a moment. Then I remembered that email I sent him.

"You don't want me to come home with you?"

"I don't have a home for you to go to. I lived in my girlfriend's house. So, I don't have a place to live."

"We can find a new home together."

Dad smiled. "I think you've already found a home of your own."

"But I don't have a place to live."

"You do with us."

Both Dad and I turned towards the door. Pearl stood in the doorway with Hannah right behind her. She walked to the side of my bed and stood next to Dad. She reached under my head and cradled it.

"Mom and I talked. We want you to live with us."

"But Pearl, you're already doing too much. You can't take care of me too."

Hannah smiled. "But you will get better. And then, you can help her help me."

•   •

Watching Dylan, Pearl, and Hannah together, I saw the love I wished Teresa and I could have given him. But I no longer felt sadness or regret. I felt joy that my son was moving ahead in his life. He found purpose and direction. It gave me a sense of warmth and happiness I never felt at any time in my life.

I reached up and patted Pearl on the shoulder. "Do you want to spend some time alone with Dylan?"

•　　•　　•

When I got the Dylan's Explorer out of impound, I had it towed to the gas station where Reza worked. Pearl drove me to the station. I paid for five gallons, enough to see if it would start. Pearl and Reza stood next to the vehicle as I got into the driver's seat. The car smelled like underarms and unwashed socks. I couldn't believe Dylan spent a month living in it.

"Will this thing start?" Pearl said.

"As long as the battery has a charge, it should turn over," Reza replied.

It was up to me to find out. I put the key in the ignition and turned it. The engine roared back to life without hesitation.

Reza and Pearl stepped away from the vehicle.

"He could have gone home anytime he wanted," Reza mused.

Pearl smiled. "He did."

I shifted the transmission to drive.

•　　•　　•

Back at Hannah and Pearl's, curiosity got the best of me, and I started looking through Dylan's things in the back. He showed his ingenuity by covering the windows with a black plastic tarp, laying a sleeping bag out over the bed, and getting a folding knife. He must have learned about the usefulness of knives in Scouts. I found his iPhone and a couple of books. One was Steven's. The other was some New Age book.

"Mom let him borrow that." Pearl walked towards me.

"I'm sure he'll want to finish this. I'll take it to the hospital for him." I glanced at the title, *The Healing Power of God's Light*. "I used to read books like this in college. I was into all that stuff. Crystals, incense, tarot cards, meditative piano music. It didn't help me."

"It helped Mom."

I set the book on Dylan's sleeping bag next to something bunched in a pile. I then turned to Pearl and looked at her t-shirt. I hadn't noticed it before.

"You play softball?"

"I did in high school."

"My daughter does too. She's at the University of Minnesota."

"Scholarship?"

"It doesn't cover everything."

Pearl exhaled. "I was offered a scholarship to Oklahoma."

"Patty Grasso has a great program there. They won the NCAA title in 2013. They say they might win again this year."

"Yeah. They say." Pearl hung down her head.

I mustered up some positivity. "When Dylan starts helping your mom, you can go back to school."

"I can't go to Oklahoma…"

"They have schools in this area. I think there's a Cal State here, and I'm sure there are community colleges. Perhaps you can get into UCLA."

"It's too late."

"It's not. Sometimes, life gives us second chances."

She looked up at me. "Like you have with Dylan."

"And you too. I know how you feel about each other."

Her face reddened, and body locked stiffly. I thought what I said embarrassed her. Then, I noticed she was looking in the bed of the Explorer. I looked in the same direction she did. I realized what was in that bundle near the book.

I smiled. "It's nothing to be embarrassed about. It's perfectly acceptable these days." I took a step towards her and whispered. "If you need any tips, there's an excellent website. I think it's called 'Hawthorne.'"

I patted her shoulder and went back to the Explorer to close the lift gate. Pearl still looked red-faced and stiff.

CHAPTER THIRTY-SIX

Reseda

"I guess you're not reading his book anymore."

I looked up from the book Hannah lent me. Mrs. Cimino stood in my hospital room.

"I can't say I blame you." She picked through the *Orange County Register* that Dad left for me on the tray.

"I'm sorry, Mrs. Cimino. I know how much Steven's book means to you. You said it saved your life."

"Did I ever tell you why, Dylan?"

"No, Mrs. Cimino."

I set the book next to me. She walked over to my bed and looked straight at me.

"Hugh was a good man, but he wasn't always a good husband."

"What did he do?"

"He worked. He got a job at Lockheed after college. I tended the house and took care of the kids. That's the way things were back then, you know."

"It's not that much different now," I said. "Mom stayed at home too, at least for a while."

"It was a lonely life, Dylan. Especially when he traveled for business, which he did a lot."

"What did you do, Mrs. Cimino?"

She gave a deep sigh. "Drink."

I stared at Mrs. Cimino. I couldn't imagine such a trim and healthy woman in her seventies wrecking herself that way. She sensed my confusion.

"You remember me telling you about Hugh's parents and their liquor store. They kept us well supplied. But drinking alone got tiring after a while. After I tucked the kids to bed, I'd go out…"

"You left your kids at home alone?"

"As I told you, unhappy people do things that cause them greater unhappiness." She swallowed hard and deep.

"Mrs. Cimino, if…" I cleared my throat. "If you feel uncomfortable, you don't have to…"

"I have to." She sniffed. "I lost something I believed in. Something that saved me. Now I have nothing to turn to."

Fucking Steven Dimity! That fucking bastard Steven Dimity! Of all the shitty things he did, the worst was to rip the heart out of people like Mrs. Cimino. People who depended on him. Believed in him! How could he do that to…

Mrs. Cimino must have known how angry I was. She stood up and started backing away from my bed.

"I'm sorry. I didn't mean to lay this on you, especially when you're recovering…"

"No." I softened my voice. "Please, Mrs. Cimino. You can talk to me. Please."

She walked slowly back to my bed. When she got there, she stood mute. She couldn't gather the nerve to talk. I had to help her.

"What happened, Mrs. Cimino?"

A tear weaved through the wrinkles on her cheek.

"What happened to your children?"

Another tear traced down her wrinkles.

"Did something happen to Bernice…"

"Bernice was my youngest. She was seven years younger than the others. And…" She hung down her head.

"And?"

Mrs. Cimino exhaled long and hard before continuing. "I met this man at a bar. His name? Hell, I don't remember his name. Hugh was away so much, it just felt good to be with a man."

"You slept with him?"

"Hugh never knew. When I got pregnant, he was just happy to have another child. He adored Bernice. He never questioned…" She exhaled hard. "A few years ago, he had gotten sick. Both of his kidneys failed. He needed a transplant. And Bernice—dear, sweet Bernice—she donated one of her kidneys. And... and..."

"That's when they found out, wasn't it?"

"His body rejected her kidney, and Hugh..." She sighed hard. "His body couldn't handle it. He died."

"And your children blamed you."

"And I blamed myself." Mrs. Cimino covered her eyes and wept.

I let her cry. I brushed tears from the corners of my eyes.

Finally, she asked in a soft, broken voice, "Do you have a tissue?"

"There's a box on the tray behind you."

She needed a few tissues to dry her eyes and clear her nose. She then held out the box to me.

"Thank you."

I took a tissue and dabbed the tears from my eyes. When both of our eyes were clear, we looked at each other.

"Is that why you said forgiveness was the hardest thing you had to learn, Mrs. Cimino?"

"Steven Dimity taught me about forgiveness." She put the box of tissues back on the tray. She then stared at the *Orange County Register*. "But I guess that's just a lie."

"Maybe it's not."

.   .   .

"Are you sure you want to do this?" I handed Dylan my iPhone.

"It's not just for me."

.   .   .

"Oliver?"

"No. It's me, Dylan."

"Dylan?"

"Yes, Mom."

Mom's voice sounded different from the last time I heard her screaming at me. Her voice was softer. Maybe sadder. But it tightened to her familiar bitchiness.

"I'm surprised your father didn't reconnect your phone."

"When I get back to work, I'm paying for the phone myself. There's a place near my work where I can buy a SIM card and minutes. I can even call Argentina at 11 cents a minute."

"Argentina sounds good right about now, except they took my passport." The sadness returned to her voice.

"Where are you, Mom?"

"I'm with your Grandma Pauline."

"And Steven?"

"He's at the house."

"You're not with him?"

"No."

"Did your lawyer tell you to stay away from him?"

Silence. Then her voice turned nasty again.

"You must be enjoying this."

"How?"

"We kicked you out of the house..."

"You're still my mom."

Silence. Then her voice turned bitter.

"Just because a woman shoves a baby out of her uterus, it doesn't mean she earned the right to be loved. Your father's grandmother didn't."

"Love isn't something you have to earn..."

"Please don't tell me you're quoting Steven..."

"It's from another book. One my friend let me borrow. It's from Reverend Patricia Williams Story..."

"One of the people Steven plagiarized. Excuse me, *allegedly* plagiarized."

"I thought you believed Steven. You said so in that newspaper article. You said you stood by him 100 percent."

"Oh, please, Dylan! Everything he said was bullshit! He didn't even believe it himself!"

"Some people believe it. One of the customers at our store, she said his book saved her life."

234

"You mean someone read Steven's book in liberal LA!?"

"It's 'the Valley.' Not 'LA.' People in the Valley hate it when you call it 'LA.'"

"Who gives a shit, Dylan!? They're all a bunch of pretentious kombucha-sipping wannabe movie producers!"

"Then you don't know what people are like here."

"Apparently not! Apparently, the Valley, as you put it, has brain-dead sheep!"

"Sheep? Is that all they are to you and Steven, sheep?"

"Damn right, they're sheep! And Steven got rich fleecing them! That's because they'll believe any bullshit you throw at them! They won't question anything! It doesn't matter how ridiculous or big a lie it is. They'll believe it simply because they want to believe it!"

"Just like you did."

Silence.

"You believed Steven too, Mom. You believed him so much you left Dad for him."

Silence. Then a deep sigh and a tense voice.

"He offered me a life your father couldn't. He had passion and wealth."

I couldn't help myself. "So much for wealth being a sign of God's favor."

"You think your father was so great?" Mom snarled, "Your father lived in the past!"

"But Steven made up his past. His wealth and fame were built on lies. But you believed him."

Silence. Then Mom blurted out furiously.

"What's the point of this call, Dylan!? To tell me what a piece of shit I am?"

"No, Mom..."

"You want to call me out? You want to tell me I'm an idiot? I'm a terrible mother?"

"Mom..."

"Maybe you're trying to get me to confess! Maybe you're looking for something you can use to put me away for the rest of my life!"

"Mom!"

"That would be justice for you, wouldn't it, Dylan!? As punishment for making you sleep in an SUV, I'll spend the rest of my life getting raped in prison! Is that what you want!?"

"No!"

Silence.

"Mom, I just want to tell you." I exhaled hard. "I forgive you."

"Forgive me? How can you forgive me?"

"Because I love you. I'll always will."

"Spare me the greeting card poetry, Dylan! I've lost everything, including my freedom and reputation. What good does your forgiveness and love do for me?"

"Just to know..." I exhaled hard. "I'm not carrying any hatred towards you. Mom, I don't like to see you suffer, even if you deserve it. I'll never stop loving you, despite what you've done. But I have to go on with my life. Whatever happened between you and Dad, whatever happened between us, I have to let that go. I have to forgive you so I can have peace. I don't want to hold on to my pain like Dad did. It's like Steven said, 'All of us are broken. All of us are flawed. All of us have sinned against God, each other, and ourselves. Until we see the grace in the brokenness in ourselves and others, we cannot receive God's grace.' Yes, Mom. I believe that."

A long silence. Then her voice turned soft.

"That was the only thing Steven wrote himself. That may have been the only thing he actually believed. It's the hardest thing to put into practice."

"I can understand that. It is a hard lesson to learn."

"I'm glad you're learning it, son. I'm a long way from learning it myself."

Silence. After a moment, I moved Dad's phone from my ear and looked at the screen. She had ended the call.

•   •   •

Dylan handed the iPhone back to me. "I thought I'd get closure."

"There's no such thing as closure. All you can do is decide how you'll move ahead."

"Excuse me." The nurse peeked her head inside the room. "Dylan needs to go for a walk."

He looked up at me. "Will you walk with me, Dad?"

"Of course."

. . .

I had to walk as part of my recovery, but it hurt like a motherfucker, and it tired me out like an old man. And to think, before I got shot, I booked it all the way up Reseda Boulevard from Victory to Sherman Way. But I did it without having a drag around an IV and a piss bag.

But Dad was walking with me. I had to keep going to impress him, even though I wanted to go back to my room. He gave me that proud papa smile, like when I made a great catch in baseball or got good grades at school. It was a smile I hadn't seen in a long time.

"Are you sure you have to go back, Dad?"

"I have to catch up with my patients. Alison said I lost a star on Yelp. But I'll be back on weekends."

"The doctor said that if my recovery continues to go well, I can be discharged soon. What does that mean?"

"It means you'll be going home. Home with Pearl and Hannah."

Home. I liked the sound of that word. I never truly had one for a long time.

Dad continued, "So, what will you do when you get home?"

"Well, Pearl and I talked last night. I want to finish my high school diploma. They have night classes at the same high school she graduated from. She's going to back to school in the fall. There's a community college nearby called Pierce. They even have a softball team."

Dad smiles. "She's a wonderful girl. You're lucky to have found someone like her. You have so many wonderful things going for you, Dylan."

"That's why I want to clean up my life, Dad. I got a second chance, and I don't want to blow it. I don't want to screw up anymore. I want to stop those hateful voices in my head."

Dad stopped. "You too?"

I stared at him for a moment. He walked over to me and put his hand on my shoulder.

"There are a lot of things you don't know about me." He patted my shoulder, and we continued walking. "It's time we got help and helped each other."

"Very good."

We turned around. The nurse had been watching us.

"You made it all the way around the ward."

CHAPTER THIRTY-SEVEN

Lake Forest

One bottle of 145-milligram tablets of fenofibrate. One bottle of 50-milligram tablets of losartan. One bottle of 81-milligram tablets of low-dosage aspirin. One bottle of 5-milligram tablets of Cialis that I had not taken since I left Rachel's house. I suppose that someday, I would take them again.

I gathered them up along with my MacBook Pro and put them in the safe in the closet. That was one of the amenities in this residence hotel room, along with a coffeemaker, iron, and a whirlpool bath. It still wasn't a home, but it would do for now.

I picked up my briefcase and headed out the door. Before I went to the office, I had something to do.

• • • •

I drove through the tall gates of El Toro Memorial Park and followed the looping driveway. I parked my SUV in the back of the Evergreen section. As I stepped out of the car, I noticed some small rocks in the gap between the curb and grass. I picked up two of them and put them in my pocket.

First, I went to Maury's grave. I took one of the rocks from my pocket, knelt down, and placed it on the black marble marker. I ran my fingers over the faded white engraving. The dates on it were too close together, and the last date happened too long ago. I stood up and bade him a silent farewell. Although I've spent many times communing at his gravesite, he wasn't the reason I came here.

Just a few steps away was Grandma Dinah's marker. She wanted to be buried in a Jewish cemetery, but the closest one we could find was in Norwalk. If only she knew how close she was to the grandson who she beat and tormented. I had only visited her gravesite once, but only because Mom begged me to go to her marker dedication.

Her marker was also in black marble with white engraving. It had a Magen David and the following inscription:

Dinah Wolfowitz Glass
1923 - 1996
The Lord is full of compassion and gracious,
slow to anger, and with much kindness.

It seemed strange that she chose that passage from Psalms, especially with how she lived her life.

I knelt down and reached for the rock in my pocket. I stayed fixed for a moment, staring at her inscription.

"Grandma, I'm letting you go. You may have thought you controlled me. In truth, that's what I allowed you to do."

I took the rock out of my pocket.

"Maybe I needed you to save me. Maybe I needed to be afraid. But I don't need to be saved, and I don't want to be afraid anymore."

I looked at the rock between my fingertips.

"That's why I'm letting you go. I'm letting you go in peace and..." I sighed. "I wish I could say love. But I don't think I loved you. You never allowed me to. So, I'm letting you go *for* love. For my family. For myself. I will not live in fear or in the past anymore."

I set the rock on her marker.

I stood up slowly and took a long look at her marker and the rock I left there. Rocks are supposed to represent the permanence of memory. I could never forget those memories of her, but I didn't have to be a prisoner of them. I turned away and headed to my SUV.

•   •   •

"You have a full schedule today, Dr. Glass." Alison handed me a printout of my calendar.

"Thanks."

"And there's someone in your office to see you."

My face scrunched up in confusion. Who would be here to see me? I handed the printout back to Alison and headed towards my office. When I opened the door, I needed a few minutes to gather my thoughts before speaking.

"Rachel?"

Instead of scrubs, she wore a polo shirt and jeans as well as an intense look of someone who had something urgent and difficult to say.

"Um…" She had a hard time gathering her thoughts as well. "Alison said you found Dylan. How is he?"

"He's fine. Actually, he's doing great. He's up in L—uh…" I smiled. "The Valley. They hate when you call it LA. How are the kids?"

"That's what I want to talk to you about." She looked down. She rubbed her hands together tightly. It took her some time to gather the courage to speak. "I came to say I'm sorry. And goodbye."

That word made my whole body shudder.

"What do you mean, goodbye?"

"I'm going back to Israel."

"But what about David and Moshe?"

"I plan to leave them with Avraham."

"Your ex who said raising kids is women's work?"

"They're better off with him than me." Her shoulder trembled. Tears gathered around her eyes.

"What about your practice?"

"Who will hire an obstetrician who screams at her kids!?" A tear fell down her cheek.

I stepped to Rachel and took her hands in mine.

"You can't give up like this! You need help!"

"I'm sick!"

"You won't get better if you don't get help."

Tears flowed more freely down her face.

"Who would want to help me?" She hung down her head. Her body convulsed in tears.

"Hey."

I moved my hands to her shoulders, then her back. I drew her close to me and let her weep on my chest. I always thought she was strong and powerful, but she was as broken as me. I kissed the top of her head and held her closer.

"I'll help."

She pulled her face away from me. "But I hurt you! I hurt my children!"

I put my hand on her face and brushed away her tears.

"I've hurt people too. We're broken people, Rachel. But no one is too broken that we can't be fixed. We can make things right." I caressed her face. "We can make things right with Moshe and David. We can make things right between us. I'm willing if you're willing."

She nodded, then wrapped her arms around me.

"Dr. Glass?"

I turned towards the office door. Alison had it partially opened and stuck her head in the opening. But she pulled it back slightly when she saw Rachel.

"I'm sorry to disturb you, but Mr. Marchenko is here for his appointment."

Rachel and I had to end our embrace. I turned and smiled at Alison.

"That's all right. Tell Don I'll be out to see him in a moment."

"Don?" Alison looked puzzled.

I was too for a moment. I had forgotten I always called patients by their last name. I chuckled.

"Have Joy check his vitals. I'll be right there."

Alison closed the door. Rachel and I closed our arms around each other and kissed.

CHAPTER THIRTY-EIGHT

Reseda

Things have been going great at Buck & Awesome. I guess I became sort of a celebrity after getting shot. People would come up to me and ask how I'm doing. Fatima's family and members from her mosque thanked me for stepping up to protect her. I was nervous about the attention at first. Quang didn't like me chatting with customers. But he seems cool with it now. He's even nicer to me.

Reza started shopping at the store. He came in for these generic Mexican candies that are both sweet and spicy. I had been paying him back for the damage I caused that night.

"So, when's your dad coming back to visit?" He put a bag of candy in his basket.

"Sunday. I'm finally going to meet his girlfriend and her kids. The oldest is really into baseball."

He grabbed a few more snacks off the rack. "You should all go to a Dodgers game."

He headed towards the register. I walked with him.

"I'd like to," I said, "But Dad's a die-hard Angels fan."

"Is there such a thing?"

"You'd be surprised."

A lot of things Dad told me surprised me, especially about my great-grandmother. I surprised him too with the things that happened to me, especially Zoey and the baby. What surprised us both was how much we have in common, and how much we could help each other. All those years we wasted being afraid, angry, and resentful. At least, we didn't have to waste any more time.

Reza and I went to Pearl's register. She was ringing up the woman I once saw at the dumpster, the homeless woman I gave all that money to. Her name is Francine. She used that money to get herself and her kids into temporary housing. She got help, and Magdalena gave her a job working at the restaurant.

"I heard they're fixing up and reopening the theater," Francine told Pearl. She was talking about the abandoned movie theater I lived behind for over a month. "That'll be great for business at the restaurant."

Pearl smiled. "That will be great for all of us. Four thirty-three, please."

The woman handed her a five. Pearl rang her up and handed her the change. Francine dropped the coins into the plastic box for United Cerebral Palsy.

"Have a pleasant day." Pearl then turned to Reza. "Hey, Reza."

"Hey."

Pearl then gave me a long, lingering glance and a broad smile.

"Dylan?" Quang's voice came from the other end of the store.

"Gotta go," I said to Reza.

He patted my shoulder and whispered, "You're lucky."

I only had a second to smile back at Pearl before rushing over to Quang. He had a hand truck and a box of books.

"Can you please put these in aisle 12?"

"Sure thing, Quang."

I wheeled the hand truck to the aisle. When I got to the shelf where we stock the books, I knelt down, slid off the box, and opened it.

Inside were copies of *Face Time with Jesus*. I took one out. There was Steven on the front cover with his perfect hair and self-satisfied smile. But on the bottom, a black mark smeared across the pages.

"Do you forgive him?" Mrs. Cimino was staring at Steven's book.

I stood up and faced Mrs. Cimino.

"Do you?"

She nodded. "It took me a while. I came to realize that despite what he did, his book still saved my life. And what he did to you, Dylan, is what helped you find the path you needed to follow. God takes us where we need to go..."

"And teaches us the lessons we need to learn." I smiled and nodded. "Thank you, Mrs. Cimino."

"You're welcome, Dylan." She stepped to her cart and continued down the aisle.

I looked at Steven's smug face again. His book was written with the hands of an asshole, but they are still words from the mouth of God. And it is a remainder. Something that seems worthless can still have value.

ACKNOWLEDGMENTS

The Remainders is my second novel published by Black Rose Writing. Again, I am grateful to Reagan Rothe and the team for their ongoing support and assistance. I appreciate what a welcoming and supportive family of authors this group is.

Part of this family are the members of the Write Or Wrong Virtual Book Club who have supported me as a published author. Special thanks go to Jackie Anders, Ella Clarke, Steven Searls, Erika Modrak, and the others for their generosity and encouragement.

I've also found support from the writing community of Orange County, California, especially Brian Fitzpatrick, Meadow Griffith, Flora Brown, Anne Moose, Lynette Smith, Katie Mathers, the Muzeo, and the Anaheim Public Library.

I am also grateful to folks in my hometown of Reseda, California. *The Remainders* began as a project for Fun-A-Day Reseda in 2016. Thanks goes to Chloe Cumbrow, 11:11 A Creative Collective, the San Fernando Valley Arts & Cultural Center, and the others involved in this annual event.

Thanks also to my beta readers, Shelley Logan, H.R. Kemp, and Maisy Menold for their time and valuable feedback.

Finally, thank you to my family for their ongoing support, understanding, and love.

ABOUT THE AUTHOR

Matthew Arnold Stern is a Southern California native who grew up in Reseda and lives in Orange County. He graduated Summa Cum Laude from California State University, Northridge. *The Remainders* is his second novel published by Black Rose Writing. His debut with Black Rose Writing, *Amiga*, was called "a brilliantly plotted, well-crafted historical novel" and "a good and entertaining read."

He earned awards for his writing and public speaking, including Distinguished Toastmaster and an Award of Excellence from the International Online Communications Competition. He is married with two children, a granddaughter, and lots of cats.

NOTE FROM THE AUTHOR

Word-of-mouth is crucial for any author to succeed. If you enjoyed *The Remainders*, please leave a review online—anywhere you are able. Even if it's just a sentence or two. It would make all the difference and would be very much appreciated.

Thanks!
Matthew Arnold Stern

We hope you enjoyed reading this title from:

BLACK ROSE
writing™

www.blackrosewriting.com

Subscribe to our mailing list – *The Rosevine* – and receive
FREE books, daily deals, and stay current with news about
upcoming releases and our hottest authors.
Scan the QR code below to sign up.

Already a subscriber? Please accept a sincere thank you for
being a fan of Black Rose Writing authors.

View other Black Rose Writing titles at
www.blackrosewriting.com/books and use promo code
PRINT to receive a **20% discount** when purchasing.

www.ingramcontent.com/pod-product-compliance
Lightning Source LLC
Chambersburg PA
CBHW010733100726
47899CB00009B/3023